the
th n
p nk
ine

lauren baratz-logsted

the thin pink line

**RED
DRESS
I N K**
™

First edition July 2003

THE THIN PINK LINE

A Red Dress Ink novel

ISBN 0-373-25030-4

Visit Red Dress Ink at www.reddressink.com

Printed in U.S.A.

For Jackie:
If it weren't for you,
I never would have come up with the idea.

"The man has a penis which he puts inside the woman and sprays things out. The things are called semen. And that is seed that makes the baby grow."

—*What We Keep*, Elizabeth Berg

planned parenthood, or the story behind the story

"Have you become a fuckwit, Jane?"

Not exactly "Last night I dreamt I went to Manderley again," or "It was the best of times, blah, blah, blah," I'll grant you, but it'll do for my life story.

"Have you become a fuckwit, Jane?"

No, perhaps it's best not to start there for a first impression.

Okay. Let's try this one last time. Deep breath here:

I didn't plan on getting pregnant, I swear, although I am certainly capable of going to great lengths to get what I want. The way I figured it at the time, it was a combination of rare animal passion and manufacturer's error. It does happen, you know. Surely, all of the world's unplanned pregnancies can't be from people silly enough to engage in unprotected sex, can it? Regarding the passion and the error, er, at least that was how things came about the *first* time I was pregnant…but then wasn't really.

Perhaps I'd better back up a bit and explain.

You see, Trevor and I had been to yet another friend's wedding that weekend, so of course I was understandably depressed afterward. After all, I wasn't an au courant Singleton or even a much maligned Smug Married, but rather, that lowest of the social lows, an inhabitor and cohabitor of that famed female limbo, an Unholy Unmarried, or UU for short, which looks kind of like a cow's udders when seen on the printed page, but perhaps that's neither here nor there. Anyway, after the wedding, Trevor, being Trevor, since he knew he wasn't ready to ask me to marry him but still wanted to make me feel better, had great sex with me.

It's always amazed me how often heartache and really great sex go hand in hand. From what I hear other women say, I think it must be different for them. Hell, sometimes I think everything must be different for other people. But for me, the more melancholy, the bigger the bang. I mean, if I'm actually happy, then I'm probably eating something and even letting myself enjoy it, and sex is the furthest thing from my mind.

But back to Trevor, great sex and pregnancy.

So there we were, having great post-someone-else's-wedding sex, and I was thinking how not only had everyone I knew been getting married lately, but they were even having babies as well, when the thought occurred to me, *What if I turned up pregnant?* Well, no sooner did the thought occur to me than Trevor hit my high note, prophylactic rubber barrier and all, and the thought flew completely out of my mind.

Until I didn't get my period when it was due three weeks later.

Of course I told my best friend David—pronounced *Duh-veed*—right off the bat.

"But this is great news, is it not, Jane?" David asked in his overly precise English.

David lived upstairs from Trevor and me. Just over the minimum height requirement for the Israeli military, in which he had served—I mean, they all do, right? Israelis, that is—he was a regular spark plug. Given to wearing muscle T-shirts and early eighties-style blue jeans, as far as I could see he was the sole item in the plus column for bringing back Jordache jeans. He also had coils of black hair that, along with his bronzed skin, gave him a Semitic Caesar profile. A former fighter pilot, make that *gay* fighter pilot, he was now trying to make a go of it as a chef in his own trendy Covent Garden bistro, still in the planning stages.

"In the Israeli military, Jane, you both ask and tell, and you take gays and women and anyone else who can handle an Uzi," he'd once told me over a shared bottle of Burgundy left over from a *boeuf bourguignonne* that a lover of his had failed to show up to share.

When David suggested that my days-old pregnancy was great news, I found myself agreeing with him. After all, it wasn't as though I had deliberately set out to snag Trevor, but this would certainly do the trick. Trevor was such a Do-Right Dudley that he was sure to marry me.

At the time, I didn't even think about what an actual baby might actually mean.

I also didn't think about the emotional consequences of telling people other than the father before I told the father. This was another one of those things that falls under the heading of I Didn't Plan It That Way, But. In this case, the "but" had to do with how gleefully David had received the news. (And him I'd only told about the news first because Trevor was away on business in Singapore for the week.) Bowled over by how happy my pregnancy had made him, I proceeded to tell a few more people. Oh, I didn't go overboard—well, maybe just a bit—didn't do anything so silly as telling my mother or sister or even the girls at work, but I did tell the Pakistani newsagent down the street ("Here, have some curry—it will bring good luck"), a policeman who helped me jimmy my lock one night when I'd locked my bag in the flat ("You can't be too careful at night now that there's two of you") and the odd stranger or two; so, just enough to give me a taste of how the other half lives. Their combined reactions were enough to make me start to experience a warm glow. I began to feel like, maybe, were I to miss out on being pregnant, that I'd miss the potential for the world to be a rosy place.

Of course, never one to do anything by halves, I started to tail pregnant women. You couldn't really call it *stalking,* but I did spend the Saturday just prior to Trevor's return trailing every prego I happened to casually encounter, until I finally settled on one who looked so close to delivery that I thought I might be called into service at any moment.

And it was amazing the things I learned! Following my quarry through a heavy doorway, I was surprised to see a man who'd been walking ahead of both of us double back to hold the door patiently for her until she'd squeezed her way through. I was still smiling my surprise when he let the door go just in time to smack me in the face. Apparently, the fact that I didn't have the equivalent of a sack of flour attached to the front of my body rendered me invisible or at least not in need of any courtesy. Oh, well. As I followed her about her rounds that day, it wasn't even so much the common courtesies she was shown that impressed me, although I was damned shocked when the drunken old sot on the tube blearily yielded his seat to her so that she could "rest yer Madonna feet, luv." No, it was more the mere fact that people actually *talked* to her, all the time; perfect strangers who might step over their own mothers in the gutter kept making comments and asking her questions in the most solicitous manner imaginable: "When're you due?" or "Do you know yet if it's a boy or a girl?" or "Spring babies're always so extra special—just like little sunny angels, they are," this last from the bleary old sot.

Why, it was as though someone had sprinkled pixie dust all over her! Her existence seemed that enchanted, and I longed to find out if my bout with pregnancy would prove the same.

The only problem was that just as I was on the verge of telling Trevor, who had returned from his trip just in time to partake of the pre-celebratory Sunday dinner that was waiting for him, an odd thing occurred. As I was teetering on the precipice of my new future, while serving up a helping of the *blanquette de veau* that David had prepared for me to pretend to prepare, I felt an unwelcome twinge of pain in my lower back.

"Fuckfuck*fuck*," I swore under my breath, just barely restraining myself from slamming the pot back down on the stove.

"What was that, Jane?"

"Nothing," I informed Trevor, ignoring the twinge. "Just a little back pain."

"Mmm," he said distractedly, still rifling through the post that had accumulated since he'd been gone. "Perhaps you should take some Tylenol?"

"No, that's okay. I'm sure it will pass." I brightened. "Ready to eat?"

Moments later, I eyed Trevor as he speared a piece of meat.

"Mmm, Jane, this is really great. It's always so wonderful when you take it into your head to do the homemaker thing."

That sounded promising.

He chewed some more—he makes it a practice to always chew each piece something like fifty-four times—and flipped open the newspaper to see what had been going on locally while he'd been gone. Eyes glued to some story about Charles and Camilla, he absently asked, "Wasn't there something you said you wanted to tell me?"

He yawned and briefly glanced my way, looking a bit knackered after his long trip. "Didn't you indicate that there was a reason why you were fattening me up for the kill?"

"I'm pregnant," I said, remembering the simple script I'd planned out earlier in the day. "I'm late and I think I must be pregnant."

Trevor didn't even bother to look up again. "Oh, that." He flipped another page. "That happened to Sam's Dolly and it turned out that she just had a bad case of anorexia, compounded by acid reflux." Then he smiled at me, helpfully, indulgently. "But if you want, why don't you pick yourself up one of those at-home test kits? That should put your mind at ease."

Okay, so maybe it wasn't exactly the reaction I'd envisioned, but it was a start.

I would have thought that, given the news that we were going to have a baby, Trevor would have wanted to make wild passionate love to me that night. I certainly wanted to make wild passionate love to him.

But no.

"Sorry, Janey." He gave my shoulder a vague pat when I made overtures to him in bed. "I'm just so tired from the plane and all. And you know how lethargic red meat always makes me. Perhaps tomorrow night?"

"That's okay," I said, watching him roll away before I even got the chance to explain just why it was okay.

And it really was okay, you see. Oh, sure, I would have liked to be physically close to him right then. But, I thought as Trevor started to snore, what did missing out on one night of passion really mean in the greater scheme of things? Trevor and I were going to have a baby together! I was finally going to have what everyone else had!

I let myself get—dare I say it?—*sentimental.*

I lay beside him, night-dreaming of our future together:

pushing the pram down the street; going to rugby games or dance recitals—or even both if I had twins; being part of that rosy world I'd glimpsed while stalking the other pregos.

Then I thought of what it would mean to me personally: I'd finally be a member of The Club. After a life lived mostly on the fringes of what constituted normal female friendships for other women, I'd finally have a legitimate reason for joining in on their discussions. We would be able to talk about—oh, I don't know—*diaper rash* or something. It wouldn't really matter what we talked about. What mattered was that I'd be one of the group.

I thought and I night-dreamed, and I thought, and I night-dreamed...

Blast! There was that damned lower-back pain again, only now it was worse and the pain had radiated frontward to my abdomen as well.

I sighed, trotting off to the bathroom, thinking to follow Trevor's earlier advice about taking Tylenol.

Switching on the bathroom light, I grabbed a glass and took two pills from the plastic bottle. Just as I was about to toss them back, however, I vaguely remembered something about pregnant women being not supposed to take certain kinds of painkillers, something about it being bad for the developing fetus. Was it just aspirin? Was it Tylenol, too? I couldn't remember. I shook my head, dropped the pills back in the bottle, set down the glass. No point in taking any chances. I could just muscle through the pain. After all, I had a baby to think about.

Oh, well, I thought. *I'm in here already. Might as well pee.*

I dropped my drawers, squatted on the toilet.

Well, of course I had gotten my period.

I'd never been pregnant at all.

I don't know why I did what I did next, but, after peeing and wiping, without even thinking about it, I balled up my stained undies, wrapped them in paper, tiptoed across the flat and buried them in the kitchen trash beneath the leavings from dinner. Then I tiptoed back to the bedroom, got out a fresh pair of undies, returned to the bathroom, attached a sanitary napkin and tiptoed back to bed.

As I crawled in, Trevor stirred.

Shh, my mind telegraphed my urgently whispered plea to him, wishing him to remain sleeping while I lay on my side, watching him sleep blithely on as I thought about how to tell him that I wasn't really pregnant after all.

I was just about to reach out my hand to rouse him in order to tell him what I'd discovered—I swear I was—when, in a reversal of the clichéd near-death experience, my future rather than my past flashed before my eyes.

Okay, so maybe it wasn't my real future: my future as still-single Jane Taylor, now that I wasn't really pregnant. No, it was my potential future as Trevor's wife, as a mother, as one of The Club, the potential future represented by that rosy world I'd glimpsed while stalking, the potential future that I knew in my heart with certainty that I'd be giving up in the instant I told Trevor the truth.

Then I thought about how Trevor had behaved when I'd told him I was pregnant, when I'd still believed it myself.

I'll never know what it was: the recollection of Trevor's offhand manner, the fact that I had set myself up by telling others first—even if one of them was David, whom Trevor never spoke to, and the others were people neither of us knew—or the position of the stars and the planets, but I did a strange thing that night. In a second, without even thinking about it, I leapt into the void.

By leaping into the void, what I mean is that when Trevor stirred once more, murmuring a vague, "Still awake? Is everything all right, Janey?", rather than telling him the truth, I simply replied, "Everything's fine. Go back to sleep."

I told myself that I wasn't doing a *hugely* bad thing by not telling him right then and there. After all, it wasn't as though he'd expressed *hatred* for the idea of our having a baby together. No, he'd hardly seemed bothered by it at all. Come to think of it, what he'd mostly been was indifferent.

I told myself again that I wasn't doing a *hugely* bad thing.

Then I snuck upstairs to consult my best friend.

"Did you tell him?" David asked.

"Yes." I hurled myself into a sling chair. The wretched thing would probably destroy my back, but who cared now.

"Then why are you so glum?"

"Well…"

"Jane." He said it as though the name itself were a caution, full stop.

"Well, the thing is, see, I'm not pregnant anymore. Actually, as it turns out, I never was."

For my part, in case I haven't mentioned this before, I loved David with a rare human passion. I mean, if a girl's lucky enough to have a gay pal, she has to be nice to him, doesn't she? After all, they're the only ones you can count on for the truth.

"Have you become a fuckwit, Jane?"

Apparently, David's idiomatic English was just growing by leaps and bounds.

"Let me get this straight," he pressed his verbal advantage, not even giving me a moment to answer his unanswerable question. "You now realize that you are not pregnant, but you are neglecting to share that teensy bit of information with the father of your nonexistent child. May one be so bold as to enquire as to what you plan to do next? It's not as if a person can impersonate being pregnant, like a trained assassin might impersonate being just a regular guy."

"Well," I shrugged, attempting a smile, "that was sort of the plan."

"Now you've got *a plan?* Oh, you're really beginning to scare me, Jane."

"Actually, I don't have the whole plan yet, just the beginnings of one."

"And what do you propose to do in nine months' time? Don't you think that eventually Trevor might begin to notice that there is no pitter-patter of little feet on the horizon?"

"Odd that you should say that. I don't think that you can actually see the pitter-patter of little feet. It's not really a visual thing at all."

"Jane."

"All right. It's not a big plan. Like I said, it's just a little bit of a plan. The way I figure it, now that I've already told Trevor that I'm pregnant and he hasn't gone through the roof about it, I might as well just go ahead and get pregnant. In a way, when you think about it, it's not exactly like I'm trapping him in the conventional sense, not since his behavior indicates that he's not terribly bothered about it. It's more like I've trapped myself."

"You could, of course, resort to the truth, Jane."

I didn't even bother to dignify that with an answer.

Then I explained to David all about the rosy place that being pregnant had come to represent in my mind. "You see," I said, finishing up, "I just *can't* give that up."

"You can't give up this *rosy place* of pregnancy? But you're not even pregnant. Don't you think that maybe you're putting the cart way too far ahead of the horse?"

I impatiently shrugged off his objection. "Details."

"Details?"

"Yes, *details.*"

"Meaning…?"

"Meaning I'll just get pregnant. So the order of events is a little screwed up. It'll work. You'll see."

David shook his head. "I'll never understand why you want to marry him so badly, anyway, that paragon of manhood. Just out of curiosity, what did Trevor say when you told him?"

the first trimester

the first month

So, you see, actually, when you really think about it, this was all Trevor's fault in a way, since he was the one who suggested that I get the at-home pregnancy test kit in the first place.

If what follows smacks a bit of being something of an apologia, I think it only fair to point out that most people never see their own tragic flaws. For my part, I am fully aware of what my shortcomings are. Does that mean I should be instantly forgiven them? Hardly. But at least I'm willing to be honest about who I am, and if who I am is a fairly small-minded person who wastes most of her days in silly-minded pursuits, nothing about who I am has ever been quite so bad as to add up to Jack the Ripper.

Anyway, I've always been what you might call a selfish person, always been fairly free about admitting it, at least to myself. Oh, now mind you, I don't mean selfish in the grab-for-the-last-slice-of-pizza-when-with-friends way; that would be bad for what little image I have. Nor do I mean selfish in the willing-to-push-old-lady-out-of-way-to-secure-last-seat-on-tube-even-if-it-is-next-to-stark-raving-bonkers-loon sort of way; ditto above. No, I mean selfish in the garden-variety, monkey-see, monkey-do sort of way that's been the bane of my existence ever since I was three years old. That was when I first saw my sister playing with a doll—a Kewpie doll, mind you, with messy red hair and a tongue that shot out at you like a snake when you poked its stomach, the kind that would normally give me nightmares—and knew I had to have one myself. Even if it meant biding my time until she was asleep and easing it out of her arms, telling her when she woke screaming in tears, "She wasn't yours anyway, you know. You only *dreamt* that Mummy and Daddy gave her to you." Here I cradled my new baby in my arms. "There, there," I lullabyed her, before looking down once again at my crying sister, Sophie. "Now that you're awake and not dreaming any longer," I pointed out sternly, "you can see that the baby isn't yours at all. It's mine."

Ah, Sister Sophie: I guess I sort of think of her as a nun—a golden, beautiful, sort-of-mean nun. One year my senior and perfection itself in nearly every way, it was in fact a rare occurrence indeed for me to get the better of her. She was a real blonde with razor-straight hair, always got good grades, always had dates, always had the lion's share of anything on offer in life, including our parents' attention. In fact, as had once been explicitly stated to me by them, the only reason they'd ever conceived me in the first place was as a playmate for her.

It is a matter of public record that I was always the more aesthetically challenged of the Taylor girls. They say she never even drooled as a baby. I, on the other hand, had a steady stream of saliva running from lower lip to chest from the get-go, family legend holding that they had to keep me in bibs pretty much well from birth until grade school. In short, then, being Sophie's younger sister was about as bad as having the Queen for one's older sister without one's older sister being the Queen. You might say that Sophie and I had the biggest case of sibling rivalry in the world since Liz and Maggie, except that Sophie didn't even appear to know about it. Am I exaggerating when I compare my lot in life to that of the Queen of England's late sister? Perhaps. But I can honestly say that, based on firsthand knowledge, I can certainly understand why Maggie drank.

But back to the Kewpie doll. It didn't even phase me when I had raging nightmares about that darting serpentine tongue every night for the next month, until the doll was finally irretrievably lost somewhere—probably into the void behind the big blue couch in the living room, the black hole of our very early childhood—and Sophie acquired the next thing that I simply couldn't live without.

Now that I'm an adult—in years anyway—working for a London publishing company, not all that much has changed. Oh, I don't mean that I'm still stealing my sister's dolls; nothing like that. I've moved on to much more mature levels of envy; I've taken to coveting on a higher plane: ohm. No, no more childish things for me. Teetering on the cusp of thirty, for the past year the object of my grasping jealousy has been matrimony—much to the chagrin of Trevor Rhys-Davies, the suspenders-snappingly handsome stockbroker I've been sharing a place in Knightsbridge with for the past two—a state that sister Soph has been blissfully wedded in for exactly that length of time. To Tony. Who cooks Italian on weekends and who lovingly encourages her to put her feet up whenever she gets tired, which she does much more often now, her being—*suck it up and tell it all now, Jane! Tell the worst!*—five months' pregnant.

So I guess that, technically, you'd have to say that matrimony was last year's rivalry problem. After all, it was last year that I won the Bad Sportsmanship Award for Inability to Throw Rice Nicely; last year that I used to sob un-controllably at all of the weddings of friends and acquain-tances, not out of happiness for them but out of sheer misery for myself; last year that I'd sniffled onto Trevor's shoulder as he led me around the dance floor after the bride had cut the cake, had a garter put on her in a sala-cious manner and thrown the bouquet to some other guest whom I'd tried to tackle. "It's not fair," I sobbed. "Why isn't it ever me?" To which Trevor would caress my fashionably spiky dark hair as best he could, sigh heavily and say, "Oh, Jane."

Technically, then, this year's problem is no longer mat-rimony. Technically, the green-eyed-monster dilemma for this year is pregnancy.

Pregnancy envy, for those of you who have never heard of it, is something akin to penis envy in that the appeal lies in what is represented by the physical shape of the thing itself. It's sort of like wanting to wear a cross around your neck without ever being at all sure that you'd want to set foot in any kind of church.

Notice that I don't say a thing about babies. This is very specific, so pay attention.

It was only April, and I had already been invited to, and guiltily felt compelled to attend, seven baby showers that year: three for people at work, only one of whom I knew in a more than passing way; two for people whose wed-dings Trevor and I had attended the year before (eager lit-tle rabbits, weren't they?); one for a woman whose name I hadn't recognized at all but whose invitation said that the shower was being catered by Food by Gloria (I love catered food); and one for a woman that I had grown up with. My mother always remembers her as being my best friend as a child and had wrangled a spare invitation for me out of the girl's mother under this pretext. I, on the other hand, remember myself as having despised the girl intensely for her Tory views—perhaps that's a slight exaggeration of my political precocity, but she was an annoying girl. Still, I went anyway, in the hopes of more catered food, and with what I thought of as a generous gift certificate to A Mother's Work: The Breastfeeding Emporium tucked inside my purse, fighting with my mother the whole way to Brighton: "She was your best friend!"—"I hated the twit!" And, even if no more showers loomed in my immediate future, I still had Sophie's to look forward to in about three months' time.

Yes, with me teetering on the cusp of thirty, you could say that technically my lust had turned toward pregnancy, except that there was really nothing technical about it and it had in fact become a fact:

I was determined, in a big way, to join the pack and fast. But how?

Well, we all know now about the first failed pregnancy and me telling Trevor that I was pregnant and him telling me to pick up a kit. Before I did that, though, I figured I'd better do some preliminary research.

First off, I bought a copy of that book that every woman who's gotten pregnant in the last eighteen years always buys: *What to Expect When You're Expecting.* In light of the book's ubiquitous popularity, one really had to hope that Eisenberg, Murkoff, and Hathaway—the book's three authors—knew what the hell they were talking about. If not, we were all up a creek.

I placed the copy in the bottom drawer of my desk at work, so that whenever I wasn't terribly busy doing anything on behalf of Churchill & Stewart, the publishing firm at which I was titularly an assistant editor ever since I'd graduated with a first in English Literature from the University of Essex, I could read up on what I could expect to expect. I was just reading about what I was most interested in at the time, The Home Pregnancy Test, on page 4, when…

"Taylor!" I heard the sound of my immediate boss, Lana Lane, calling my name.

Lana Lane was the kind of woman for whom misogynists like Chandler and Hemingway first designed sentences that began with the portentous writing-school words: "Madame X was the kind of woman..."

In Lana Lane's case, Lana Lane was the kind of woman other women hated, strolling around in the kind of clingy sweater dresses that made her look like a cartoon knockout come to life, and all men feared. In fact, it was a good thing that my physical appearance was one of the few things I felt secure about, since Lana was the impossibly drop-dead-gorgeous kind of woman who could make Cindy Crawford start looking for zits. And, as far as men went, they feared her not only because she was far more beautiful than anything they could ever hope to be worthy of in their wormy little lives, but because she was also more successful than any of them in what had once upon a time been a man's game. For all of her sins, then, the men had christened her Dodo, and the women in the office all went along with them. Since she was a gorgeous blonde and since all gorgeous blondes were historically stupid but she was not, they guffawed about it as if it were some kind of flatteringly ironic pet name. I, for one, am not sure that I get the joke.

Truth to tell and feminism be damned, Dodo was not an entirely inaccurate sobriquet for Lana. For despite the fact that she had the kind of publishing acumen that would have made Bennett Cerf and Monsieur Gallimard tip their respective hats and *chapeaux,* when it came to real life she was something of a social moron. Never having had a genuine girlfriend in her thirty-five-year-old life, I was the closest she'd managed to come. And, if she was going to have to rely on me, whose boss she'd been for the past seven years, to teach her social skills...

"Taylor!" she screamed again from her office to mine, the receptionist that all of us in Editorial shared having called in sick because it was Friday morning and Dodo being as inept with the new office phone system as she was with social skills. "Do you think you could pick up line two? It's Colin Smythe. He's going something fierce about his latest while doing what I *think* is meant to be some kind of a John Wayne imitation, and *I* can't make heads or tails of it. Could you please, *please* take this one?"

I tucked the Lion Bar wrapper that I was using for a book-mark in between the pages on home testing and lab testing. Intrigued by what I'd read about the former, I stowed the book back in my drawer before picking up on Colin Smythe. He was the respected author of five scrupulously researched historical bestsellers on Regency England, none of which had even a smidgen of romance in them but which had oddly struck a nerve with a book-buying public who clearly felt that they were getting enough sexual stimulation these days from the daily newspapers. He'd also written a sixth book, against all of our best editorial advice, about a California surfer who moves to Chicago and finds love in a spectacu-larly odd place. Loosely based on a story he'd heard while attending the Windy City wedding of one of his wife's rel-atives, it had been published here last year and had *not* be-come a bestseller, although the critics had for some reason liked it. Now it was due to come out in paperback here at the same time it was due to come out in the States for the first time in hardcover. It was hoped that sales in the U.S., where Colin had a respectable following among the Maeve Binchy set, would be favorable enough to give the paper-back sales here a shot in the arm. After all, the Americans were quite good at persuading the rest of the world into wanting something that it hadn't occurred to them to want before; just look at what they did for Arnold Schwarzenegger.

"Yes, Colin." I always felt as though I should be calling him *Sir* Colin, and he clearly thought so as well. Still, in spite of the fact that his readers thought of him as a male Dame Barbara Cartland minus the kisses and pink robes and cats, the Queen, though she was a fan and had invited him to more than one of her garden parties, had not as yet made him a knight. "Jane Taylor here. What can I do for you today?"

"Have you seen the *Times* yet?"

"Yes, of course I have. I can't believe that Blair really said that. Don't you think sometimes the reporters just make some of this stuff up?"

Each word came out like a bullet. "I'm—not—talking—about—our—*Times*." He resumed a more normal speech cadence although one could still detect the strain. "I'm talking about their *Times,* the *New York Times.*"

"Oh dear," I said, consulting my watch as if the minute hand might help. "Have I got my dates mixed up? Did the book come out already?"

He didn't exactly begin his sentence with "you ninny" but it was definitely in the air. "Yes and yes. And the *Times,* their *Times,* has already gotten their hooks into it. Sometimes I swear they assign books to be reviewed by reviewers they know will hate them just so that they can be provocative. Did you see the hatchet job they let the editor-in-chief of *Briefcase Woman* magazine do on that first mystery where the sleuth was a housewife and former cheerleader?"

"Yes. It was positively cruel."

"And did you ever notice how if their daily reviewer loves a book it gets trashed in the Sunday edition and vice versa?"

"I believe it has been commented upon in the trade before." Much fun as this was, I wanted to get back to the crux of why Colin was calling because the sooner I did that, the sooner I could get back to *What to Expect.* "This really is loads of fun, Colin, as always, but what exactly did the *Times* say about *Surf the Wind*?"

I could hear the newspaper rustling over in Duck's End, Colin's country weekend estate, and the little throat-clearing cough that I knew always accompanied the donning of his reading half glasses. "Are you ready?"

What could I possibly say? I knew it was going to be awful. "I can't wait."

"By the way, the reviewer is an American historian, educated at Oxford. His name's not familiar to me. I think he might have some sort of ax to grind. Anyway, here goes— 'It is always a literary crime evincing the highest hubris, when a citizen of one country presumes to set a story in another country of which he has never been a resident. Such a circumstance is certainly egregious enough when the author is content to confine himself to a strict narrative form; however, when he commits the further, grosser, offense of assuming to understand the nuances of speech patterns native to the country he is purloining, he makes it impossible for any serious reader to take his efforts seriously. Such is the case with Colin Smythe's most recent effort, *Surf the Wind,* a preposterous romance so seasoned with the word *reckoned* that one can only assume that Mr. Smythe erroneously believes all Americans to be equally at home on the range. If anyone who knows Mr. Smythe happens to read this review, kindly do us all the favor of disabusing him of this notion. Contrary to the beliefs of certain Caribbean countries and, apparently, a small percentage of Englishmen, every American is not from Texas. We do not all walk through life talking around the hay stalks we have jammed in our mouths. Nor does each region of the United States speak in the same idiomatic fashion any more than one would expect, say, a Liverpudlian and a student of Cambridge to make the exact same verbal use of the letter *h*—' Do you need me to go on?"

I had to admit that the American reviewer had something of a point there. It seemed to me that the idea of an English person trying to impersonate Americans was potentially just as offensive as if, say, an American were to think that he or she could mimic an English novelist merely by throwing in a handful of "ex-directory" and "off-license" references every now and again. But I couldn't very well point that out to Colin Smythe, now, could I?

"Was that the daily *Times* or the Sunday *Times*?" I asked instead, sympathetically, the implication being that whichever one had trashed him, it surely meant that the other one would canonize him. Hopefully, it was the daily, since the Sunday carried more weight with booksellers.

For once he didn't sound a bit bombastic; more like deflated, really, as I heard the sigh that accompanied the removal of his glasses. "Both."

"How is that possible?"

"I spliced the two reviews together and read them to you as though they were one. The Sunday reviewer added something to the effect that 'it would be a relief to see Mr. Smythe turning his attention to something other than those insipid historicals he usually writes if only one could persuade him to remove the ten-gallon Stetson he is metaphorically wearing while doing so.' I thought I'd leave that part out because it depresses me so." Sigh. "I did so like America when I was there, and I had thought that it liked me. Don't they understand that I wasn't trying to mock or imitate anybody? Don't they understand that we all talk like that all the time, and that it has absolutely nothing whatsoever to do with Western drawls, six-guns, or corn in Nebraska when an Englishman says 'I reckon'?"

"I reckon not."

Colin sighed. "I wish that either you or Lana had picked up on this during the editorial process. It would have saved me so much bother."

I neglected to point out to him that he had been the one who had actually traveled to the United States, where he should have had ample opportunity to study the speech patterns of nontourist Americans. I, on the other hand— although I would have dearly loved to go to California or Chicago or even Texas, where the latest governor was reportedly still executing death-row inmates fairly regularly—had never hardly been any farther west than Gloucester. Instead, I promised to do whatever I could in terms of damage control from my end and rang off after only a handful more sighs out of him.

Now it was my turn to sigh, not with dejection, however, but with relief. It was time for me to get back to *What to Expect.*

There were so many things to worry about, I began to learn as I read on.

Oh, I don't mean things to worry about as far as the baby's health; after all, that would go without saying if a person were actually pregnant. No, what I'm getting at here is all the things that could go wrong if, say, a person didn't quite know what they were doing and weren't really pregnant, a person like me who had told her boyfriend that she was pregnant but wasn't quite there yet really. For example, what if someone were to ask a person how they first suspected they were pregnant? A person might take the easy way out and say, "Well, I missed my period, didn't I?" But if a person didn't want to just go with the obvious, if they wanted to maybe spice things up with a splash of authenticity, they might want to say, "I've been tossing my cookies all day long," or "I was beginning to think I'd turned into a greyhound, I've been peeing that much," or "My vaginal and cervical tissue's been changing colors lately." Of course, the problem with that approach is that a really swift person might come up with alternative medical and nonmedical causes for those signs. They might easily counter with, "Have you considered that it just might be food poisoning?" or "Well, there have been those diuretics you've been addicted to for the last year," or "You know, Jane, you're not supposed to study yourself down there with a handheld mirror on a daily basis—cut it out!"

No, it definitely seemed to me that the only conclusive proof to offer Nosy Parkers should they ask would be the results of an official test, which was pretty much well what Trevor had indicated already.

★ ★ ★

On the way home from work, I stopped off at Mr. Singh's and ordered a take-away curry to appease the cravings that I was sure to be having soon. While waiting for my order, I popped in next door at Boots the Chemist. I studied the display of at-home pregnancy tests available, reading the backs of each until I found one that claimed to be effective anytime during the day; no point waiting for first morning pee when a girl could do it anytime she felt like it. Then I selected a package containing a colorful assortment of fine-point Magic Markers, paid for my purchases, picked up my curry, and completed the journey home.

It wasn't as though I'd gone out of my way, per se, when Trevor and I had first moved in together, to select a paint color for the majority of the apartment that would clash so with his beige personality. It was more, I told myself, that I genuinely enjoyed salmon pink and, anyway, it's always good early on in a new relationship to push the envelope so hard that you know just exactly how far a man is willing to go in terms of concessions to keep you happily in his bed. I'd heard girls at the office tell about pressuring the men in their lives to buy them gemstones as big as their heads, to take them vacationing on Necker, to let a second man play in their beds. By contrast, having your beige man paint the walls pink seemed like comparatively small potatoes to me.

And it wasn't as though Trevor hadn't been doing his own share of envelope pushing which, in his case, came in the form of a horrible orange beast he loved that went by the name of Punch the Cat. I don't know why I hated Punch the Cat so much, whom I always wanted to kick every time I entered a room as he slinked out at me from around some corner, because I've always adored cats in general. I guess it could be because he came across as some kind of smugly malevolent Puss in Boots or maybe it was just the color orange.

Anyway, on that particular evening, my knee-jerk reaction upon entering the apartment and seeing Punch the Cat slithering toward me, moving like the Grinch when he's going after the Christmas decorations and appears to not even touch the ground, was no different than any other: I wanted to swing out with one of my two-inch chunky-heeled burgundy suede Joan & Davids and send him flying into the fireplace. But I couldn't do that tonight. Not if what I was hoping to do was launch the campaign to get Trevor to start looking at me as the future mother of his child.

"Hello, Punch." I juggled chemist and curry bags so that I could reach down and pet my enemy. "Is Daddy home yet?"

Well, of course I already knew that Trevor was around here somewhere; his car was parked out front. Why else would I be sucking up to the cat?

"Hello, there," Trevor said, using a towel to wipe his wet ears, wearing blue jeans and nothing else as he strolled toward me from the direction of the bathroom.

Trevor was a two-shower-a-day man and whenever I saw him walking around suspenderless, in addition to wanting to swat him on his perfect behind, I always found myself marveling at the fact that I'd somehow managed to wind up with a man with light-blond hair and dark-blue eyes, the color combination I'd have least pegged myself to settle down with.

"Darling!" I gushed. Perhaps I was overdoing it? Tossing my packages on the table, I threw my arms around him, slightly damp chest and all. "Lucky me to come home to you." Well, at least I had the grace not to guffaw at my own inanities. "Tough day at work?" Could I get any more situation-comedy wife? "Hope you didn't have to deal with any Nick Leesons."

"Nah, it wasn't too bad," Trevor said, disengaging, but in a gentle way. He peeked in the bag from Mr. Singh's. "Hey, curry! Great!" He looked up at me. "You don't know how many times today I thought to ring you to see if you'd like to split one, but I kept getting interrupted, and then I thought to stop on the way home, but I also thought, that if you'd already stopped someplace first, it'd create a food conflict, so I ended up not doing anything." He smiled. "You're the greatest."

God. Sometimes it was just so damned easy.

"I'm glad you're happy. Tell you what. Why don't you lay out the plates and things while I just pop into the bathroom to wash my hands and—" I patted the chemist bag I'd retrieved "—attend to some girl stuff."

Trevor was so instantly preoccupied with the curry bag that he didn't even remark on the chemist's bag. What an odd man. He'd as much as told me to pick up what amounted to a ticking bomb at the chemist's. I now had it in my possession and was about to detonate it, and rather than showing any outward signs of anxiety, he had his nose buried in the chicken *tikka masala.* Oh, well.

Once I'd safely managed to lock behind me the door we usually never bothered to lock, I tore into the bag, pulled out the pregnancy kit, and reread the directions. Well, I thought, I could just dismantle the plastic wand thing and use the pink Magic Marker to make my pink line right away. But then I figured that I should at least pee onto the thing first so that it would have that authentic urine aroma.

Dropping my drawers and squatting over the toilet bowl, I did so, only to discover, after getting pee all over my hand as well, that when I finally dismantled the thing and applied the pink Magic Marker to the damp surface, the line came out all smudged-looking and not at all like the "you are pregnant" diagram depicted on the back of the box. It didn't help matters any that, not ever having been what one might term "good" at art class, my line had come out on a very strong diagonal and thus not like anything pictured on the box, not even like the "you are not pregnant" diagram. Good thing I'd purchased one of the few brands containing two tests. Perhaps its manufacturer had anticipated that some women might be overly cautious or that some, like me, might do something truly bizarre with the first test.

I hastily shoved the botched test into the cabinet beneath the sink for now, dropping it behind a package of sanitary napkins—after all, it wouldn't do to have Trevor see the odd-looking botched test sticking out of the refuse basket by the toilet, would it?—and removed the second test, deciding not to take any chances by peeing on it this time. If I blew this one too, then I'd have to wait until the following evening to try again, and I was getting anxious.

"Jane?" I heard Trevor's voice calling. "Are you all right in there? The curry's getting cold."

Trevor might not have been the kind of knight in shining armor that I'd wanted him to be that last year, the kind that would have asked me to marry him so that I'd at least have one less thing to envy everyone else for, but he did have the most uncommonly gracious table manners; I knew that even if he'd decided to turn Muslim all of a sudden and began observing Ramadan, that even if he'd been fasting all day long he'd never sneak one forkful past his lips until I was also seated at the table.

"Coming!" I shouted. "I'll just be one more tick in here."

Again not to take any chances this time, having already most emphatically *not* peed on the plastic wand, I dismantled it, lined the box up perpendicularly over the top of the wand to function as a ruler and made my mark less than a finger's distance apart from the control line that was already in the test window for women to compare the color of their own results. Then I shoved the marker back loosely in the bag that my purchases had come in, shoved the whole thing to the back of the cabinet where the botched test had already taken up residence behind the

sanitary napkins that I would, theoretically, not be needing for the next nine months, and shouted, "Trevor! I
think you'd better come in here! There's something you're
going to want to see!"

I heard the sound of his chair scraping back from the
table, accompanied by the kind of sigh that clearly said,
"But I'm hungry!" Still, Trevor was too well mannered to
say anything direct about it.

I heard him jiggle the handle of the locked door. "I'm
afraid that you're going to have to unlock this door, Jane,
if you have something you desperately want me to see."

"Look!" I enthused, having opened the door to allow
him to join me in a bathroom that was really only fit for
one. Out of the corner of my eye, I saw Punch the Cat
sneak in behind Trevor, the sly feline obviously not spotting out of the corner of her eye that I had spied her out
of the corner of mine. "Look!" I shouted again, holding
the test with its dual "yes, you are pregnant" stripes up
across my chest as if I were some sort of quiz show hostess displaying a much-desired prize. "Look! We've created
the matching pink line!"

"Good God, Jane." He involuntarily grabbed onto the
doorpost for support. "Does that mean what I think it
does?"

"If what you think it means is that you're going to have
to be nicer to me for the next nine months because I happen to be bearing your child, then yes."

He swallowed hard. "Oh, God, Janey." He looked
slightly horrified but determined to eat his Brussels sprouts
like a good Gordonstoun boy would as he hugged me to
him. "Of course I'll stand by you."

For my part, as I allowed him to hold me, my face positively wreathed in the beatific smile of one Madonna or
another, I used my toe to give Punch the Cat a healthy
shove out the door. There just wasn't room in that bathroom for three beings.

According to the calculations that I would be giving out to family and friends as the next few weeks and months wore on, at the time of the bathroom hugging I was a scant two weeks late. For his part, Trevor was as good as his word. He did stand by me. What he hadn't specified, unfortunately—although, to be fair to him, he didn't have all the facts—was just how long a period of time that standing would last for. In fact, it lasted for exactly two months and thirteen days, leading me right up to the threshold of my second trimester, at which point we were planning a small wedding and at which point events conspired to give Trevor the rest of the facts.

But that's getting ahead of my story.

My story was still in its first month; my baby was still smaller than a grain of rice, a little tadpolish embryo, getting ready to sprout arms and legs from things called buds in about two weeks' time, along with the neural tube— later to become the brain and spinal cord—and the heart, digestive tract and sensory organs; Trevor was treating me like I was either made of glass or plutonium; and I was about to embark on the next exciting phase in my procreative journey.

the second month

The morning after I'd first confirmed the "news" for Trevor, I woke, stretching languidly like any cat other than Punch the Cat. I snuggled up next to the yet fitfully sleeping father of my unborn child but was unable to assume the position for very long.

My sanitary napkin needed changing.

Rushing to the bathroom, I dropped my champagne-colored panties from the Victoria's Secret Satin Collection, only to discover that I was still sporting the telltale scarlet stain of the unpregnant. Good God! I'd been so excited about telling Trevor that I was really pregnant that I'd completely forgotten that I still had three days to go on my period.

Two nights before, after I'd initially told Trevor that I was pregnant and David that I was not, I'd crawled back into bed and lain awake, plotting what I would do to camouflage my own menstruation until such time as Trevor's sperm finally took and I really became pregnant.

The biggest stumbling block, as I saw it, was the sanitary napkins themselves. So the person to blame for what might end up ruining what should be the happiest days of my life, again as I saw it, was my mother.

After my father had died, when Sophie was seven and I was six—I was sure that it was the state of being married to my mother that had killed him—all my mother had seemed fit to cope with was spoiling Sophie and enjoying the rather substantial inheritance he had left her. She certainly hadn't gone out of her way to provide me with any of the skills I might need to get on in the world, not least of which was the ability to use a Tampax.

Let me just point out here that I am not one of these dirty-laundry-in-the-wind type of women who likes to lay the responsibility for everything she's ever done wrong at the feet of everything her parents did or did not do. Even I, in my craziest moments of what others might term "diabolical plotting," am aware of the fact that if I take out a loaded gun and pull the trigger, it really is me making the choice. As a matter of fact, as I grow older, I find myself having increasingly less patience with acquaintances who whinge on about not being able to have proper relationships, about being passive-aggressive, about needing to be a child before they can be an adult, blah, blah, blah, all of it being the fault of Mummy and Daddy. I sometimes find myself wanting to shout, "It's not your bloody mother's fault you can't get laid on Saturday night! It's because you're a bloody whiner!"

But back to the Tampax. For it is true that I don't believe it's my mother's fault if I choose to fake a pregnancy until the real thing comes along, but parents can most definitely be blamed for some vacancies of knowledge and, in my case, it is definitely my mother's fault that I never learned how to use a Tampax. Being the old-fashioned daughter of an old-fashioned mother who hadn't helped her out either, when my mother's generation finally made the change from belted napkins to the more convenient type with the adhesive strip, it was like taking a major evolutionary step; Tampax was a Mount Everest they'd never dared ascend. I never knew what Sophie had done about the situation later on in life. I suppose that, if the two of us had been closer, we might have been able to figure it out together; we could have helped to modernize one another. As it was, I had a mother who was useless, a sister who was as good as, and, as far as any girlfriends I'd had over the years, they were never the kind of overly chummy types of relationships that you see depicted in girls' mystery stories all the time, the kind in which you might envision one young heroine saying to another, "Oh, Sally! Could you give me a hand with something? My mother's hopeless when it comes to feminine hygiene products and, well, I'm worried that if I don't know exactly what I'm doing, I'll manage to lose the Tampax inside of my pancreas or something."

As for me then, not having a Sally, I was, quite frankly, scared of the things.

But I couldn't keep dwelling on my mother, Sophie, Tampax and my lack of a Sally. I needed to come up with a plan.

The problem was that at home, when I disposed of my napkins, I used tin foil to wrap them in afterward. And Trevor, even though he certainly was not obsessed with the details of feminine hygiene, would most definitely notice if a presumably pregnant lady began piling up foil-wrapped packages in the bathroom trash. As a matter of fact, he'd always somewhat affectionately referred to these little packages as my "rat packages."

So what to do to solve this problem that would definitely be a problem five days a month until I could somehow make it become no longer a problem?

The only solution that I had been able to figure out was that I would have to purchase and learn how to use Tampax, which would be much easier to hide from Trevor when I needed to dispose of them than the rat packages.

Since I'd forgotten, what with the excitement and all, to do it yesterday, I'd just have to remember to do it today.

Then, too, there was the further problem of me not being able to have sex with him until my period stopped, because if I did he might notice that something was amiss. But that was another bridge—I could always claim to be too nauseated or something—and I would cross it, like all others, only when I had to.

Besides, oddly enough, even though Trevor was usually hot for sex whenever he returned from a business trip, there hadn't been a peep out of his southern region since he'd been back. Perhaps the idea that sex could somehow lead to babies had put him off his feed for the time being.

Great. By the time my period was finally over, I would probably end up having to do naked back handsprings to seduce the father of my child so that there would be a child.

I had decided to make Dodo my new best girlfriend.

It had been the process of elimination really. Now that I was going to be pregnant, I needed to have a best girl-friend at work, a gal pal to confide in and complain to, and Dodo presented all kinds of advantages in that area. For starters, Dodo was older, if only by about a half decade or more, but older meant that she could be called upon to do maternal for me if I needed it. Then, too, she had no sisters and was hated by almost every woman at the office because she was so unconscionably beautiful. (Of course, I was hated by almost every woman in the office too, given that they saw me as a minor appendage of Dodo, like a middle finger or something, but this was okay with me since—sour grapes here? you might well ask—they weren't the kind of people I wanted to engage in chitchat with around the water cooler about television programs anyway.) If I could co-opt Dodo, I could have all the appearances of having a normal pregnancy—i.e., having a girlfriend to share the experience with—while keeping the other females in the office at bay.

It was really amazing to me sometimes how much planning and sheer energy went into being a dishonest person.

Anyway, up until that point, I had been a paragon of restraint. Sure, I'd wanted to blab my good news to the world once I'd drawn that first pink line, but I knew from experience that prospective mothers did not behave in such a devil-may-care fashion. I knew that they traditionally played the coy game, that they tried to wait ten to twelve weeks before talking about it, so as to have safely hurdled the time most likely for their fetus to become part of a sad statistic.

As I say, I was a paragon of restraint. By the sixth week, absolutely determined that this was one baby I was not going to lose, I began to tell people, caution be damned.

Dodo was so surprisingly, touchingly happy for me that she swore to stop addressing me as Taylor on the spot. On top of that, since it was a Friday afternoon, and since Fridays were the accepted day for all the full editors to leave work early and stop off at the local pub for drinks and a rehash of the week, Dodo, who was only included because she had more successful authors than anyone else, impulsively said, "Oh, why don't you come with us today, Jane? I'd love to help you celebrate!"

No sooner were the words out of her mouth than I was reaching for my bag. Yes! Me and the full editors, out for a friendly pint or two, maybe a slimline and gin. The next thing I'd know, I'd finally be one of THEM.

No sooner had my hand grasped my bag, however, than I heard Dodo's breathy exhalation of disappointment. "Oh, how stupid of me, Jane," she said, literally hitting herself on the side of the head, "of course you can't go out for drinks with us. You're expecting!"

I let the strap on my bag slide down over the back of

my seat again. So much for celebrations. Apparently, there were going to be problems with this pregnancy that I hadn't anticipated yet.

Dodo gave me that disappointed "Bad luck, old girl" look again while readjusting the strap on her own bag and squeezed my shoulder. Then her face brightened considerably. "Tell you what. Next week, you and I'll have lunch, just the two of us. We can have salads and yogurt and—oh!—everything else that's good for the baby. How does that sound?"

It sounded a treat.

I still wasn't pregnant. I really was going to have to do something about that.

On the way home from work I picked up a couple of steaks and two bottles of pricey red. Not much for meat myself, I'd often remarked in the past that, unless a man is a vegetarian, it's amazing how chewing on meat that's still pink in the center can put an otherwise civilized man in mind of ravishing the nearest breathing body that has even a smidgen of estrogen coursing through its veins. True, the night I'd initially told Trevor that I thought I was pregnant, he'd begged off having sex by using meat making him tired as an excuse, but I'd known it had just been that: an excuse. Red meat usually makes men horny as hell. (David claims that for gay people this theory only works with filet mignon, but then of course it's just testosterone on both sides all the way.) As for the matching bottles of wine, these were also for Trevor, since, as Dodo had pointed out to me—rats!—I wasn't supposed to be drinking anymore. Just to enhance the pretense that this was a real meal and not a base seduction, I tossed in some frozen potato thingies that I could zap in the micro and a few mangy garden veggies to toss in a bowl. Dessert? I wasn't planning on us needing any.

Yes, I know that my life had become a cliché: Girl Tries

to Get Pregnant to Snare Man. But, honestly, at this point, what choice did I have? And, anyway, how many times do I have to keep pointing out that he thought I was pregnant already? So it wasn't as though it was some kind of black-and-white case of entrapment.

"My, that's a rather large glass of wine you've poured for me," Trevor pointed out.

In my overeagerness, I'd used the biggest goblet I could find as opposed to something more delicately suitable. Okay, truth time: I used a brandy balloon.

He took a sip. "Mmm, it's good though. Aren't you going to have some?"

I made a vague gesture in the general direction of where I thought my womb might be, but his head was already bent over his plate.

"Mmm, these potato thingies are top-drawer. What did you say you call them?"

"Potato Toss." The potatoes looked so *not* tossed, what with their tiny squared-off shapes and their fried casings, that I felt moved to embellish, "It's a recipe I got from David."

"Oh." He frowned at his potatoes. "Him. I always have trouble figuring out what you see in him."

"Well, he is my best friend. So there is that."

This really wasn't going as I had planned. I topped off Trevor's brandy balloon. "How's the steak?" I asked brightly, poking a fork against my own steak that I hadn't taken a bite of yet. "Is it, er, pink enough in the center for you?"

"Mmm. Perfect."

"Would you like mine as well?"

"Hmm…what?" Trevor raised his eyes from the evening *Times.* Okay, so maybe he was squeezing in a bit of reading smack-dab in the middle of my big seduction scene, but it was just the headlines. I was sure of it.

"My steak. I asked you if you'd like mine as well."

"But don't you want it yourself?"

"Oh, that," I poohed. "No. I only made two because I thought you might be really hungry after a hard day at work. And, anyway," I couldn't resist one last embellishment, "I don't think that a lot of red meat is such a good thing for the baby."

"Oh. The baby." His eyes returned to Tony Blair's recent credibility problems.

I poured out the last of the first bottle into his glass and cracked open the second.

In any event, it turned out that the best laid plans of assistant editors named Jane Taylor were about as effective as those put out by mice and men.

"I'm not really sh-sh-shure that thish-sh-sh ish-sh-sh sh-sh-shuch a good idea tonight, Janey."

"Course it is. You just need to loosen up a bit." I loosened his tie for him, hoping that might help.

"Too loosh-sh-sh. Too loosh-sh-sh. I think that'sh-sh-sh the problem—I'm too loosh-sh-sh!"

And he was right of course.

I tried pulling it...

"I don't believe it'sh-sh-sh meant to sh-sh-shtretch that far, Janey."

...and pushing it.

"Wrong direcsh-sh-sh-way. But it feelsh-sh-sh good!"

I watched as it dangled uselessly over me....

"Not working."

...and sat over it.

"That'sh-sh-sh a sh-sh-sh-shtrong maybe."

In the event, it wasn't much of a sexual experience as sexual experiences go, but I was pretty sure that something happened on that last go-round.

True, I mused as I listened to Trevor's snores, Shakespeare had been proven right yet again regarding the correlative nature of wine and performance, but all I needed was for there to have been just one strong swimmer on my side.

Just one strong swimmer and then I would have what I wanted. Then my dreams would all come true.

It was one of those perfect London days that every tourist secretly prays for. Oh, I don't mean the odd day in August when the sky is just as perfectly blue as a robin's egg and the temperature makes people walk around the city as though it were San Diego. No, I mean the kind of day in May where the rain comes down so relentlessly that, if not for the barely visible modern conveniences glimpsed through the fog, you'd swear you'd just been dropped into the middle of one of those old Sherlock Holmes movies with Basil Rathbone and Nigel Bruce, the ones with all of the historical and literary inaccuracies. The kind of day that is so atmospherically awful that it enables every tourist to later return home from their vacation and say, "Yup. It really is just as damp there as they say. And the people really don't know how to cook—can't get a decent steak to save your life."

So it was one of those perfectly miasmic London days and I had been looking for Dodo, hoping to suss her out on what to do about the latest Colin Smythe emergency, only to find her huddling outside beneath the arch of the cement building which housed our offices, only partially successful in her attempts to keep both herself and her extra-long cigarette wholly dry.

This insanity had all started about six months ago, when an American businessman from Seattle had flown in at zero hour on his white horse in order to save our company from being swallowed up by a bigger company, a pattern of acquisition that had become the norm in publishing in the past decade or so. In fact, some dire souls predicted that one day, there would just be five companies left; and that the day after that, there would just be one. Anyway, the man from Seattle's name was Steve Johnson. It was rumored that his mother had enjoyed a wartime affair with the original Churchill of Churchill & Stewart, and that it was sentiment over this, plus the fact that he believed Mr. Churchill to be his real father, that had caused him to invest such a large sum of capital into the then shaky company. The only stipulation that had accompanied Mr. Johnson's largesse—well, aside from the insistence that we make him a full member of the board whose vote would always count twice to everyone else's once—was that we declare our offices to be wholly *smokus non grata*. This dictum from a man who did eat the London meat, and enjoy it, as well as the Stilton cheese and any pastries he could get his hands on during the entire time he was here; well, at least he wouldn't have to worry about contracting lung cancer while he was in the midst of having his full-blown coronary. This dictum from a man who hadn't set foot in the country since we'd waved him off at Heathrow at the end of that one week he'd spent here six months ago. This dictum that all of us still followed religiously, despite the fact that there was no sign of Mr. Johnson's imminent return, because who knew when he might suddenly fly in again on his white charger.

So now we knew what Dodo, who would have still been a chain-smoker were it not for Steve Johnson's position, was doing outside. As for me, now that I'd found her and was ready to talk Smythe, I extracted a Silk Cut from the packet in my purse, placed it in my mouth, rooted around in my purse for my lighter, and...

"You're pregnant, Jane! You're not going to smoke that, are you?" Dodo asked, her own cigarette dangling a long ash that was so damp that it threatened to make the whole thing go out. Not bothering to wait for a reply, she reached out and yanked the cigarette from my mouth, grinding it beneath her heel.

I gave her my patented combination horrified-askance look and said, "Course not! Don't be daft. I just pull one out now and again and hold it, unlit, as a metaphoric eternal flame of all that I am willing to sacrifice for the health of my unborn child." Ugh! Where did I get this crap?

Actually, I got it from the bloody Yanks mostly. It wasn't enough that they beat our arses in one war and then, worse injury, saved our arses in another; now they had to export all of the worst of their godforsaken grasp of culture and social mores "across the pond." This meant that no one anywhere was allowed to enjoy smoking or drinking anymore, that expectant mothers spent nine months suspended in the purgatory of waiting to be accused by any Tom, Dick or waiter who thought that what they were doing to their unborn babies must be against some kind of law and that if it wasn't, it should be. These being always the same people who believed that, following a smokeless and alcohol-free pregnancy, it was perfectly okay to have one's offspring raised by strangers, never mind if the well-nourished former fetuses one day grew up to kill their own classmates. And, as for Walt Disney, well, you couldn't swing a dead cat anywhere within the borders of the European Union without hitting Mickey bloody Mouse square in his eternally grinning face. Phew! Still, due to the ever watchful eye of the Pregnancy Nutrition Police, I was probably going to have to abandon the diet of twelve smoothies a day that I'd been strictly adhering to for the past few months.

I watched Dodo suck on a rain-spattered Benson & Hedges and thought about how good it looked.

"Doesn't Trevor worry when he sees you walking around with an unlit cigarette dangling out of the corner of your mouth?" Dodo pressed. "I mean, that you might start up again?"

I thought about it for a moment. Actually, the cigarette Trevor was used to seeing me with was always lit, and no, actually, he never said a word. Oddly enough, so long as I said that the doctor reported everything was going okay, he didn't ride me at all about what I was doing with my body.

"No," I said virtuously, going all Joan of Arc. "He knows I'd never do anything to hurt our child."

Blast. Now I was going to have to give up public smoking too.

Well, I supposed, I'd have to give it up in private as well soon, anyway, once I was really pregnant.

"Was there something you came out here to talk to me about, Jane?" Dodo prompted, lighting a fresh cigarette off of the end of the other. "Surely you didn't come out here in this damp, and risk giving the fetus a cold, only to keep me company."

Actually, I came out here to have a bloody cigarette, you stupid twit, was what I wanted to say, but I couldn't very well say it now, not with Dodo being my new best girlfriend and me being pregnant and all.

"Oh," I sighed. "I just wanted to talk to you about the Smythe situation. But it can wait." I smiled tightly, patting my flat belly. "Mustn't let the fetus get wet."

Then I went back inside.

To cheer myself up, I manufactured a tilted uterus, culled from *What to Expect,* and tossed that into my sympathy-garnering bargain.

"A tilted *what?*" asked Minerva from Publicity.

Legend had it that Minerva had been with the company for so long that when the original Mr. Churchill had put his key in the door for the very first time, she'd already been there waiting for him. Since she was always the last one left in the office each night, it reinforced the image that she was merely this being who existed only in the Publicity department. Minerva had an honest-to-God beehive hairdo that was spun out of a yellow-red color that was improbable on a woman of her years and wore harlequin glasses that had a safety chain and an abundance of rhinestones on the corners.

I had been trying to get her to do some damage control on the Colin Smythe "reckon" situation, perhaps send out copies of all of the favorable prepublication reviews he'd received from other magazines (i.e., British ones) that hadn't had any trouble understanding what he'd meant by peppering his text with so many "reckons" that to American readers the book was like a bowl of chili with too much chili in it.

As a ploy to enlist Minerva's sympathies, no sooner had I mentioned Colin Smythe's dilemma than I began rubbing my own lower back and wincing—but not too much—as though bravely covering up a pain, only mentioning the tilted uterus as though I were reluctant to do so after she asked me if I were having some kind of nervous attack.

"A tilted *what?*"

I explained to her how, statistically, one in five women had the top of the uterus tilted toward the back rather than the front.

"It's really not that big of a deal," I went on bravely. "They say that in most cases, it should right itself by the end of the first trimester."

"And if it doesn't?" she prompted.

"Well, in those rare cases, it becomes stuck in the pelvis, puts pressure on the bladder something fierce, and sometimes, they have to insert a catheter to drain the urine and push the uterus back into its proper position."

"Ouch," said Minerva, but her "ouch" somehow lacked sympathy. "Well," she said, turning back to the stack of press releases she needed to get out, "let me know if it comes to that. As you say, though, it'll probably tilt itself back into place before your first trimester's up. Good luck. In the meantime, no on the Smythe. It's just not in the budget."

Perhaps one can catch more flies with honey than with vinegar but, apparently, a tilted uterus simply wasn't worth squat.

★ ★ ★

Shitshitshitshit*shit!* Still not pregnant!

I exited the bathroom in David's flat, tossed the useless at-home pregnancy test kit into the trash bin under his kitchen sink and helped myself to the extra-large bottle of vinegary Australian in his fridge.

We'd mutually concluded long ago that there was no point in wasting the good stuff on depression. We were only going to wind up pissed anyway, so why punish ourselves by throwing a lot of money into the bargain? On the other hand, it *was* worth paying the price of a hangover that a lot of cheap wine always bought a person, if only so that we'd have the reminder in the morning of why not to become alcoholics.

"Shitshitshitshit*shit!*"

"Why don't you tell me what you really think, Jane?"

"It's just that I'm so tired of not being pregnant when I want to be!"

He snapped his fingers and pointed an accusing finger at me. "Okay, now what you are doing right now, now that is really gross."

"What?" I'd taken a container of ice cream out of his freezer and was eating from it with a spoon.

"That. Mixing wine with ice cream. It's gross. You'll be sick."

"Oh, that." I went back to spooning the ice cream. "As if it would matter if I were. I'd just tell Trevor that it was morning sickness in the evening." Spoon; eat; sigh. "As if he'd care."

"What do you mean?"

I filled him in on the fact that Trevor had been less warm since he'd learned about the baby.

"To be 'less warm,' Trevor would have to have been warm to begin with, a concept that fills me with grave doubts."

I followed him to the bathroom where he commenced

to shave. David's hair grows so fast that if he doesn't shave twice a day, he begins to look like an Orthodox who's somehow wandered his way into a Calvin Klein ad.

"Oh, you're always so hard on him," I said.

"Perhaps because I still do not see what you see in him."

I leaned in the doorway, concentrating on my ice cream. "Oddly enough, he says the same thing about you."

"Yes, but in my case my conclusions are the result of rational thought." He waved the razor dismissively. "In his case, it's just a matter of meanness."

"Oh, you just don't know him. He's really very sweet."

He eyed me in the mirror as he scraped one lathered cheek. "Perhaps for a homophobe."

"How many times do I have to tell you? Trevor's not homophobic. He's just very conservative. And he doesn't particularly like Israel."

He tapped his razor against the side of the sink. "Oh, well, if it's just a matter of the entire country I come from presenting a problem…"

"Could we please not do this right now? *I* have problems!"

He wiped his face with a towel. "Oh, well, of course, Jane, if *you* have problems…"

I nearly choked on my spoon. "What does that mean? Do you think I'm self-involved?"

"Well, maybe just a smidgen."

"I'm…I'm…I'm… Fine. Tell me, how are the plans for your restaurant coming?"

"Wonderful. Thank you for asking."

"Architect's behaving?"

"Today."

"Backers haven't backed out?"

"No."

"Still don't want to give me the details? You know, I could always meander through Covent Garden and figure out which building it is for myself."

He hit the lights on his way out. "No. And, yes, I know you could, but you won't. Curiosity might kill you, but missing out on a chance to experience the other end of the element of surprise for a change would prove devastating for your personality."

I grimaced. "You know, you're beginning to do some rather weird things with the English language."

"True, but I am only just getting started. By the way, you're doing an impressively good job of impersonating a real person."

"Oh, God," I groaned, tossing the empty container of ice cream into the trash and reaching for the wine bottle again, "then I really am self-absorbed?"

"Yes." He put his arm around my shoulders and squeezed. "But don't worry. I still like you."

"But *why* do you like me?"

"Because there is nobody else like you. Because you are a natural force."

"Well, if I'm such a natural force, then why can't I get pregnant?"

David shrugged. "I don't know. Perhaps you don't really want to get pregnant."

"What an absurd thing to say. Of course I want to get pregnant. What do you think I've been going on about for the last several weeks?"

"I don't know. But it seems to me that if you really wanted to get pregnant, you would not keep putting up stumbling blocks in your own path."

"Like what, for instance?"

"Like getting Trevor drunk before sex. Anyone who has ever read the complete works of Mr. William Shakespeare knows—"

"Yes, I know all about wine, desire and performance, but I didn't intend on him getting completely inebriated. It just happened that way."

"Yes, well, I just think that if you were more serious

about having a baby, you would take it all more seriously.
You wouldn't drink.... You know, just because no one but
I can see you doing it when you're in my place, it still
doesn't make it the same as if you weren't doing it at all.
You wouldn't smoke...." He snapped his fingers. "That's
it!"

"What's it?"

"You don't really want to have a baby at all! You just
want to be pregnant without necessarily being pregnant."

"That's insane!" I puzzled over it for a moment. "And
what exactly do you mean by that?"

"Tell me, Jane, if you could be pregnant without really
being pregnant, would you?"

Of course when, not long after I'd told the girls in the
office about the baby, I further told them about Trevor's
plans to marry me, my cachet ratcheted itself up another
notch.

"You're never!" said Louise, giving me a playful swat
across the shoulder. It had never occurred to me before
that Louise, who had always appeared to hate me with a
chartreuse passion, could do playful.

Louise was the definition of "cool blonde" in every
sense of the phrase. She was cool to the point of iciness,
presenting too scary a challenge even for Stan from Accounting. As for the blond part, she was another one of
those with knife-straight hair parted on the side. (There
have been periods in my life when I've been so surrounded
by knife-straight blondes that I'd swear England was man-
ufacturing them in some little cave somewhere or something.) Louise's position at Churchill & Stewart placed her
lateral to me, meaning that she toiled in the shadows created by the greater glory of an important editor, much as
I toiled under Dodo. If Louise had been a different person, or if I had been a different person, we might have become like comrades in the trenches. But we weren't

different people. She'd hated me on first handshake and I'd responded accordingly.

"Oh, am I ever!" I returned now, swatting her shoulder for all I was worth.

Then the other women crowded around me again, just like they'd done when I first told them about the baby, and we all started schoolgirlishly jumping up and down with enthusiasm as though the solid earth were a trampoline; until, that is, Dodo pointed out that this kind of leaping wasn't good for the baby, but not before Stan from Accounting walked by and, taking in the synchronous-dancing sight of our bouncing breasts, remarked, "There's a fond sight I only normally get to see when I pay for it at female mud wrestling."

For the record, we all hated Stan from Accounting, who was slim in a nonphysically fit way, wore suits that were more expensive than his job warranted, had a brown crew cut, steel glasses with squinty blue eyes hiding behind them, and looked as though he'd gotten beat up at school on a regular basis for being gay, even though all of us who'd ever been pinched on the arse by him could testify most emphatically that he was not. Were it not for the fact that his ruthless mathematical juggling was able to save Churchill & Stewart barrels of money each year, we probably could have collectively filed suit against him and gotten him the heave-ho he deserved.

But back to my impending wedding.

Unfortunately, when Trevor had spoken to me about his intentions to marry me, it hadn't been quite the romantic proposal that my girlish exchange with Louise and the others would make it out to be.

We'd left Punch the Cat at home alone and gone out to a favorite restaurant of Trevor's, where they specialized in eggplant parmesan cooked just the way he liked it. The candle was burning, the melting pink wax dripping down in rivulets over the blues and greens that already adorned the side of the Chianti bottle. Trevor had a second bottle of Chianti, sans candle and dripping wax, that he was having no problem putting away all by himself. The salad dishes had just been removed and his eggplant was on its way. In short, everything was nearly right as rain in Trevor's world, save for the absence of Punch the Cat and the presence of a pregnant girlfriend. For my part, I'd ordered the pasta primavera over Trevor's objections that it wasn't Italian enough and, as for the Andrea Bocelli coming through the speakers, I probably wouldn't have minded it so much were it not for the fact that I heard the same bloody song blaring at me every time I tried to do the food shopping and had come to associate it with picking out fish.

"You know, Jane," Trevor said, taking a large sip from his third glass of Chianti within the half hour and picking up knife and fork to attack his eggplant, "when I said I'd stand by you, I meant every word."

Well, that certainly had a vaguely reassuring tone to it.

"Did you have anything specific in mind?" I asked, idly twirling my pasta.

"Well, you know, I was thinking that it might be doing right by the little tyke if we were to think about taking on the marriage thing as well."

"Really?"

"Yes, of course."

"But didn't I hear you once say at a cocktail party that you'd no sooner walk down the aisle before you turned thirty-five *and* had something like a gazillion trillion pounds saved up before you'd take on a wife?"

"I might have done. But that was before this happened. This changes everything."

"How so?"

"Well, for starters, it's as though the future is here, it's now. Kind of as though it came at us from the wrong direction on a conveyor belt, though, isn't it?"

"Not really."

"Okay. Fine. But if it were, then the only approach for us to take is to meet it head-on. We can't very well turn tail and try to run in the opposite direction, can we?"

"Are you asking me a serious question?"

Trevor's head snapped up. "Excuse me?"

All of a sudden, I wondered why I was resisting so. Why was I giving him such a hard time? After all, wasn't this what I'd wanted all of last year, for Trevor to ask me to marry him? At the thought of that, of finally getting my way, I felt my expression soften. I reached across the table and stilled the hand that was wielding the knife again on the eggplant, twining my fingers through his.

"Never mind," I said. "If you really mean it, Trevor, of course I'll marry you." I must have been experiencing the effects of phantom pregnancy hormones, like someone who's had to undergo a leg amputation (except that in my case I never had the leg in the first place), because I'd gone from reticent to over-the-moon enthusiastic in about zero seconds. "When were you thinking about? Right away? If we elope now, before I'm too far along, I won't have to suffice with wearing a gown with an Empire waist, like that poor woman in that famous Van Eyck painting teachers were always going on at us about in art class when we were at school."

"Good God, no, Jane!"

I wondered at his strange reaction, but reacted in my own fashion nonetheless. "Well, you may have something there. I know we didn't go to the same schools, so I'm sure it's possible that your teachers focused on some other painting."

"No, of course I didn't mean that, Janey." He removed his fingers from mine and made that irritated swatting-flies gesture he had, the one that irritated me so much. "Of course my teachers went on ad nauseum about the Van Eyck—they all do. No, what I meant was that, while I do insist on standing by you and doing the right thing, I see absolutely no reason why we should marry before the child is actually born."

It had more typically been my experience in life that it was me who usually caused another person to choke on their food; now, as I felt a little green pea stick in my throat, I got to find out firsthand what it was like. I gulped some water. "You mean that literally, that we should wait until after the child's born and get married while I'm still bloated up like a boa constrictor having a meal or something?"

"Well, of course, if you want to, we can wait—no pun intended—until you've lost all of the weight. Just so long as it's after the delivery, it doesn't matter much to me when it is."

"And why is that so important to you, waiting until after the birth before getting married?" I was beginning to feel very hard done by.

"Oh, well, you know." He dabbed at a red spot beneath the corner of his mouth but missed getting it all. "*You* know. There are all of these things that might happen along the way. Things might not work out with the baby, you know, coming to term and all. Why, look at what nearly happened to Princess Niquie."

"Let me get this straight. You're willing to marry me in order to give our child a name, but only after I've actually given birth, so that you can make sure that the child survives and you're not wasting a good wedding for nothing?"

He at least had the good grace to look mortified. Not that it helped.

"Well, Jane, of course when you put it like that it sounds as crass as can be. All I meant…"

But as Trevor's voice droned on, my mind began to drift back to earlier in the evening when, even before I'd rudely been made to realize how pragmatically the prospective groom was hedging his bets, I'd felt reticent about "taking on the marriage thing as well," as Trevor had so romantically put it. Perhaps the reason I'd felt so hesitant had something to do with the niggling feeling that had been plaguing me ever since that day in the bathroom when I'd proudly revealed my twin pink lines. Even then, all that talk about standing by me, while somewhat noble in a shotgun-to-the-head sense, had smacked of being not quite the level of enthusiasm one would hope for under such circumstances.

Still, I'd always been something of a pragmatic girl myself; a make-do girl, actually. Ever since I could remember, it seemed as though I'd always had to make do with whatever life dealt me, always had to settle. True, I had been rather defensively aggressive with Sophie when we were little, but that had been born of necessity. Making the transformation from being a make-do girl to being a monkey-see, monkey-do girl really takes no more effort than a hop, skip, and a jump, the two being only one evolutionary step removed from each other. So now I'd had my fling with the monkey-see, monkey-do part, in relation to the as yet faux pregnancy, but even I could see that if I also wanted Trevor to marry me, I was going to have to morph back into the make-do part. Well, when push came to shove, I could settle with the best of them.

"Fine," I forestalled his torrent of words with a tight smile. I no longer cared exactly what he'd meant. "Fine. I accept your proposal. Under your conditions."

He smiled the smile of the greatly relieved. "You won't regret it, Jane. You'll see. It'll be best this way."

Not long afterward, he excused himself to the facilities as the tuxedoed waiter came to clear our plates. The moment by myself gave me a chance to think about the months ahead.

Well, when I really thought about it, I realized that it wasn't too bad the way things were turning out. So I'd had to settle a bit. Big deal. It wasn't as though, even if Trevor were to marry me tonight, I'd seriously expect him to want to stay married to me if it turned out that I never got pregnant after all and he learned that I never was in the first place. This way, at least, I'd get the fun of planning a wedding over the next several months. The other way, *my way,* I'd have gotten married now with the knowledge that I might have to let him divorce me less than a year down the road. Still, it did rankle that he was in no rush to marry me for *me,* making me feel just a wee bit bitter.

While Trevor was still using the facilities, the waiter returned with dessert menus. "Do you think that the *signor* will be interested in having a sweet this evening?"

I didn't even bother looking to see if they had Trevor's favorite chocolate mousse. I reached across the table and drained the rest of Trevor's Chianti glass, depositing it on the waiter's tray. "Only if the *signor* feels like wearing it on his head."

I had survived the critical first two months of my pregnancy with my baby still intact. By now, he or she was much more human looking and far bigger than the grain of rice it had represented just one month before. It was approximately one and one-quarter inches long from crown to bottom, one-third of which would be its big head, and weighed about a third of an ounce.

It didn't seem like very much, really; in my university days, there had been times when I'd smoked that much marijuana, single-handedly, on any given Thursday evening.

My baby now had its very own beating heart, and real arms and legs where formerly there had been only buds. Now it was working on developing fingers and toes, or pointers and piggies as my uncle Jack used to call them just prior to giving Soph's and my piggies a tickle that neither of us were ever sure we wanted. Bone was starting to re-place cartilage.

We definitely had a solid start of something going on here.

the third month

Surprisingly enough, to hear me tell it, I didn't always hate my sister Sophie.

Once upon a time, my own behavior during the Kewpie doll incident notwithstanding, I'd actually dreamed of having a big sister who could generously help me figure out the ins and outs of life on this crazy planet; a big sister who could be a best friend as well as a blood relative; a big sister who wouldn't crow over her own successes and smile at my defeats with condescension or, worse, confirmation.

But I'd gotten Sophie instead.

There had been one twelve-hour period there, however, about five years after our father died, when I didn't hate her at all. Our mother had gone out on the first and last date she would ever go on, and she had left us without a baby-sitter, having decided that Sophie, now well into double digits, was sufficiently mature to take charge of me, especially since Soph was "the dearest angel who ever lived." According to our mother, who told me this and told me often, I could do worse than to adopt Sophie as my role model.

No sooner had the red lights on the car of Chance Reynolds, our mother's date, disappeared around the corner of the gravel drive, than I turned to Little Miss In-Charge. "I've got an idea for a game," I announced.

Sophie bit her lip. "Will it get me in trouble?"

"Nah. You're gonna love it. You'll even like the taste."

"Oh dear." She'd picked that one up from our mother and, I must say, it sounded ridiculous coming regularly as it did out of the mouth of a twelve-year-old.

"Isn't that the key to Mother's liquor cabinet?" she asked, as I dangled something on a chain hypnotically before her very eyes.

"You *are* a clever girl. We, my dear Soph, are going to play a little game called Bartender and Patron." I led her through the house and to the cabinet in the entertainment room, just like you'd lead a seal at a water show.

With her just-washed straight blond hair, knife-parted on the side, her fresh white cotton granny nightgown and her yogurt complexion, she looked just like an advert for the perfect English child. This put her in stark contrast to my own ill-advisedly sunburned cheeks, self-cut hairstyle that didn't quite work, and low-cut leopard pajamas I'd talked my mother's sister Harriet into buying for me when no one else was around.

"I think it's safe to say that I should be the bartender, don't you?" I asserted, taking my position behind the mahogany bar and bending over to unlock the cabinet. "After all, my attire makes me more suited to the position, while yours, well, makes you look like someone who could use a drink."

This, of course, was back in the days when it was still acceptable for people to drink beverages other than wine and beer openly, and so our mother's cabinet was stocked admirably, particularly since most of the stocking had been done by our late father, a man who'd never been known to say no. The time period meant that there were also cushioned leather barstools set up in front of the bar, as though people might freely indulge in our household at any time, although no one ever did since we'd put Father in the ground. I indicated that Sophie should pull one up and she carefully did, hopping on, her clean feet with their neatly trimmed little toenails dangling over the side.

"So," I said, pulling a crystal tumbler out and dusting it off for her, "what'll it be, madam?"

"Umm…" She hesitated, pulling on her lower lip, but then brightening after a moment. "A sherry?" she requested hopefully.

"Can't you do any better than that? Why, you can have a taste of one of those practically any time you want to, so long as Aunt Harriet's visiting. How about something you haven't had before?"

More lower lip pulling and umming on Sophie's part while I rooted around among the mostly dust-covered bottles in the cabinet.

"*Aha!*" I gave the cry of the newly resurrected as I rose with my find. "Well—" I placed it on the bar "—what do you think of that?"

Sophie studied the label on the bottle I'd drawn from the back, peering closely at the reassuring pictorial depiction of a cluster of blackberries on the vine. "Blackberry Snaps," she misread slowly, as though she were a bit of an idiot instead of twelve years old. She looked up at me with a weak smile adorning her lips. "How bad can it be?"

"That's the spirit!"

To be fair to myself, it wasn't as though I knew how much I was giving her when I filled her tumbler to the brim and, as for the percentage of proof listed clearly on the front of the bottle, well, at that stage in my life such a figure meant almost nothing to me.

She took a sip, grimacing at the first strongly alcoholic

taste. "Ghastly," she pronounced, wiping the residue from her lips with the back of her hand, as if in doing so she could make the flavor go away altogether. Instead of pushing the tumbler disgustedly away, however, as I might have expected her to have done, she grabbed onto it again, studying it closely, as though it were some kind of schoolyard nemesis that she could overcome only by staring it down. "That's odd," she commented. "At first, it really does taste ghastly. But then, after you've gotten past the horrible part, the blackberry part begins to hit you and then it's really a bit of all right."

I'd never heard buttoned-down Sophie use the "a bit of all right" phrase in her life. This was getting interesting, and going right according to my plan. (Actually, there wasn't any set plan, per se, save a general plan in which I merely wanted *something* to happen.)

Sophie took another sip, a bigger one this time, then gestured in my direction with her now half-empty glass. "Aren't you going to have any yourself?"

"Course. Just wanted to set you up right first, that's all. You know, that *is* how you play Bartender and Patron."

I made a show of looking inside the cabinet for another large tumbler like hers. There were the remaining eleven of a matched set there, but instead, I selected a single-shot glass. After all, I may not have known what exactly a particular proof implied, but I wasn't stupid about liquor. "That's odd," I informed her as I filled her tumbler to the brim and poured the single shot into my glass, "it appears that there was only the one like yours under there. Oh, well." I saluted her with my shot. "I'll just have to keep refilling mine more often."

But I didn't. As the evening wore on, I kept refilling our glasses at the same rate, so that the rate roughly fell that she was consuming four ounces of "snaps" to my every one. By the time we were each on our third, I began to feel like someone else completely. The thought vaguely entered my mind, just once, that if I were being so affected, God knows what was happening to four-to-one Sophie.

Apparently, what was happening to Sophie was that she was beginning to feel like someone else as well.

Sophie lay on the couch in reverse position like one of those tarot cards, perhaps The Hanged Man or something. Her back was on the part where her bottom should have been, with her now tangled hair dangling over the side until it grazed the carpet. There were purple stains on her white cotton granny nightgown, which was somewhat rucked up about her hips. As for her bare legs, they were straight up in the air, ankles leaning against the top of the couch while her toes danced to their own tune, one that looked remarkably like the Charleston. Every time she tried to slur something else at me, which was often, she gestured with her right hand, the half-filled tumbler she held on to metronoming wildly over Mother's new cream-colored couch.

"Do you know, Jane…" she began.

"Watch the glass, Soph," I cautioned for the umpteenth time, steadying her hand with my own.

I was seated cross-legged on the floor beside her in such a way that I could keep an eye on her dangerous glass, her face upside down to me. In that position, with some real-live color on her cheeks, I found her to be almost pretty.

"Do you know, Jane," she began again, more deter-minedly this time, "I don't particularly like being Mother's favorite. I don't know how this all ever started. Do you really imagine that it's ever any fun, feeling as though one has to be perfect at all times?"

And it was at that exact moment that the feeling that had been growing in me all night long fully crystallized, for it was at that exact moment that I first loved my sister.

"You really don't like it?" I asked trepidatiously, for once the cautious one.

"Cor, no," she shook her head in time with the glass,

dropping idiomatically back into that linguistic black hole in her personality from which she'd dragged that "bit of all right" line earlier. She burped, covering her mouth with her hand far too late. "Hate it." Now Sophie the Virtuous wasn't even speaking in full sentences anymore.

The bonding just got better from there.

We baked a lopsided cake, making a mess of the kitchen as we dyed the frosting with all of the colors in the dye box, meaning that it finally ended up being a brownish-black with bits of blue, green, yellow and red on the edges where we hadn't mixed it in thoroughly. This brownish-black color was very deceptive since it would make eaters think that the frosting was chocolate fudge when in reality it was meant to be vanilla buttercream. Still, I don't think it mattered much since, to my recollection, no one ever ate any.

Then we arranged the furniture throughout the public parts of the house to our own liking.

After that, Sophie threw up some of her Blackberry "Snaps" while I held her hair out of the way. For the first time in my life, I felt like a sister.

Then we went to bed.

"Night, Jane," Sophie said sleepily as I tucked her in. "Love you." Then she rolled over.

I studied the white cotton back before pulling the cord on her lamp. "Night, Soph," I spoke softly, proceeding with the utmost caution. "Like you too."

Then I retired to my own room next door.

The next morning, when our mother discovered the damage and the unlocked cabinet, having not turned on the lights upon her return the night before but having done so in the stark light of early day, she went immediately to Sophie's room next door. I heard the sound of murmuring voices, but was unable to make out words until Sophie's voice pealed out: "And it was all Jane's idea!"

The fact that I heard her wretch up the schnapps for the

second time not long afterward did nothing to mitigate the circumstantial fact that I was now back to hating my sister.

Nearly two decades later, my feelings toward Soph had changed little.

It was a clear Saturday in June, early on in my "third month," and I'd invited my mother and Sophie over for elevenses. I'd figured that, having already told everyone that I worked with (including those that I hated like Stan from Accounting), as well as the man who was in fact supposedly the father of my child, I might as well tell my mother and sister before news reached them first in that telephone-line sort of way that this kind of news always seems to have. I'd laid in a vast supply of decaf teas, in honor of Sophie's virtuous-pregnant-lady eating patterns, as well as enough pastries the size of a small person's head for my mother. Never mind fairy cakes; I had giant napoleons, gargantuan éclairs, and I'd even purchased a full-size pink-and-blue cake in the shape of a baby rattle.

So naturally, my mother didn't show.

"What do you mean she's not coming?" I fishwifed at Sophie as the rest of her body followed her swollen belly into my living room.

At any other time, I would have been pleased to note that the hormones of pregnancy had dulled the normally bright sheen of her hair, leaving it flat and stringy compared to my own healthy cut; but I was too busy having a childish meltdown to take satisfactory note of that or the fact that pregnancy had clearly caused her to take leave of the extraordinary fashion sense she'd always possessed, the oversize smock she wore with its little bow at the collar proving once and for all that too much progesterone can be a very dangerous thing in the wrong hands.

"What do you mean she's not coming?" I demanded a second time as Tony deposited her on my sofa, kissed her on the top of the head and promised to return to collect her in an hour, before escaping.

"I'm sorry, Jane," she said, not really sounding very bothered about it at all as she sought to adjust *my* pillows for *her* comfort. Anyone would have thought that I was practically hopping from foot to foot in front of her for my own benefit. "But Mother really couldn't make it. She said to give you her apologies, but when she originally told you she would come, she'd forgotten that Saturday morning at eleven actually means Saturday morning at eleven and that's when she prefers to have her nails done."

"Her *nails?* But this is important!"

Now it was Sophie's turn to sniff with indignation. "Oh. Important, is it? Well, you could have said as much on the phone, instead of being so mysterious about it as you were. I mean, do you have to always be so Mata Hari? 'If you're free at eleven on Saturday, I'd love it if you could pop by.' Why can't you just say it's urgent if it's urgent? God!"

"What's the matter with you, Soph, maternity bra too tight?"

"No. I've just got to pee again for the fortieth time today. Do you mind?" she asked, returning to the state of dull mildness that generally characterized her personality as she struggled to her feet, one hand to her lower back as she slowly made her way down the hall. Good God, you'd think she was ready to pop at any moment, instead of being only something like seven months gone.

"Ah," she said as she came back into the living room a few moments later, hand to belly with the beatific smile restored. "I feel ever so much better now." She resettled herself on the sofa as I poured her a beaker of chamomile tea. "So tell me, Jane, what was so important that you wanted us both here so badly today? You know," she leaned toward me, more reasonably now but also not giving me a reasonable chance to answer the question she'd just posed, "if you had told Mother that you had something important to tell us both, you know she probably would have tried to find another time to get her nails done."

This last comment made me feel so unreasonably exasperated that, if I hadn't known better, I would have sworn that I was pregnant, too. "When," I demanded with deliberate steel in my tone, "was the last time I invited you both to come round?"

She made a considering face for a moment, then answered, eyes wide, "Never."

"And how long have I been inhabiting this flat?"

She considered again. "Mmm…couple of years?"

"Close enough. So if I've lived here a fair length of time and I've never invited you both over, then if I did it must be because of something…" and here I left a blank where the last word should be, making a rolling-along motion with my hand as though she were a semi-bright child who might be depended on to guess if given enough time and encouragement.

"…important?" she finally filled in after a lengthy pause.

"Bing." I applauded. "Give the girl a cake," which I tried to do but she declined, claiming it wasn't wholesome for the baby and did I have any radishes instead.

"Don't be ridiculous," I said.

"What's so ridiculous about radishes? You are a fairly health-conscious person. Anyway, I've been having an uncontrollable urge for them lately. That and cake. But since I mustn't have the cake—"

"Never mind that now," I said, picking up Punch the Cat from the dining table and tossing him back on the ground where he properly belonged. I didn't know where he'd been hiding all morning but, apparently, he'd developed an uncontrollable urge for cake as well, as evidenced by the healthy serving of buttercream frosting he'd managed to swipe off of the pink side of the rattle cake. I smiled what I hoped was a sincere smile and took a seat beside Sophie, determining to do things nicely. "What I wanted to tell you was——"

"You know, pregnant women aren't supposed to be around strange cats *or* change litter boxes."

I rubbed the bridge of my nose, praying for patience. For this, I'd given up a glorious Saturday morning that I could have been spending with the father of my child, biking through the park? I'd traded the park for, of all things, *toxoplasmosis?*

Of course, truth to tell, I wouldn't have been biking with Trevor if Sophie weren't there. Even though it was a Saturday, he'd left early to attend to some pressing work that he said he could do even though the office was closed on Saturdays. He'd been doing that a lot lately: working. And, of course, if Sophie weren't there, I'd be working, too. Since the slush pile that accumulates on the metaphorical shores of publishing houses never really ebbs back to the ocean where so much of it belongs, and since Dodo had additionally been entrusting me with more of her work lately, my pregnancy having earned me an odd kind of office status, I'd been taking more and more work home, too. Still, I told myself, I had invited Sophie for the purpose of bonding....

"Yes," I said, trying to fight off the residual feeling that I'd rather be reading bad writing than discussing litter boxes, "I believe I remember reading about that somewhere."

"It has something to do with a disease they can carry. They pick it up when they go outside and kill and eat rats and other things."

"Yes. I know. But Punch the Cat isn't a strange cat, not really. Well, I mean, he *is* a strange cat but not in the sense you mean. Anyway, he never goes outside, much as I'd like him to, so there's really no worry that he's——"

"We still had a cat when I was first pregnant."

"You did?" This was news to me. But then, Sophie hadn't been to my flat since I'd lived there, so why on earth should I have known that she had once kept a cat in hers?

"Yes," she replied, clearly not bothered at all herself by our mutual lack of knowledge regarding each other's lives. "Bugles, she was called."

"For any reason?"

"Reason? I don't know. Tony named her and I never asked. Anyway, when I got pregnant and he wanted me to give up work, he said it wouldn't be good for me to be around Bugles and her litter box all day, even though all the books say that if you have the cat already there's probably no need to get rid of it. So we put an ad in the paper and the cutest little girl came to the door with her parents and with her very own box—"

"For herself or for Bugles?"

"Excuse me?"

"Was the box for the cat or the cute little girl?"

"Why, for the cat, of course. I don't see why you would ever think—"

"Oh, would you just be quiet!" I shouted. "Can't you see that I'm pregnant?"

"No, of course I can't, because you're so skinny. But anyway, getting back to the cat—" But before I could cut her off this time, she did it to herself, as her hands flew to the sides of her face in disbelief.

"You're never!" she cried, oddly echoing the girls at the office.

"Oh, am I ever," I replied, fully versed now in my lines.

"My God," she said in a hushed tone, and then she did something that she'd never done before. She reached out and hugged me, tenderly pulling me to her as though she were my older sister by far more than one year.

Nearly twenty years ago she'd said she loved me but, much as I had wanted to attribute it to reality at the time, I'd known it was just because I'd kept her pretty hair out of the vomit. Now she wasn't saying it, but her actions were showing it; only this time, it wasn't for something I had done for her. This time, if it wasn't necessarily for who I was, it was for something she thought I was capable of doing, something in me. Perhaps one of my most secret dreams was finally going to come true. Perhaps I was finally going to achieve a sisterly relationship with my own sister.

"My God!" she said again, more gleefully this time. "Do you know what this means?"

I shrugged noncommittally: no, for "not really"; yes, for "what do I look—stupid?"

Sophie accepted the no. "It means that our children are going to be the same age and they're going to be cousins!"

I caught on to the possibility that a new generation brings, the extended hope of second chances. I impulsively grabbed her hands. "Maybe they'll even like each other!"

"Oh," she said, "*this* calls for a celebration. We need cake."

"But you said—"

"Oh, to hell with perfect nutrition. We can start being nauseatingly good again tomorrow. In the meantime," she said conspiratorially, "let's split an éclair. And a napoleon. And maybe a piece of that nice rattle cake, if you can make it just big enough to include both the blue and pink parts but staying away from the part that the cat swiped because that probably wouldn't be too good. Oh," she ohed again, only this time solicitously, "that is, of course, if you're feeling up to it. God knows *I* know that the first trimester can be a pretty wonky time for a woman's stomach."

"Oh," I brushed off the morning sickness I wasn't having as I cut a massive slice of cake, "I haven't been bothered much by that. Must have been lucky enough to inherit Gran Taylor's genes. Remember what she used to say? About how she'd rather give birth to a houseful of children than go on one trip to the dentist?"

Sophie laughed. "And remember what Mother used to

say? That the only reason Gran Taylor could make that claim was because back then they used to knock women out, before Lamaze got into the act, and that anyway Gran Taylor was a drunk?"

"I remember."

At Sophie's insistence, we ate off one plate, using two forks.

"Oh," she sighed, "this is going to be just heavenly."

"Our babies being the same age?" I asked, thinking she was still reading from the same page. "Them being cousins and maybe even liking each other?"

"Well, there is that. But also," she conceded coyly, "there's the added bonus of your being pregnant taking a lot of the pressure off of me."

"Oh?" I put my fork down.

"Well, with both of us being pregnant now, and you more newly so, Mother's bound to transfer some of the attention she's been smothering me with onto you."

So, similar to the incident nearly twenty years before, Sophie had an ulterior motive for her enthusiasm for me.

To distract myself from this unpleasant notion, I told Sophie about the plans Trevor and I had for getting married.

She smiled conspiratorially again. "Mother might even begin to finally like you," she nodded knowingly.

Gore Vidal once said, "Every time my friend succeeds, I die a little death," a perfect encapsulation of the writing life that I frequently found myself quoting to my colleagues in the publishing world. That said, in actuality I made it a practice to see my friends' successes as my successes because, really, if one didn't adopt that approach, at the end of the day what point was there in living?

"Tell me again about Christopher," I said to David, practically scampering along beside him as we neared the kebab takeaway on Tottenham Court Road. "It is Christopher, right?"

"Yes, that's right, and he is the most wonderful man I have met since I have been living in your country. He is English, but not at all English, if you know what I mean, and he's a real rakehell."

"You mean he's a libertine?"

"No, I believe he votes Labor."

"That's not what I meant." He walked through the door and then held it for me. Always the perfect gentleman, had it been a pull, he'd have just pulled and waited. "And I don't think that's what you meant, either."

"Then perhaps I meant that he is a rapscallion."

"No, I really don't think that's quite the word you want."

"Fine." He held my chair for me, wiping the seat off first. The Tandoori Crown had a whopping two tables and was nothing if not marginally filthy, but they did the best curry around. This was only true, however, if you were in the know enough to know to order it to stay; if you really did order it to take away, they might throw just about anything into your bag. "Then let's just say that I love him more than I love anyone I've met in this country since I met you. I love him like Bibi on a good day when Bibi still had good days."

"That's saying a lot."

He merely nodded emphatically.

As I looked at him, a change came over his features, his face opening up with a sheer uncomplicated joy that I had rarely seen, except on the faces of very small children who were fortunate enough to have wonderful parents. When David rose out of his chair, I turned to see the object of his untempered delight and came face-to-face with his Christopher for the first time.

I had been vaguely expecting something along the lines of the femininely male opposite of David, but what I was confronted with was another David minus the accent.

"You must be Christopher," I said, holding out my hand. "You and David met when he needed to replace the architect on his restaurant."

"Yes, I did know that," he said, giving my hand a shake that was warm enough to leach the sarcasm out of his words, transforming it into the basis for a future familiarity. "And you must be Jane. You and David met when he was first moving into the Knightsbridge flat and he needed to borrow a wrench and you answered the door nearly naked and you thought that he was trying to make a pass and you grew offended when he didn't, but then you realized he was gay and you both became the best of friends and have been ever since, not that homosexuality or wrenches have anything to do with it."

"Yes, I suppose I did know that, too." I could see what David meant about Christopher being English but not at all English. "Are you sure you're not American?"

"No," he said, opening his menu, giving it the most cursory of glances and then placing his order. "Why? Were you expecting someone more mincing than I?"

Well, I couldn't actually say that I had been, could I? "No, it's just—"

"You know, we don't all mince. It's not a prerequisite or something."

"I know that. It's just—"

"Sometimes two men that are a lot alike, like David and I, fall in love. There doesn't have to be a 'woman' partner involved, even though books and movies would have you think so."

"Yes, I am in publishing and I do know—"

"There's no reason—"

This time I cut him off. "All I meant was that you talk an awful lot for someone other than an American."

"Oh. That. Well, my mother was from New Jersey."

Then he let out a huge laugh, a bark of a laugh really, the kind of laugh that must have originally given the name to the guffaw. Perhaps the fact that it was literally right in my face was what made me jump back in my seat.

"Excuse me," I began, "but I don't really see—"

Pound, pound, pound. Christopher pounded his open palm on the top of the wobbly wooden table as David guffawed right along with him.

"You should see your face!" David roared, wiping at his eyes with the back of one hand.

"When David first told me about you," Christopher supplied in halting starts as their mutual hilarity dribbled down, "you know, the story about you nearly naked at the door and the wrench—"

"Yes," I interjected, versed by his example in my lines, "I do still remember that incident."

"—I also told him—" David picked up Christopher's narration "—that in spite of the bizarre circumstances of our first meeting, that you were the toughest woman I had ever known, and that included all of the women I had known back home who carried Uzis, and that you were nearly impossible to take the piss out of."

"To which *I* said," Christopher continued, "'Just watch me.'"

"So we made a bet," pinged David, handing Christopher a wad of crumpled notes that looked like low denominations, but still...

"And I won!" ponged Christopher, accepting the money and roaring off on another tearing laugh.

I had finally recovered. "Then you didn't mean that whole tirade about mincing and everything?"

"Oh, of course I *meant* it, but just the words and not as a tirade."

"And your mother's not from New Jersey?"

"Well, actually, that part's true too."

Oh, well, so long as it worked for them.

Over steaming plates of chicken samosa and *aloo* samosa—we were in a very samosa mood—they told me again about the details behind Christopher replacing the architect on David's project. Sure, I'd heard David's version of it before, but they were still in the stage where they

were new to each other, still in the stage where they wel-
comed the chance to relive aloud any of the details of their
coming together, and I was happy to be the excuse for their
happy retelling.

David was still reluctant to give me too many details on
his project, claiming that he wanted it to be a total surprise, which made me wonder what he could possibly be
doing with food that would seem so new. But Christopher couldn't keep himself from bringing it up, since it was
their original common ground, and at one point he teas-
ingly suggested to David that he rethink the name as well
as the theme. "You could call it Fish! *Fish! FISH!!!*" he
roared, writing it out on the paper tablecloth for me so that
I could fully appreciate the punctuation, although I failed
to grasp the joke. It didn't bother me, though, because
David got it, roaring right along with Christopher. Apparently, my best friend was in love.

I looked at David and his Christopher laughing, and as
I looked at them, I thought wistfully of Trevor. Birds did
it. Bees did it. Even Israelis with hairy knees did it. If they
could do it, why couldn't I fall in love?

"Surely you're not planning on going to the gym today,
are you?" Dodo pointedly asked, gesturing at the nylon
bag I'd pulled out from under my desk, preparatory to my
early four-thirty departure.

"Er," I responded astutely.

"Don't you think that by now you should be thinking
about giving up weight training and running? After all, that
bending and pounding can't possibly be good for the
baby."

Rats. I kept forgetting about the blasted baby.

Being pregnant in the twenty-first century, I was fast
learning, was an experience something akin to standing in
the middle of an overloaded minefield with your fetus and
saying, "God, I hope this turns out all right." If it wasn't

that smoking resulted in a higher risk of low birth weight—a statistic that one couldn't help but be sure was blown to pieces by the very fact of Frank Sinatra since it was impossible to picture Frank's mother *not* being a smoker and since anyone who knew anything about Frank knew that he'd been born weighing thirteen pounds—then it was that drinking turned your baby into an alcoholic. Okay. Fine. Even I had to admit that if the host body weighed something like sixty times more than the guest, it probably made sense to stay away from substances strong enough to intoxicate the larger of the two. But then there was all this other stuff about cat litter (which actually worked to my advantage), about hot tubs and saunas, about electric blankets and heating pads, about caffeine, about X rays, about household hazards—including lead, bad tap water, insecticides, paint fumes—about, apparently, as Dodo was presently pointing out to me, something called the Valsalva maneuver.

"What the hell is that?" I asked her.

"Holding your breath and straining. If a woman wants to continue weight training during her pregnancy, it's permissible to do *light* weight lifting—notice the stress on the *light*—but she must remember to breathe out upon lifting and must always, always avoid the Valsalva maneuver."

"How the hell do you know all this stuff?"

She hoisted a copy of *What to Expect* from her desk drawer, waved it at me and announced, "I couldn't let you go through all of this alone, could I? I mean, I know from what you've said in the past that you consider your mother and Sophie to be useless as far as any form of support goes, and as for other girlfriends..." She let her voice trail off here, being too polite to point out overtly that I had none. "Anyway," she continued brightly, "I thought that, since you and I have become such good friends, it was only fair that I arm myself with the appropriate knowledge so that I can be as supportive as possible."

Great. Here I had singled Dodo out because she had no sisters, had no girlfriends, was thirty-five and had no intention of ever having any children, and now she was declaring her determination to become a know-it-all on the subject of pregnancy, and all for my sake.

Great again, I further thought as she embraced me in a girl-power hug. Now I had the Valsalva maneuver to worry about, along with everything else.

Was it any wonder that the modern pregnant woman—in the first pregnancy, at any rate—appeared to glide through the world like a victim of shell shock? There were so many millions of little things she had to worry about that could go wrong, so many things that she could later feel responsible for, that it was as though she lived in a constant state of dread and fear, at war with the elation that people kept telling her she must be feeling—usually the same people who had her worried that she'd precipitated a potential problem by eating a piece of fish without first contacting an environmental protection agency to find out if it had been contaminated with PCBs, which, if the fetus is exposed to, can possibly lower IQ. No wonder the modern expectant mother needed extra coddling just to get through it all without having a complete breakdown of nerve. What did women in previous times experience?

I'll tell you one thing. At the risk of sounding like my mother, in the good old days, people didn't worry about all of this stuff. Ignorance was indeed bliss. True, the infant mortality rate was much higher back then, but surely there were other contributive factors. The typical farmer's wife, the way I see it, got pregnant a number of times, didn't even think that being exposed to cat shit could be a problem since she was exposed to so many other kinds of shit, drank the water, used as much heat as she could find to keep warm, drank some of her husband's whiskey occasionally for medicinal purposes, took puffs off hand-rolled cigarettes if she felt like it, lifted all kinds of heavily weighted things all the time without worrying about what breathing method she was using, lost some babies, kept some babies, and died herself without ever once feeling personally responsible for her household's survival rate.

But I knew, in the sensible part of my brain, that those times weren't these times, and that if a pregnant woman today were to behave blithely about what the public perceived as safety issues, she'd probably be arrested on charges of negligence before the outcome concerning her baby's health had even been determined.

Anyway, I had other things to worry about. For, according to Dodo, I had an obstetrician to pick out.

"What do you mean you haven't picked an obstetrician out yet for the baby?" Dodo nearly shrieked in my ear, which meant that anyone in the office who was within earshot got the same earful that I was getting, only less painfully.

I don't know how getting the name of an obstetrician had managed to slip my mind. After all, I, like Dodo, had read some of *What to Expect* and so should have known that by the time a woman was into her third month, it was pretty much well considered SOP to have found someone who would commit to delivering one's baby. Whenever Trevor asked how the pregnancy was progressing, I made up a recent doctor's appointment and said that everything was going fine. What more did people want? Details?

"Er," I said, intelligently, "did I actually say I hadn't picked one out yet?"

"Actually, you did," said Constance, our overpaid and almost underaged receptionist who, it being Tuesday and therefore not Friday, was at her desk. I had always suspected the overpaid part since she wore the season's latest over her waifish frame, had funky accessories, such as a whole bunch of different colored contact lenses, including violet and turquoise, and had her black hair coifed in an ultrachic short style that looked like she had it trimmed each week at a high-end salon. And, as for the underaged part, all you had to do was look at her; for, despite her expensive trappings, she looked more like she was just a guest at Churchill & Stewart, having come in with her mother as part of some Take Your Daughter to Work program, than someone with a legitimate right to any pay.

"Er." There it was again. Who the hell did I think I was, bloody Hugh Grant? "That may have been what I said, but it was not necessarily what I meant."

"Do tell," said Louise, the saucy git who was assistant editor to the editor who was most jealous of Dodo's success, as she played with the office copy machine. Louise always pretended an urgent need to copy something whenever she wanted to listen in on other people's conversations, the dead giveaway being when she tucked her long and straight blond hair behind one elfin ear, the better to hear us all, my dear. Now she turned her back to the copier, leaned her butt against it as though it was the bar at the local pub, crossed her arms in front of what can only be described as scary breasts, and said, "Do tell us all, Jane, what you necessarily meant."

Yes, this was the same Louise who had jumped up and down with me so enthusiastically the month before when I'd told her of my impending marriage. Since then, however, the ardor of the women in the office regarding my procreative and matrimonial double coup had cooled somewhat and I couldn't quite place my finger on why. Could it have been jealousy over this embarrassment of riches my life was providing me with? Were they, too, longing for morning sickness or, even better, the extra-special treatment that came with it? Did they also want to become engaged, with the Pollyannaish hope that, like heroines in a Shakespeare comedy, they could end their stories poised on the edge of bliss rather than continuing on into an Act VI where, inevitably, marital fights began to break out over rights to the remote control, whose turn it was to take out the garbage, and whether or not it was really necessary to visit in-laws every weekend? It was amazing, really, how quickly women could turn the worm. Even being a woman myself, I found that I could never predict with any statistical certainty which way they'd come down on anything.

Constance lined up beside Louise, although the effect was somewhat lost since her breasts were, well, nowhere near as competitive. "Yes, do, Jane."

"Could you excuse me for just a tick?" I winced a smile. "I promised one of our more neurotic authors that I'd call her back promptly at—" I hurriedly consulted my watch "—*now,* and I'm worried she'll put rocks in a burlap sack, rope it around her waist and walk into the Thames to die if I don't call on time." I winced another smile. "You know the type." I backed toward my office. "Really. I promise. Won't be a tick."

Safe in my office, the door closed, I picked up my mobile and punched in the number for David's mobile. No point in risking the use of the office phone, I figured, since who knew what kind of record the company kept of calls. Besides, I thought as I waited impatiently for David to pick up, I did have all of those fucking free minutes to use up.

"Shalom?" he said.

"Do you always answer like that for everyone," I asked, "or do you just reserve it for when you see my number flashing on your caller I.D.?"

"It's just something I do for you, Jane. I know how much you like getting the full ethnic treatment."

"Thanks so much for always thinking about me, but I haven't got time for that right now. Are you busy?"

"I can't believe you just asked me that."

"How come?"

"Because you never have before."

"Oh." I shrugged, even though I knew he couldn't see

me. "It must have been an aberration. But, really, are you—busy?"

"Well, I am working here on attaining my lifelong dream—"

"Oh. That. Well, that can certainly keep—" I lowered my voice to a hissing whisper "—because I need your help."

"For what?"

"Dodo and the girls are pressuring me to name an obstetrician."

"So?" He was whispering too now. "You're resourceful. Just make a name up."

"I can't just make a name up."

"Why not? You've made up an entire pregnancy so far. How hard can it be to pick a vaguely medical-sounding doctor's name out of a hat?"

"Yes, but what if they bother to check? These women are very nosy." I paused. "And why are you whispering too?"

"I'm just trying to be companionable," he whispered again. "Seriously, though, Jane, I really do need to go now. There are some decisions about the restaurant that only I can make."

"Oh, fine," I said, exasperated. "If you really need to get back to your own blasted lifelong dream…"

"Yes, I really do, Jane. But I have every confidence that you'll think of a solution—however insane it may turn out to be—all on your own."

Click.

How rude. I hate it when people click off without saying goodbye first.

Oh, well.

I straightened my skirt and steeled myself to go back into the breach.

"I'm back," I announced.

"Yes," said Louise, "we can see that. Author still alive?"

"Yes."

"Isn't floating at the bottom of the Thames?"

"No."

"Good. Then can we go on?"

"Yes," I said. "What I *meant* to say earlier was not that I hadn't picked an obstetrician out yet. What I *meant* to say was that Doctor…Doctor…Doctor…"

"Yes, Jane?" From Louise again. "Doctor who, Jane?"

All of a sudden a name came to me and, before I'd thought to think through the consequences, it came flying out of my mouth. "Dr. Shelton is to be my obstetrician and—"

The man I had just named was a very famous obstetrician whom I'd named simply because he was the only one whose name I knew. The problem was, since he'd just successfully attended to one of the lesser Royals in a troublesome pregnancy that had garnered lots of media attention (From the *Globe:* "Will Princess Veronique's Baby Be Born with Two Heads?"), everyone else knew his name, too. And all of the ones in the office who knew it were suddenly clouding around me like flies.

"My God, Jane," gushed Louise, as if I'd just been anointed by God or made a dame.

"Why didn't you say anything before?" asked Constance, her adoring eyes making it clear that I was her new heroine of the moment, at least until she started hating me for having good fortune that was wholly undeserved.

"Well…" I lowered my eyes in modesty. "Anyway," I went on quickly so as not to overdo, "what I was starting to say before was that it isn't that I've not seen an obstetrician yet. It's merely that Dr. Shelton and I haven't finalized our plan of action, should this pregnancy turn out to be as problematic as, well, Princess Veronique's."

"Maybe you should sit down," suggested Louise.

"I'll get you a footstool for under your desk," said Constance.

"You know," said Dodo, tapping her lower lip with a finger once I'd been thus enthroned. "You know," said Dodo, the woman who wasn't supposed to know "nothin' 'bout birthin' babies, Miss Scarlett." She stopped tapping her lower lip to point her finger at me. "I had a friend over at Random House who knew someone who had a baby once, and this person she knew also used Dr. Shelton as an obstetrician. Anyway, just the other day, after all of this stuff about Princess Niquie came out? Well, she told me that her friend said that this Dr. Shelton, whom everyone's treating as though he were the second coming of obstetricians or something, was perfectly beastly to her friend. Said that right from the start, from the very first pound she put on, he berated her up and down for letting herself become, and these are supposed to be his words, 'a fat cow.' Said he told her that the optimum weight gain charts had been put on earth for a reason and that if she couldn't play by the rules, she shouldn't be allowed to procreate. Can you believe it?"

I thought about my own gym-hardened stomach. Here was a part of pregnancy that I could definitely excel at. I was hoping to win the award for Least Pregnant-Looking Lady that anybody'd ever seen, leaving all the others behind in the pickles-and-ice-cream dust.

"No, actually," I said, "I have a tough time believing that of sweet old Dr. Shelton. He's been very kind to me. More like a grandfather really than anything else, save for the fact of course that he makes me put my feet up in stirrups whenever I see him. No, Dodo, I'm sorry to say that it's my guess that your friend's friend was having one of those bulimic pregnancies you hear so much about now."

"I haven't heard of them at all, never mind hearing so much about them," puzzled Dodo.

"No?" I yawned. "Oh, well, it must be that I keep seeing it mentioned in those pregnancy magazines I read now. Maybe it's not a matter of public domain yet. At any rate—" and here I couldn't resist the urge to pat my rock-hard abdomen "—Dr. Shelton says that in all his years of practice, he's never seen an expectant mother do so well at not gaining too much weight. *He* says that some people take pregnancy as a license to eat and begin ballooning up from the minute their urine makes that pink line on the wand. *He* says they should send me on the talk-show circuit or something as an inspiration to others."

I could tell that this last really rankled Louise and Constance. I knew that, were these normal times, they'd never let me get away with what they surely saw as pomposity. But these were no longer normal times. These were pregnant times and this had given both of them pregnant pause, for, after all, if Dr. Shelton said a thing was so...

I accepted everybody's extra attention that day but, for once, kept a clear eye on the future, at least as far as Dr. Shelton was concerned. After all, I couldn't very well have him be my obstetrician of record when I was surrounded by people who knew people who knew him, people who might, in that tell two-friends-about-it way that life seemed to go, create a situation in which the truth was revealed concerning the fact that he had no clue as to who I was. I would bide my time, spin out the Dr. Shelton fantasy for a few more weeks so as not to make everyone suspicious by making a too abrupt change. Then, when the time was right, I would make a change, claim it was a matter of personal philosophy. Although I hadn't read the chapters on selecting someone to deliver the baby in *What to Expect* thoroughly, because I hadn't really seen the need yet, I did vaguely recall there being options other than the traditional "man who specializes in making woman lie flat on table with feet in stirrups while telling her to push." I knew that some people used a family doctor and I knew that some people used a midwife. Perhaps this last was the answer to my dilemma.

Time would tell. At any rate, for now, my feet were comfier than they'd been in years.

★ ★ ★

"You do realize, Jane, that even were you to get pregnant now, by the time you actually gave birth, it would appear to the world as though you had undergone an eleven-month gestation period? That might be difficult to explain, unless of course you elect to pass Trevor off as being part pachyderm."

The speaker of course was David. The place was the Serpentine in Hyde Park, where David was keeping our little rower afloat, while I lay on my back, eyes closed. The time was smack in the middle of an indescribably beautiful crystal blue marble of a Sunday afternoon.

But all of that was irrelevant now since my best friend, the heartless bastard, had just burst my bubble.

"What do you mean?" I scrambled to an upright position, reaching up just in time to save my straw hat from sailing into the lake.

"Just do the math. Even disadvantaged as you are, without my military training, you should be able to handle simple addition and subtraction."

I did as he instructed, all the while marveling at how calmly he was able to keep rowing as my fantasy world collapsed. Then I double-checked it, this time reversing the process by going from left to right on my fingers.

"Actually, you're wrong," I pointed out, as if it mattered. "Actually, given the date I originally told people I conceived and given how far into what is supposed to be my third month I've gone, if I did conceive now, by the time I delivered people would naturally assume that I had been pregnant for twelve to thirteen months."

"Perhaps the math skills of the Israeli military are not what they once were." David shrugged it off and went on placidly rowing.

"Could you stop rowing, *please?* I'm in crisis here!"

But he didn't stop. "You've been in crisis ever since I first met you, Jane. The only difference is that this time you are much more flagrantly so."

"But what am I going to *do?* I've told everybody that I
know that I'm pregnant. Trevor, my mother, Sophie, the
girls at work—they all think I've got a baby coming sometime around the end of the year. What am I going to do
when the calendar flips over and I don't have a baby to
show for it?" All of a sudden, a horrible thought occurred
to me. "Never mind six months from now, what am I
going to do when it's time for me to start showing and
I'm not showing?"

There it was again, that shrug. "So, you'll tell everybody
that you made a mistake."

"A mistake?" I shrieked so loudly that it caused the
eavesdropping American in the rowboat closest to ours, the
one with the ultrafaded T-shirt with Arkansans for Im-
peachment printed on it, to let his oar get hopelessly away
from him. "Serves you right, you self-righteous git," I
muttered.

"What was that, Jane?" David asked.

"Never mind. What I really meant to say was," and
here I shrieked again, *"a mistake?* Are you out of your
can't-add-worth-shit Israeli military mind? I can't tell
everybody that I made a mistake! What am I going to do,
say, 'Oh, uh, oops, excuse me, I thought I was pregnant for
the last three months, but, dur, er, I guess I'm not?' You
don't think that too many of them might try and have me
locked away if I do that, do you?"

"There is really no need to be quite so sarcastic, Jane.
No, of course you are not going to do whatever that insane thing is that you just described. What you're going
to do is you're going to tell everyone the truth. Of course
that is what you'll do. You have no other choice."

I thought about the idea of coming clean with Trevor.
But how can you come clean with someone who's never
around? Each week, he was home less and less. True, we
lived together. True, on paper at least, we were having a
baby together. But, lately, he'd not been around to discuss,

well, anything. Lately, he'd been little more than a slightly warm body in bed, and on some nights not even that. Besides...

"You're starkers! I can't tell everyone the truth!"

"Tell me, what other choice do you have?"

The words that David had spoken to me in his apartment some weeks ago had been percolating in my mind ever since: *If I could be pregnant without really being pregnant, would I?*

True, I didn't think about it in his garbled-English sort of way, but there was a kernel of something in what he'd said, an essence that had been haunting me ever since he'd said it.

"Maybe you were right," I said now, realizing that the decision had been made in my subconscious long ago, although of course there was no way for him to know what I was referring to as yet.

"You mean about your baby being thought to be eleven months old when you finally get around to having it?"

"No, of course not. Your math skills still suck." I waved him off, idly thinking that he really did look like Michelangelo's *David* with his T-shirt off like that, save that there was no marble and he already needed a shave. "No, what I meant was that maybe you were right a few weeks ago when you said that I wanted to be pregnant without really being pregnant."

"Jane." He finally stopped his rowing. "What's going on in that little head of yours?"

"Think about it," I said, suddenly all excitement about my prospects for the future.

And that was when what had started out as "a plan" three months ago, what had evolved into "the plan" in the months since, finally crystallized as "The Plan."

"Think about it. Everyone is expecting me to be pregnant for the next several months. I've wanted to be pregnant more so that I could experience what everyone else seems to be experiencing than because I've given any thought to actually having or raising a real-live baby. There's nothing in the slightest bit warm or fuzzy about me, nothing maternal—perhaps Dodo could do maternal, but I certainly couldn't—so there's no reason to think that if there were a real baby involved that I'd be any sort of good mother—"

"We don't know that."

"—or that Trevor would be a good father."

"Well, we do know that."

"So, it's probably just as well that Trevor and I aren't expecting a baby together, because he never seems too terribly keen on the idea anyway. But Trevor has already asked me to marry him, so now we have this whole wedding to plan."

"Which you could always cancel."

"But I don't want to stop being pregnant!" I let the other shoe drop on him. Still, he was my best friend and a part of me couldn't help but think that he of all people had known what was coming all along. "Wouldn't it be great if I could go on having this experience, even though there would be no baby at the end of the line? I've already got three months under my belt. Wouldn't it be great if I could finish out the whole term, *if I could impersonate being pregnant for the whole nine months?*"

"Now you're the one who's barking mad!" His idiomatic English was doing that leaps-and-bounds thing again. "This you cannot do, Jane. This is too much insanity even for you."

"No, it's not. Besides, you always said you were my best friend. Won't you stand by me now in my hour of need?"

He picked up the oars and began rowing again. "This really is too much," he reiterated, but then he smiled. "So, what are you going to tell everyone when the nine months are up?"

"Constipated?" asked Constance, placing a couple of what looked suspiciously like unsolicited manuscripts onto my desk. Damn Dodo for always dumping things that were addressed to her onto me.

"Ex-*cuse* me?"

"I just saw that really big frown on your face when you were staring off into space there, and I began wondering if you were trying to maybe solve the riddle of the Sphinx or if you were maybe constipated."

I was tempted to throw the dwarf with the weird violet-red eyes out of my office but then thought better of it; for all I knew, there might be something here that I could use.

"Why do you say that, Constance?" Actually, I'd been thinking about what to order for lunch.

"Well, see, I saw this show they did on Beeb 4… Oh, maybe I should just start with Cindy Crawford."

"Cindy Crawford?"

"Yeah. The American model."

"I *know* who Cindy Crawford is, Constance. What I don't know is what she has to do with constipation."

"Well, you know how she's had two kids and everything? Well, although she was better with her second, I really didn't think she handled her first pregnancy in a way that was very positive for womankind."

I knew I was going to regret helping her out with one of her digressions but, like the hypnotized Mina Harker letting Count Dracula in, I found myself powerless to resist. "Oh? And what did Cindy do to womankind this time?"

She looked at me as though I were a mental defective. "Oh, yeah, I keep forgetting. You never read magazines." She shrugged off my inexplicable behavior. "Anyway, in the beginning of her first pregnancy, she was telling people that she was going to lay low throughout, that she didn't want people photographing her when she was no longer attractive, or something to that effect. *Well,* let me tell *you,* that set women back to before Virginia Slims came out. Who did she think she was, implying that pregnancy is anything other than the beautiful and natural condition it is? It's people like her who create anorexic pregnant women. Of course, once things got going and she got used to the idea of being considered the world's most attractive baby machine, she started capitalizing on it. No more keeping it in the closet. In no time flat, she was going the Demi Moore let-it-all-hang-out-and-then-some route. I tell you, these exhibitionists. If they were doing it on the cover of *Playboy,* it'd be an embarrassment, but because it's *Vanity Fair,* it makes it art. You would think that at the very least, they'd give some thought, prephoto shoot, to how their child would feel about it once he or she—"

"Constance. Constance. Constance."

"Hmm?"

"What does any of this have to do with constipation and the BBC?"

"Well, I was getting to that if you'd've let me, wasn't I? There was so much about Cindy and her pregnancy in all of the magazines, that *you* never read, that the BBC decided to jump on the bandwagon. In honor of Cindy's public pregnancy, they did a four-part series on the nine months of pregnancy, narrated by Helena Bonham Carter. In it, in addition to going over all of the joys, they also talked at length about the downsides. One of the big ones, it would appear, is constipation. It seems that the added hormones produced—the progesterone?—slows down the metabolism. Plus, you've got the pressure that the growing uterus exerts on the bowels, inhibiting normal activity. Anyway—" she began to look a bit embarrassed "—that's how I got from Cindy Crawford to constipation."

"Interesting," I said, pencil to lip. And, believe it or not, I thought it was.

"So? Are you?"

"Am I what?"

"Constipated? You know, the frown you had?"

"God, no. I was just trying to decide what to eat for lunch."

I encouraged her to leave, promising all the while as I was ushering her out that I had found her information most informative.

And I had. I would most definitely be filing it away for future use. After all, who knew when I might suddenly need a spa day.

"Have you heard the baby's heartbeat yet?" asked Dodo.

"Hello? What's that?"

"The baby's heartbeat. I read somewhere that with some special instrument thingy called a Doppler you can sometimes hear it as early as the tenth week."

"Nope. Haven't heard it yet. But I have been having the most marvelous sex."

"Do tell. That friend of my friend was so sick the entire time she was pregnant that she swears that she didn't have sex from the time she conceived until the baby was weaned and her breasts stopped hurting. Of course I've heard that pregnant women sometimes feel really sexy, but I've never met any who did."

So here was something else that I could excel at.

"*Well,* let me tell *you,* I have been having so many multiples, that it's as though my multiples are having their own multiples."

"No!"

"Yes! Course, I don't expect it to go on forever."

"But why shouldn't it?"

"Oh. You know. The whole fluctuating-hormones thing." After all, I didn't want to be so happily orgasmic that other women would hate me. "By the time I'm into the second trimester, I'll just probably want to have my feet rubbed."

Later that afternoon, while boning up on *What to Ex-*

pect during my midafternoon break, I came across a section called "Twins and More." For a while there, I briefly debated the idea of, when I finally did "hear the heartbeat," claiming that there was more than one. There could be definite advantages built into the exaggerated symptoms that accompanied a multiple pregnancy, the kind of symptoms that might entitle me to more days off whenever I felt like it. Then, too, there'd be the added hoopla that doing something a little bit extra, like two or who-knew-how-many more babies instead of one, would bring along with it. Of course, the downside would be that, once I did start finally showing, I'd have to gain sufficient weight to ensure the health of each child, and I really didn't like the idea of getting too big.

Oh, well. There was still time to decide. I could always say that it was thought that there *might* be two heartbeats, and just see how people reacted.

It was easy to see that Trevor had stumbled across something he shouldn't have.

"What the hell is this?" he demanded, swearing at me for the first time since he'd met me, believe it or not, while waving a pink Magic Marker in my face. "And how about this?" He waved the plastic wand which, amazingly enough, still bore its weird diagonal line.

"Would you believe—?"

He cut me off at the lie. "I don't want to hear your lies, Jane! You must think I'm stupid."

"Not really. How did you find out?"

I knew what was coming next, formed a mental picture of myself that first night I'd "discovered" my pregnancy, gleefully stowing the incriminating evidence—pink marker, the original botched test—in the back of the cabinet, fully intending to dispose of them when the coast was clear. But I'd never done that, had I? Good God, I thought, what was I—the most self-destructive woman who'd ever lived? Fucking Freud would have a fucking field day with me. But I couldn't be bothered with fucking Freud right now. Trevor had bigger things than my own questionable sanity for me to worry about.

"My electric razor died on me and I was looking for a disposable one beneath the sink when I came across all of this." He looked angry at himself for having bothered to answer me. "But that's not the point."

"No. I suppose not." I sat down on the edge of the couch, hoping to marshal my energy. "What exactly is the point, as you see it?"

If my approach was to sit and conserve, his was to pace and explode. "The *point,* the way I see it, is that you should be explaining to me just what exactly you had hoped to accomplish with this crazy scheme, rather than grilling me on how I managed to find you out. What did you think, that I'd never notice that anything was amiss?"

Well, I thought to myself, he hadn't noticed up until the truth smacked him in the face; hadn't noticed that I kept getting a period; hadn't noticed that my body wasn't changing at all. But I didn't think that this was a good time to point out the shortcomings in his powers of observation.

"Good God, Jane." He waved the incriminating wand in my face. "Here I was thinking that I was soon going to become a father, and instead it turns out that my child is no more than a fake pink line!"

"Well," I said, a trifle defensively, "you never did seem all that excited before about the prospect of becoming a dad. As a matter of fact, this is the most energy you've shown on the subject since—"

"Oh, will you just shut up, Jane! Don't you understand? This isn't about whether or not I showed the optimum measure of preparental enthusiasm, this is about what you did. And why." He sank to the couch, beside me but not touching, spent for the moment. He rested one elbow on his knee and massaged his forehead and closed eyelids with his fingers. "Just tell me, Jane. What was going on in that head of yours?"

So I told him.

Odd, but when I'd originally conceived The Plan it hadn't seemed nearly as, well, *diabolical* as it did when I tried to lay it out before Trevor. Was it so awful that I just wanted the kind of attention that every other woman seemed to take for granted as her God-given right? Well, apparently in Trevor's book…

He leapt to his feet, no longer exhausted. "You must be starkers! You'll never get away with this!"

"Only if you tell people!" I shouted desperately, leaping to my feet as well.

Before I knew what was happening, he was in the bedroom we'd shared for years, tossing items haphazardly into leather suitcases, not even bothering to obsessively fold things as he normally would.

"Where are you going?" I asked.

"Well, I'm not staying here with you anymore, now, am I?"

"But why not? Surely we can go on living together. We're supposed to be getting married in six months' time, don't forget."

Okay, so maybe I was in denial.

He came round the bed, gripped me by the shoulders. "Think, Jane. Even you can't possibly imagine that we'll still be getting married after this. Use your head and look around you. I'm leaving you."

I thought about the years we'd spent together, about the hopes I'd entertained for our future, about how I'd miss even his obsessive folding habits.

Obsessive folding habits may not seem a likely trait to hang one's love on, but I suppose a part of me had secretly hoped that we would somehow spend the rest of our lives together, in which case it would be helpful to delude oneself into believing that annoying traits were really some-how endearing ones.

Could it really be over?

I collapsed onto the bed next to his open suitcases. "But where will you go?"

"Does it matter? Anywhere but here. I'll stay with peo-ple I hate from work if I have to."

"What will you tell people?"

"About this insanity? Nothing. I want no part of it. Be-sides, you can't keep this charade up indefinitely, not un-less you're planning on maintaining the longest-running pregnancy in all of England's history. Before the day is done, you'll find yourself hoist by your own petard. Your kind always does."

Suddenly, I found myself feeling not quite so sorry to see him go.

"Anyway," he went on, "I won't be around to have to worry about it."

"Oh?"

"No. The firm's been after me to do a year in the Tokyo office, see if I can do anything to help salvage the situa-tion there, but I've been putting them off. The way I fig-ured it, with you being pregnant and all, I didn't feel it was right to ask you to up and move during such a fragile time, but now..." He allowed the thought to trail off as he fin-ished packing.

A moment ago, I'd thought I was no longer sorry to see him go. Now that the moment was imminent, however, I was back to feeling reluctant again. Casting my eyes about the flat, I sought an excuse to keep him there, if only for just a little while longer.

Pointing to the two suitcases, I said, "Don't you want to take anything more than that? Some CDs or pictures, per-haps? The couch we bought together?"

Trevor looked thoughtful. Perhaps he was thinking about the couch in question, remembering the cold Saturday in January two years back when we'd struggled with it up the stairs together?

Then he shook his head, abruptly, like a dog coming out of water. "And have reminders of *this?*" He shook his head again. "No, thank you. And, besides," he added, considering, "it'd probably cost more than we spent on any of this junk, paying the air freight to Tokyo."

Trevor snapped the locks on the suitcases and hoisted them off the bed. "Goodbye, Jane," he said. "I can't say that it hasn't been interesting." He looked as though he were going to kiss me one last time, but the moment never materialized. "And may I say, good luck. Because God knows, one way or another, eventually you're going to need it."

And he was gone.

It took me a moment to realize the finality of it all, but the sight of Punch the Cat lurking in the corner brought the perfect coda home to me. Picking up the detested orange puffball, I rushed to the door, opened it, and half hurled the feline in the general direction of Trevor's retreating back.

"Fine!" I shouted. "Desert me if you must. But if you're going, you're taking your awful cat with you. I've always hated that cat. And I don't care if he has to spend the entire time you're in Tokyo in quarantine!"

Then I slammed the door.

With both Trevor and Punch the Cat gone, there was now no one here but me. Well, that wasn't so bad, was it? After all, now I could repaint the flat so that it would no longer be the omnipresent salmon pink that it was, now that I didn't have anyone around who had to be made to pass tests.

The important thing to do now was to make myself a nice soothing cup of tea, even if I didn't like tea very much. I needed to gather my thoughts, make sure there would be no holes left in my plan once I told people that I'd been deserted by the baby's father.

Would Trevor be true to his word? Would he abstain

from telling people the truth about our breakup? The more I thought about it, the more I realized that it didn't even matter all that much if he didn't. During my two-year obsession with him, I'd made the cardinal error that many other women before me had made when faced with the notion of a steady boyfriend: I'd become socially removed from the people I formerly spent time with, willingly drifting away. In my case now, though, my estrogen-driven silliness had resulted in a happy state of affairs. Since the girls at the office had never really known Trevor, except by name, they'd never notice he was gone. And as for any mutual friends we had, well, he could tell them whatever he liked since they'd always been his friends more than mine anyway and no one from his suspenders set was the type to mix with my book-reading set. Hell, if I wanted to claim to still be getting married in six months' time—having bridal showers, going shopping for shoes and a dress—I could probably get away with that, as well.

But did I want to?

After all, being a single mom might not be so bad, not if one took into consideration all of the extra praise for bravery that would accrue to one's character for having toughed out a tough situation.

I would just have to wait, and everyone else would just have to see.

And, I thought, with an oddly contented sigh, *even if Trevor had left me, at least I still had the baby to dream about.*

The tiny human which had been theoretically growing within me was now a fetus. It was two and a half to three inches in length and weighed about half an ounce, so more now than any quantity of pot I'd ever smoked single-handedly. More organs were in the process of developing. The circulatory systems were up and running. The liver was producing bile. The reproductive organs were already developed but, from the outside, it would be difficult to tell yet if my fetus was a girl or a boy.

Well, I still had time to decide about that, didn't I?

the second trimester

the fourth month

As the first step in my campaign to get over the trauma of Trevor having dumped me, I did what any other self-respecting girl would do. I put on my not-so-glad rags, found the darkest pub in the neighborhood and, as my late father used to say, endeavored to see the bottom of every glass in town before the sun came up.

Okay, so maybe I wasn't exactly *traumatized* by having lost Trevor per se. After all, I'd had a few hours to reflect and in that time I'd come to terms with the startling truth that while I had long been in love with the idea of marriage as a whole, I'd never exactly been in love with Trevor. And perhaps, if I were really being honest, I'd have to admit that he'd never been in love with me, either. Would a man in love insist on waiting until his child had been successfully born to marry its mother, if he were in fact in love with her? I think not. Wouldn't a man in love, whether there was a child involved or not, take the first opportunity to propose to his beloved, if for no other reason than to keep other suitors from snatching her away? I like to think he would.

Sour grapes? Perhaps. But it does work for me. Not to mention that, being no Scarlett O'Hara, I've got just enough of the realist in my soul that I recognized that Trevor was never coming back to me, not after this.

And, yes, I did still need to go out and get drunk, because it *is* traumatizing being the one dumped, no matter what one's true feelings for the dumper.

The Valley of Fear, once one got inside, was something less than the emporium of Sherlockiana that its name implied. In fact, probably the only thing it had in common with the Doyle story was the concept of fear, in this case inspired in patrons by the notion of ever eating anything from the glass jars of eggs and pickles and unidentifiable (in?)edibles that lined the front of the bar and served as the chief nod to interior decoration. The pub was sufficiently dark that one could try to convince oneself that the wood on the wall-to-wall bar was authentic mahogany, the gleaming something-or-other real brass. What was undoubtedly authentic, however, was the barmaid, who had the kind of loose stomach that came from multiple childbirths combined with no discernible exercise regimen, and yellow hair that even in the dim lighting was unmistakably the color of pee. Also authentic were the hunched-over patrons, who looked like they'd come with the lease, and the publican, who was Uriah Heep with just a wistfully fleeting dash of Mr. Darcy.

He made a pass at wiping the bar in front of me with a damp rag that had seen better centuries. "Know what you want then, miss?"

"Mmm…"

"Come on. Haven't got all day."

Well, actually, looking around at the scant patronage, who would tip in shots if at all, it appeared that he did.

"Mmm…better make it a pint of Guinness."

"Fine choice, miss." He began to move off.

"And a shot of Glenfiddich."

"Very well."

"No. On second thought, make it Laphroaig. Might as well treat myself well."

"Might as well."

"But make it a double. No point in you having to run back and forth more times than necessary. Heh, heh." Good God, where did that oil-less laugh come from?

"Is that quite everything, miss? Or would you be wanting me to park the whole distillery in front of you?"

"No. Heh, heh. I can always order another round later."

"He's not the most polite bartender in all of London, but at least he doesn't water down his drinks."

"Excuse me?" I asked, turning to the man who'd suddenly taken up occupancy on the barstool to my right.

If I were to have to describe him for a lineup, I'd say that he was of medium height, medium build, was a handful of years or so older than me, had dirty-blond hair that was beginning to inch its way backward and eyes that were the shade of brown that I'd always pictured myself looking at over morning beverages for the rest of my life. Obviously, I would probably not ever make the ideal witness to a crime, but I know what I like. In short, he was no pretty boy like Trevor, which was fine because I wasn't naturally given to pretty boys. The only problem that I could see with the man before me was that he had a long, droopy mustache which, oddly enough, was drooping much lower on one side than the other.

"I said, he's not the most polite—"

"Yes, I heard you," I cut him off, frowning. I outlined the area where my own mustache would be if I had one. "Do you know that one side of your mustache is drooping down far lower than the other? If you don't do something about it soon, I'm afraid you might lose part of it."

"Oh, blast," he swore mildly, shocking me when he

ripped the mustache off, shoving it in the pocket of his tweed jacket. "I'd forgotten I had it on."

"That's much better," I commented, for underneath the preposterous mustache, there was a second mustache, much nicer than the first. "Are you coming from a costume party?" I asked skeptically since, outside of the double mustache, his tweed jacket, light-blue oxford shirt and tight jeans looked quite regular, although it was a little early on a summer evening for tweed.

"You could say that," he said without elaborating. "And yourself?"

"Sorry?"

He indicated my all-black ensemble, which had the unmistakable look of statement-making. "Are you sort of coming from a costume party as well? The Valley of Fear doesn't often get women other than Sue coming though its doors—" he nodded at the pee-haired barmaid "—much less one who looks like she's supposed to be something."

"Oh. No." I imagined an imaginary party. "I left my broom and hat at home so they wouldn't let me in."

"I see," he said as the bartender brought my drinks and placed a pint of ale before my companion without his having to ask.

"They know you well here?" I asked, having tossed back half of the double shot and a healthy pull on the Guinness.

"You could say that this is the only place where they *do* know me."

"How sad."

"Not when you consider what most people are like."

"What a peculiar thing to say."

"But true."

"What a truly peculiar thing to say." I knocked back the rest of the shot, followed by more Guinness, and paused, considering. "What a peculiarly true thing to say." I slammed the glass down and ordered another round. "And one for my interesting friend here," I added.

"It's not very often that I'm bought a drink by a woman, much less one who's so attractive. Lack of hat and broom notwithstanding, of course."

"Of course. But, my heavens, there are an awful lot of things that don't happen very often in your world, aren't there? And most of them much less no less."

"Yes, it is a small world, but it's my world so I try to make do. Might I ask for your name, so that I can tuck it away somewhere within that small world?"

Well, *I* was willing to be charmed. I thrust out my hand for a shake. "Jane Taylor. Assistant Editor at Churchill & Stewart. Jilted lover. Twenty-nine." Might as well get the worst of it out up front, I figured.

His hand was satisfyingly warm in mine. "Whoever he was, I'm glad he's gone, but he must be the biggest idiot who ever lived."

"Goes without saying."

"Tolkien Donald, by the way, at your service."

Okay. So I didn't laugh directly in his face, but near enough. "Tolkien Donald? Are you having me on?"

Apparently, he was used to small-minded people like me who had nothing more amusing to do with themselves than laugh at other people's names. His answer sounded like it had been given with the near regularity of extraordinarily tall people responding to the old "How's the air up there?" query, although I sensed he was putting a little more energy into it than usual for my sake. "Actually," he said, "I think that it was more of a case of my parents having *me* on. Course, now that I'm grown up and they're both gone, it seems a bit silly to hold a grudge."

I tried to look appropriately sober, at least after I was through hiccupping. "Dead?"

"No. Barcelona."

Well, that wasn't that bad then. "So," I prodded, "are you

going to elaborate on the name thing, or is this going to be another one of those *mysterious* things like the fake mustache thing, where you just shove it in your pocket and pretend it was never there?"

"Oh, no. I'm willing to talk about the name thing. Quite used to it, really. See, my parents caught the sixties bug a little late in the day, so when I was about four, they suddenly went all hippie and everything, discovering peace and incense and *The Hobbit* and all of that other groovy stuff. Up until that point, my name had been Donald John. But they decided to convert, see, and just like some people at that time were switching religions, they decided that we should all change our names. My father went from Ron to being Elrond, which wasn't too bad, but my mother went from Claire to Galadriel which was awful hard for some people to spell. It didn't help the postal service people any when they gave up on last names entirely. Course, me being their only child, they renamed me from Donald to Tolkien, after the man who'd started it all."

"But you said *your* last name is Donald."

"Oh, yeah, well, the grandparents were confused enough as it was, so my parents let me keep that just for people who couldn't handle change very well."

"And your parents? In Barcelona? They still go by Elrond and Galadriel while being, what, in their fifties? Sixties?"

"God, no. They went back to Ron and Claire John about twenty years ago, about the same time they gave up tie-dyeing and got into the bond market."

"But you never thought to go back to Donald John?"

"No. Why would I? I'm used to it, aren't I."

And, oddly enough, the idea that Tolkien Donald should have learned to adapt to such an oddity, to come to take it as commonplace, made me fall in love with him on the spot.

Two hours later, still in the same spot, still feeling in love only more so, I sat on the same stool contemplating life (mine), love (someday mine?) and the amazing man I'd just met (could *Tolkien* some day be mine?).

Okay, so maybe I'd budged from the stool at least twice during the evening for absolutely necessary visits to the loo, but still...

Watching Tolkien's back as he exited the Valley of Fear after he'd reattached his mustache and told me he needed to get back to work, I was basking in the rosy glow of new love.

Had I ever felt this way so quickly before? I wondered. *About any man?*

No and no.

I was still doing that rosy-glow thing, moonily gazing at the space he'd so recently inhabited, when for the second time that evening I was startled by a voice coming at me from the side.

"I thought you were supposed to be pregnant? Why, not only are you not even showing, but here you are out drinking as well!"

The voice belonged to Alice Simms, an acquaintance of mine who edited for Quartet Books Limited.

As I swiveled sharply to face the body that the voice was coming from, I saw that Alice was still...

Oh, good God! Do you really need to know what she looks like right now? This woman was about to burst my mendacious bubble! I had no time for pithy descriptions. Suffice it to say that she'd never been asked to model for any glossy covers, but no man had ever asked her to put a bag over her head, either. Alice was medium; in almost every way imaginable, she was medium.

No sooner had I relegated Alice to a lifetime of mediumness, however, than the thought occurred to me: would it really be so bad to end my charade now? Surely, even I could see that it was insanity to try to impersonate a pregnant woman for nine months. Yes, the positive attention would be nice. But I had originally wanted to trap Trevor, and yet now had lost him. Then, I had wanted the experience of being pregnant to continue, with no threat of a real baby at the end of the line. But now that I had met Tolkien—okay, so maybe I'd only *just* met him—what good did my faux pregnancy serve me?

I decided there and then that confession would be good for my soul; a first baby step, if you will, toward coming clean with everybody. So I told Alice *everything*. After all, she was a reasonably even human being—okay, medium—surely, if anyone could understand and forgive my actions...

"Has anyone ever told you, Jane, that you're insane?"

We had retreated from the bar to a tiny corner table for more privacy, as if we really needed it in that deserted hole. Now I put my finger to my lips as though in deep thought. "Now, let me see... What is it about your unfortunate choice of wording that leads me to believe that you won't take no for an answer to that unspeakably rude question?" I had decided to take offense. "Of course they have," I replied with some asperity, "more and more often as time goes on." Belligerent now, arms crossed: "So? What of it?"

The expression on Alice's face showed that she had clearly decided to take offense, too. Well, who could blame her, really? I was behaving in an impossible way for someone who was so patently in the wrong in so many ways; even *I* could see that.

But then, a curious thing happened: Alice laughed.

"Oh, Jane, what a wonderful story your story would make!"

Then, an even curiouser thing happened: Alice got a positively devilish gleam in her eye that reminded me shockingly of, well, *me.*

"Oh, Jane," she gushed some more, "I've just had the most *wonderful* idea!"

I was almost afraid to ask. "Which is...?"

She leaned in conspiratorially. "*Don't* stop your charade now."

"But I just told you—"

"Continue faking being pregnant for the whole nine months, see if you can pull it off. You can consider it as research."

"But—"

"Then turn it into *a book*."

"Wha—?"

"Just think about it for a moment. You know yourself that all of us in publishing are always looking for the next great thing. Well, let me tell you, nothing could be more bizarre than what you're telling me you've been doing. Think of the book it could make—Woman Fakes Pregnancy for Nine Months."

My practical side was kicking in. "Well, as far as titles go—"

"Never mind that now." She brushed me off. "We can work out the minor details later. For now, just think about it. I know my publisher would pay a lot of money for such an unusual story. Hell, we'd probably have to bid against several other publishers to get it. Although," she added, an ingratiating note creeping into her voice, "I would certainly hope, that since this was *practically* all my idea—"

"How much money are we talking about here?" I was now officially in full-fledged practical mode.

She couldn't have emphasized her next utterance more if she had been the person to originally invent italics: "*Lots.*"

Mmm, that did sound like an awful lot.

"But wait a second," I objected. "What am I going to tell my family and friends when the nine months are up?"

She shrugged it off. "Well, you'll have a big book contract by then, won't you? You'd be amazed… Well, maybe *you* wouldn't…but it truly is amazing how quickly people forgive and forget all kinds of things when there's a published author around."

What she said was true.

"Yes, but—" I was still stuck in objecting mode "—if I make it nonfiction, people might object to how they're portrayed. I don't want to get *sued* for this."

"Then write it as *fiction,* if you must, Jane. Really, I don't care. *Just write it!* Honestly, fiction, nonfiction, like I said, we can work out the details later. Put it to you like this— if you *don't* write it, *I will.*"

I was a little shocked. "You mean that *you* dream of being a writer, too?"

"God no. A person would have to be *insane* to choose to be a writer if they could possibly help it. No, it's simply that I can't bear to have a good story go to waste. *Write—the—book—Jane.*"

She certainly was persuasive.

Within the body of every editor beats the heart of a would-be writer.

Okay, maybe not *every* editor. I'm hyperbolizing a bit here, but bear with me.

As with many another editor before me, I had initially got into publishing in the hopes of getting a leg up on my own writing career. I wanted to write novels; not necessarily *important* novels, mind you, but I did want to get paid for telling stories. The problem was, as is often the case in these situations, in performing the mechanics of the day-to-day grunt work that was supposed to move me closer to my ultimate dream, I lost sight of the dream. Oh, sure, there were mornings when I still dragged myself out of bed early enough to take a stab at writing a cohesive story. But, as time wore on, those mornings had dwindled down to the status of few and far between. I, who had never really wanted to settle—at least not in my working life—had learned how to settle: settled for a job that gratified me in some small sense; settled for being part of the stratosphere that other would-be authors wanted to float in; settled.

I took a moment out for sensible thought, a moment to

reflect on possible outcomes of this harebrained scheme of hers. If I went along with it, then I wouldn't have to come clean just yet with everyone I knew—a definite plus. In addition, I'd finally be what I'd longed to be before I'd become A Woman Who Settles: I'd be A Published Writer. To carry it further, if I made my story nonfiction, people might sue me. But even if I made it fiction, there was still a chance—a fairly large chance—that people would be angry with me for lying to them for so long.

Well, I finally concluded, in a sense Alice's plan would leave me no worse than before. In fact, what with a book contract and all, it would leave me a lot better. Oh, sure, at the end of nine months, unless I could somehow produce a baby, people might be so mad at me that I'd have to leave London forever. But now, instead of just being any old exile, I'd be a successful exile. And anyway, I had never known before what I was going to do when the clock ran out on me, and yet I'd proceeded. Why not proceed now, then, with a far greater incentive?

Still, wanting to object at least one last time, I half-heartedly reiterated my concerns to Alice about everyone hating me in the end.

"Well, you did always say that you wished you were a paid storyteller," she pointed out.

I had indeed.

Then she made me be quiet—no small task—as she outlined the way she saw the next several months as going: me keeping a diary of daily events regarding the fake pregnancy, then distilling it down to the funnier parts and e-mailing it to her for her approval.

When she was done, I had one final question. "How much did you say again that you were sure they'd pay for this story?"

"*Lots.*"

"A more exact number might be nice."

Holding my gaze as if we were expert bluffers involved

in some kind of poker match, she rifled through her purse, located a pen, scribbled a figure on the bar napkin and pushed it across the table to me. She'd never once broken eye contact and yet she'd managed to write her figure out legibly. God, she was good!

I studied the figure, swallowed. "This must be a mistake," I said. "I'm fairly certain you must have absentmindedly added an extra zero or two here."

Alice smiled confidently, and just shook her head.

"Are you authorized to make an offer this big?"

"Well," she conceded, "there are a few formalities I'll need to go through at my end. But, basically, yes."

"*God,* you've got so much more power than I do."

She merely shrugged.

"Okay, I'll do it. But only if I can have a contract now."

"Now?"

"Yes, *now.* I'm certainly not going to go on with this charade—and possibly fuck up my entire life in the process—in the mere *hopes* of there being a contract at the end. I need a guarantee."

"And what's in it for us?"

"You get to sign me up now, without having to run the risk that there might be a bidding war involving other publishers, a bidding war that *you might lose.* After all, if you're waving these kinds of figures under my nose merely upon hearing the idea…" I paused for a moment, thinking about how betrayed Dodo would feel that I'd sold my book to someone else. But I *couldn't* tell her about the fake pregnancy, not just yet. Oh, well, I sighed. Maybe I could just dedicate the book to Dodo. Didn't people usually forgive all sins when books were dedicated to them?

"Yes," she said. "I see your point. But tell me something."

"Hmm?"

"How do I know that you can write?"

"I'm an editor, for chrissakes. Of course I can write."

She stared at me until I relented.

"And you're an editor, too," I conceded. "So if it turns out I can't write, you can always fix it."

"True."

"When do I get the contract?"

"A few weeks?" She shrugged. "Just as soon as we can agree on the details and draw it up."

"And then I'll get...?"

"What everyone else gets—one-third upon signing, one-third upon delivery of a satisfactory proposal, one-third upon delivery of a satisfactory manuscript."

"So, then, when I sign this contract in a few weeks, at that time I'll get one-third of...?"

"Yes, Jane. You'll get one-third of *lots.*"

Well, I couldn't very well walk away from that, now, could I?

So now at least there was a financial motive to my madness.

I couldn't wait to tell David my good news!

While strolling the few blocks home from the bar, I pulled my mobile from my purse and punched in his number. Sure, I might've waited until I got home and then gone upstairs, but I was pretty sure Christopher wouldn't appreciate my popping in on them so late.

So, naturally, it was Christopher who answered the phone.

"Oh. Jane." He sounded peculiarly short and groggy. "David's right here."

David was on in an instant. "Jane? What's wrong? Are you okay? I saw Trevor leave earlier with his suitcases, but I never got the chance to come down and see how you were. And then when I did finally make it down, you were gone already and I had no idea where you went. Are you okay?"

"Yes!" I danced down the street. "I'm fine!"

I could almost see him hold the phone away from his

ear in shock, before bringing it in closer again and reply-ing, "You *are?*"

"Yes, I really–really am!"

"May I ask…why?"

"*Why?* Because two *stupendous* things happened to me this evening! I fell in love——"

"*You* fell in love?"

"You sound so surprised." I gave it a brief moment's se-rious thought. "Yes," I said, thinking of Tolkien, "I think that I did."

"That's amazing, Jane. If it's true, then I'm very happy for you."

"Thank you."

"And the other stupendous thing that happened…?"

I hesitated. For some reason, I was reluctant to tell him about the book contract. For some reason, now that I had told him about Tolkien, the book contract didn't seem like as big of a deal.

"Nothing," I said softly, stopping on the sidewalk and tilting my head backward in the hopes of counting the stars beyond the city lights. "Isn't one stupendous thing enough for one evening?"

"Yes." I could hear him smile through the phone. "One stupendous thing is quite enough."

I smiled back. "Yes."

"And you should be coming inside soon. I can see you down there from the window. I'm glad you're safe, Jane."

"Thanks."

I heard a muffled voice in the background. "David?" It was Christopher's voice, calling out to him from across the room. "Aren't you ever coming back to bed?"

"I've got to go," David said.

"I know," I said.

"See you tomorrow?" he asked, waving down at me through the window.

"Yes." I lifted my own hand, waving in reply. "See you tomorrow."

★ ★ ★

According to the pregnancy books, the variety of things I might be "feeling" in the first month of my second trimester was mind-boggling. There was, on the physical front: fatigue; constipation; heartburn, indigestion, flatulence and bloating; continued breast enlargement, although, thankfully, this was usually accompanied by a decrease in tenderness and swelling; occasional headaches; occasional faintness or dizziness, especially when suddenly changing position; nasal congestion, occasional nosebleeds, ear stuffiness; "pink toothbrush," meaning bleeding gums; increase in appetite; mild swelling of feet and ankles, occasionally affecting the hands and face; varicose veins in the legs and/or hemorrhoids; a slight white vaginal discharge called leukorrhea (in case there have been no other signs, now one can have smelly discharge seeping out of orifices); fetal movement by end of the month, but only if one is very slender or this is not one's first pregnancy.

Oh, dear! I was very slender. Would people be wanting to touch my moving baby?

If none of that was enough, of course, there was always the emotional: instability comparable to premenstrual syndrome, possibly including irritability, mood swings, irrationality and weepiness; joy and/or apprehension, provided one has started to finally feel pregnant (oh, I think that the constipation and leukorrhea would have clinched that for me by now, leaving me a bloody manic-depressive); frustration, if I *don't* feel pregnant yet but can't get into regular clothes while still being too small for maternity clothes (not going to be a problem in my case); a feeling of being not quite together, of being a scatterbrain, accompanied by the tendency to forget things, drop things, and have trouble concentrating...

It was at that point that I took the book and hurled it across the room from where I'd been lying on my living room sofa, whereupon it made a satisfying crash against the wall which had the unsatisfying effect of causing the Marcuses down below to thump on the ceiling. Oh, well. I guessed that, being the scatterbrain I now was, I'd forgotten what I was doing and somehow dropped the wretched thing. Now where was I?

Oh, yes.

I poured myself the rest of the bottle of wine I'd been killing while boning up on pregnancy and drank a toast to all of the poor slobs who really were pregnant. Good God, I thought, with all of that happening to a woman's body—and those just the tip of the symptom iceberg for the fourth month alone—it's a wonder that women still bother to have babies at all.

When I finally told the women at work that the wedding was off, their reaction made me wish that I hadn't.

"But this is no time to be alone," Dodo said.

"I think you're brave to be a single mom," Louise said, "even if there are so many others doing it."

"You know it'll be tough for you to find a man who'll take you on under these conditions," Stan from Accounting said, intruding as he passed through on his way to pester Minerva in Publicity about a trifling matter that he'd undoubtedly never win. "Most men are hesitant enough as it is to start anything with a woman who's thinking about turning thirty any minute, never mind having to contend with soiled nappies as well." He put his arm around me, protectively. "You might come to find your Uncle Stan starting to look pret-ty attractive—"

"Shut up, Stan!" everyone shouted.

After Stan'd been chased back under a rock, the youngest country was heard from. On that day, she was wearing contacts that were more golden than brown, lending her eyes an otherworldly quality which, when taken in conjunction with the words she spoke, would be having me in nightmares for a week.

"You know, Jane," Constance said, reaching up toward my shoulders so that her hand replaced the warmth where Stan's arm had been, "I've been meaning to move out of my parents' house for some time now. It's just that I've never managed to find the right situation. If you wanted, I could—"

"God no!" I fairly recoiled out of her embrace. "I mean, I think it's so unimaginably kind of you to offer that I don't really know how I can say no—" her eyes brightened briefly, so I rushed on "—but I must. You see, part of the new spirituality I've found since this all started has had to do with taking full responsibility for my life—a feeling that Trevor clearly doesn't feel for his, I might add. Nevertheless, despite his poor example, I am determined that I should hoe the row I've been given alone or die trying." It might have been my imagination, but I could have sworn that I heard "Rule Britannia" swelling somewhere in the background as the RAF boarded fighter jets. From the looks on their faces, apparently the others were hearing it as well.

"So brave," went the half-heard murmurs of the little people who surrounded me.

"But won't it be an awful financial burden for you," Dodo pointed out, "having the expense of the flat all on your own shoulders while you have so much else to financially worry about?"

Ah, the voice of reason.

Not that I had so much else to worry about financially, not like they thought. True, it would normally have been a strain, footing the entire rent each month for the flat; except that now it wouldn't be, not once I received that first advance check.

In order to distract people from the Trevor-deserting-me-in-my-time-of-need issue, which really wasn't the kind of undeserved sympathy I preferred to cultivate, I thought it was as good of a time as any for me to make a switch in my obstetric arrangements. Having learned a trick or two from observing the other women in the office, I ripped a page out of Louise's book, sauntering out to the copier to copy something that didn't need copying. I timed my trip perfectly to coincide with Dodo being in the common area as well by leaving my door open and watching obsessively until she crossed by, meaning that I would only have to pull this particular mendacious stunt once, allowing the gossip line to do the rest for me. For good measure I whistled so as people could not help but notice my passing, although, since I've never been much good at it, the result was more a hard blow than a twittering cheep.

"Oh. Jane." Constance eyed me with that day's aqua eyes as if she'd not seen me before, like maybe I was a new species or something, before returning to her daily feigning of typing skills. "Any news?" she asked, not looking up as her hands flew across the keyboard with what I was sure would look like fhygoy;yhgjvgjdkty if anyone bothered to check. Whenever Dodo was around, she made an extra effort to look as though she actually did something for the company.

"Oh, nothing much," I said casually. But then, when no one pressed me for any further details—like asking "Have you felt the baby kick yet?" or "How's that tilted uterus coming?"—I realized that I was going to have to be more direct if I wanted to get them to worm the false information out of me.

"Oh, nothing much," I said again, turning my back on the copy machine à la Louise, although when I tried to further imitate her by giving my hair a nonchalant flick the move failed to have the desired effect since she had long hair while I did not. "Nothing much, that is, if you count firing the great Dr. Shelton as nothing much." I studied my nails, which had nothing particularly right or wrong with them, letting my bombshell sink in.

"You did *what?*" practically shrieked Louise, scandalized. "People wait in line to get him to attend them. They say that there are some women now who actually refuse to go off the pill until he's signed a contract stating that he'll be their obstetrician."

"It's true," put in Constance, who was an avid reader of the *Globe* whenever there was no pressing need to pretend to type. "I read that even Princess Niquie timed her conception so as to ensure he'd have a vacancy in his schedule."

"Actually," I said coolly, always willing to compare my lot with that of the Royals, even minor ones, at the drop of a name, "Princess Niquie's horrifying experience is part of the reason why I've given old Shelton the boot."

"You don't say," oohed Constance, rising from her chair and drawing closer.

"Yes," I said dryly, "I do say."

"But I thought her experience was only horrifying *before* Dr. Shelton swept in to save the day."

"Not quite. That's just the part of the story that's printed for public consumption."

"Do you mean that there's another part?" asked Louise as she drew near as well, her interest now piqued nearly as much as Constance's.

I looked over at Dodo. "Do you remember what you told us about that friend of your friend? You know, the one who was told by Shelton that she'd used pregnancy as an excuse to turn into a big fat cow?"

"Well, I don't think that those were my exact words...."

"*Well. I* heard that *she's* not the only one he pulled that stunt on."

"Oh?" Dodo's proximity as she asked this proved that I'd finally caught her as well.

"Yes," I said cagily, "that's right."

"Well, tell us," said Constance, aqua eyes flashing. "Who else did he pull it on?"

"Would you believe Princess Niquie?"

"No!"

"Yes! That's what was so horrifying about the entire pregnancy-childbirth process for her. Well, outside of the fact of that multiday labor period, et cetera, yawn. But what she really said was the worst was how, the whole time she was pregnant, he kept riding her about every pound she put on. Told her that just because a woman has a hereditary right to put a crown on now and again is no excuse for gaining an ounce over the accepted limit."

"He didn't!"

"He did!"

"Wait a second here," said Constance, hands on hips. "This was never in the *Globe*."

"Course not. You don't think that either the Royals or Dr. Shelton would allow a story like that to leak out, do you? After all, it does neither of them credit now, does it? For his part, it makes him look like an unfeeling old misogynistic pisser and, as for Princess Niquie, it makes *her* look as though she has no self-control."

"Well, she doesn't."

"True."

"But if neither of them would ever allow such a story to leak out," pressed Constance, enquiring mind ticking away every second, "then how did you come by this unknown knowledge?"

I wanted to point out to her that her last two words formed one of the oddest verbal constructions I'd ever heard, but I was worried that I'd only confuse her. Instead, I said, "Because I'm one of his patients, aren't I? Or, I was anyway, before I fired him in a show of solidarity to other women laboring—all puns intended—under the patriarchal system that has been oppressing them for so long."

"I don't even understand what any of that means," said

Constance. "What I want to know is—where did you hear this?"

"From the nurses in his office, of course. They all gossip something dreadful, don't they."

"Really?" asked Louise. "I always thought that it was part of their job to keep things as confidential as possible."

"That's just what they *want* you to think. In truth, they're worse than a bunch of magpies."

"No!"

"Yes! Why, one day, when they were doing the blood pressure thingy with me, right next to me was this teenaged girl, about five months' gone, who had this older woman with her whom I assumed had to be her mother since they both had the same nose only on different faces. Anyway, the nurse says to her, cool as you please as she reads right off of this form, 'It says here that you were pregnant once before?' Well, believe you me, it would have taken something a lot less heavy than a feather to knock that poor mother over and I sure wouldn't have wanted to be her daughter when they got home to Soho."

"But that's not gossip," Louise objected. "That's merely indiscreet."

"Close enough," I shrugged.

"Getting back to Dr. Shelton," prodded Dodo, going all practical on me. "You can't really mean that you gave the heave-ho to the most sought after obstetrician in all of England. Can you?"

"Oh, yes, I can." As a matter of fact, I'd been giving the matter considerable thought, ever since I'd first made the mistake of laying claim to Dr. Shelton. Knowing that I couldn't possibly continue under the care of such a public figure, I'd been working on an alternate birthing plan for the past two months. I'd figured that, if a person could get an at-home pizza delivery, there was no reason why I couldn't get an at-home baby delivery.

"I've decided to go with a midwife," I announced firmly.

Dodo eyed my obviously still slender frame. "But I don't understand. Surely Shelton can't be giving *you* a hard time for gaining too much."

"Course not. Matter of fact, he's mostly given me a hard time for being in *too* good of a physical condition. Apparently, the man's got some kind of bizarre fetish concerning women's weight. But that's neither here nor there. I'm certainly strong enough to take it. Stronger than poor Princess Niquie by a long shot, I can tell you," I couldn't resist adding. "No, as I was starting to say before, about the show of sisterly solidarity—"

But before I could go on, Constance cut me off midgloat. "Well, I think it's just marvelous!" She clapped her hands. "A midwife! It's just…brilliant!"

"Well, I *guess* it won't be *too* awful," said Dodo. "I mean, I seem to recall reading in *some* reasonably non-Stone Age publication that *some* of these private group practices have even taken to keeping a midwife on staff. And, of course, since the baby *will* be born in a legitimate hospital…"

"No!" I nearly shouted. "No, no, no, no, no. Why, that's part of the reason I've selected a midwife. I mean, apart from the whole female-solidarity thing. *I* want to have my baby at home. You know—natural lighting, soft music mimicking wave sounds, squatting in the corner if you feel like it. I don't want some institutional setting. That's why I've employed Madame Zora."

"Madame *Zora?*" Dodo appeared skeptical. "Sounds more like a tarot-card reader than a midwife."

"It's funny you should say that. Actually, Madame Zora is both."

"She's both a midwife *and* a tarot card reader?"

"Oh, yes. And you have no idea how convenient that's going to make things. I don't know if I've mentioned this before, but ever since I've been, well, *enceinte,* I find that this newfound sense of spirituality has overtaken my life." I did some hand embellishments in the air to help illustrate. "It's just that, with this new being growing inside me…"

"Oh, yes, I've read about that," eager Constance cut me off. "They say that, if you haven't been real religious before, it really gets the old God thing going."

I tried not to glare at her too much for interrupting. "As I was *about* to say, ever since this whole—dare I say, *unbelievable*—process started, I've found that the whole Judeo-Christian thing isn't quite enough anymore. I feel as though there's something otherworldly going on in my life as well and only forms of alternative spirituality seem to fit the bill." I finally let my gesticulating arms drop. Like Will Shakespeare seeing the finish line, I was now sprinting for it, talking double-time. "And *that's* where Madame Zora comes in. You see, the perfectly marvelous thing about her being both a midwife and a tarot card reader is that she brings her cards to the delivery and, at any time during all of that panting and pushing that I feel like it, she just whips them out and does a reading for me right there. Want to know how much longer or difficult the labor will be? Done. Want to know if it's going to be a boy or a girl? Done. Grow up to be a criminal or a Cabinet minister? A harlot or a talk-show host?" I folded my arms across my chest and nodded my head twice for emphasis. "Done and done."

Constance, who was occasionally given to wearing healing crystals, regardless of their individual prescriptive properties, but rather merely because they matched with that day's outfit and eyes, clapped again. "It's just…too brilliant for words!"

Louise was not quite as enthusiastic as Constance, but she certainly seemed glad that there'd be something different to talk about, while Dodo was clearly dead set against.

"And does this…*Zora* person have any legitimate medical qualifications?"

"Course not. If she did, what would be the point?"

"Well, then, what do you suppose is going to happen if things *don't* go perfectly, if it turns out to be *not* a matter so simple as shaking a package of voodoo herbs around the birthing chair and chanting to the baby, 'Come out, come out wherever you are'? What will you do if something goes wrong that Xena, Warrior Princess isn't able to handle with her mood rings?"

"Oh *that*." I flicked my wrist in perfect pooh-pooh form. "That's what the flying squad's for."

"The flying squad?"

"Yes," I said, showing unwarranted exasperation at her lack of knowledge, when I myself had only gleaned this information from *What to Expect*. Since she had her own copy, supposedly she should have been aware of this herself. But I guessed that, since she thought I was using Dr. Shelton, she hadn't figured on it being necessary for her to read up on alternative birthing options. "Don't you know that, for us Brits, it's not at all uncommon to want a home birth? Why, we do it all the time. Just to be on the safe side, though, we like to keep the flying squad at the ready. That's a fully equipped ambulance to you laypeople, ready to take me and baby to hospital should the need arise. Course, in my situation, it won't."

Dodo put her hand to her chest. "Well I *am* relieved to hear that, Jane. To know that competent medical help will be nearby will give me a lot of comfort."

"Glad to be able to relieve your mind so easily. But really, girls, I think I can guarantee that this is one delivery that will go off without a hitch."

I had high hopes for this lunch. Perhaps, after nearly thirty years, my mother and I were finally going to bond.

My mother and I had just been seated at our table at

Meat! *Meat!! MEAT!!!,* a new restaurant she'd insisted we check out.

What an odd name for someone to choose to give to an eating establishment, I thought.

"Isn't it a bit—let's see—crass? Or is *vulgar* the word I want?" I observed aloud, rubbernecking to see the handsome waiters strolling around in butchers' uniforms with suspiciously authentic stains which were, hopefully, ketchup, on their aprons. "Aren't the sides of beef hanging by the menus in the front window just a tad bit *de trop?*"

"I'll have you know, Jane, that this restaurant is considered by all the best guidebooks to be very trendy right now." She arranged her napkin in her lap at the same time rearranging her buttocks on the chair by doing one of those lift-one-cheek-and-then-the-other moves that never failed to annoy me. It was as though she had gas and was expressing it in a prissily obvious sort of way.

"What guidebooks have you been reading? *Butchers Monthly?*"

"Don't be absurd, Jane. There is no such magazine." Couldn't fool her. "No, I meant real guidebooks, not imaginary ones. Anyway, the critics say that Meat! *Meat!! MEAT!!!* is just the high point of the cultural backlash they've been forecasting for some time now. After all, you can't expect people to be excited about dining on healthy cuisine indefinitely. Radicchio, my foot. It's just not natural." She leaned in closer and whispered, "They predict that drinking's going to make a comeback too, and that soon people will be donning buttons that say, I'm a smoker and I'm proud of it." She did the shifting around thing with her buttocks again in her chair. "Anyway, I know what a crazy diet you always eat and I'm worried that, now that you're pregnant, you won't get enough protein."

"Yes, I suppose it would seem to be a crazy diet to others, the attempt to avoid unnecessarily large quantities of animal fat."

"Now there's no need to get huffy. There was that bizarre smoothie phase of yours not too long ago."

"True."

"And the cantaloupe-at-every-meal phase during your university years."

"Guilty."

"And the first diet you ever went on, when you were ten. Wasn't that Dr. Sitwell's Sit Well and Live Longer Diet, the one that guaranteed you a long life and eternal slimness if only you did all of your eating before noon? The one that said it was okay to eat five thousand calories a day, even if you ate it all in the form of sticks of butter, provided you did it all before the clock struck twelve?"

"Fine. All right already. Point made."

"I seem to recall you actually gaining quite a bit of weight on that one."

I sniffed. "Well, that was just because I started getting too hungry late in the day, what with not eating or drinking at all during the eleven hours between noon and bedtime. It was like a sort of Ramadan in reverse. It got so bad that I took to going to sleep at four in the afternoon, around the time that everyone else was enjoying the tea I couldn't have. Then I'd get up at midnight, declare it to be a new eating day, and eat my way straight through to noon."

"No wonder you turned into such a little butterball that summer."

"You have such an endearing way with words, Mother."

Just then the waiter came and I observed her as she placed an order for a sirloin steak—not terribly original—which I noticed she placed by weight.

This maternal cross I'd been bearing for nearly three decades was still quite pretty in a well-preserved way. She tinted her hair champagne-colored just often enough that no one would ever guess it was still a very pretty black underneath. Her blue eyes had the confidence shown only by women who have lived without a man for a long time, deciding that they like it that way just fine. And her body was in just the optimum good shape for people to think that she was genetically lucky rather than desperately spending hours in the gym in an attempt to beat time. In fact, were it not for the fact that she made me stark-raving bonkers any time I had to be around her for more than five seconds, I might have admired her.

"I'll have what she's having," I informed our waiter, Butcher Brad according to the red script that was embroidered on his uniform, handing over the menu, "but half."

Now it was my mother's turn to sniff, proving from where genetically I'd acquired that nasty little habit. "I knew that you'd object to red meat, probably say something about too much of it not being good for the baby, but it had been my hope that, if I just got you here, I could persuade you to eat enough in one sitting to carry you through the next several months. You are," and here she cast a severe eye on my form, "looking remarkably slender for a pregnant lady."

This from a woman who had bandied about that dreaded word *butterball* only moments before.

"Isn't there something else we can talk about besides food, Mother?"

"Fine."

I was consigned to mineral water as she took a sip of wine poured from the split Butcher Brad set down in front of her. For the first time I registered that there was something awfully familiar about this Butcher Brad, but I only got a glimpse of his face, overwhelmed as it was by his floppy big chef's toque, before being distracted by my mother's next words.

"Have you given any thought to what you might like to name the baby? I was thinking that naming him after your late father might be a nice gesture."

I spewed water all over the tablecloth, which was actually large sheets of butcher's paper. "Do you really think the world needs another Hugh Pugh Taylor getting the shit kicked out of him at public school?"

"Watch your mouth and lower your voice, Jane. Your paternal grandmother's family name isn't that bad."

"Not when it's paired with anything else, Pugh's not that bad, which certainly isn't saying that it's ever good. But when it's paired with Hugh, well…didn't you ever think it was suspicious that Daddy used to introduce himself by saying to people, 'Please just call me Taylor. Really, Taylor's just fine'?"

Butcher Brad set our hot plates before us, my mother's slab of meat stretching over the edges, while mine just took up most of the plate. There was a halfhearted attempt at some roasted potatoes and a mixed veg squeezed onto the plates, too, as if in concession to the delicate sensibilities of those diners who needed the illusion that they were eating an omnivorously balanced meal. I took up my serrated knife and fork with an odd feeling of relish and tucked in. It's amazing how cannibalistically tempting a juicy piece of meat can look at times when one's mother is sitting across the table.

"Well," she said, her own bold knife and fork already going to town, "if you're not going to name the baby—if it's a boy, that is—after your father, and I'm sure you won't be naming him after Trevor, not after he did a bounder on you, then what are you going to do about a name?"

God, I hated it when she put it like that; ever since I'd told her about my canceled wedding plans, just two hours after telling her about the baby and impending marriage in the first place, she'd been insufferable. Then, too, there was sister Sophie, who'd also been insufferable of late. After her initial sisterly surge of sentiment regarding our nearly parallel pregnancies, the fact that she was four months further along than me went straight to her head, resulting in near-daily phone calls to see that I wasn't doing anything stupid. It'd gotten to the point where I didn't even bother answering the phone with a "hello" anymore, preferring to cut straight to the meat of "No, Sophie, I haven't been using any mod-cons like the microwave lately" and "No, I haven't been inhaling any aerosol cans."

"It's not as though Hugh Pugh and Trevor are the only two boys' names in the world, is it?" I said now. "Anyway, I've already selected some strong candidates."

"Oh?"

"Yes, I was thinking either Balthasar or Attila."

Butcher Brad paused in his duties in order to pat my choking mother on the back. As he patted her, he made eye contact with me and the other shoe finally dropped. Good God, it was David's Christopher! What the hell was he doing here? But before I could query the ostensible architect as to what he was doing dressed up as a waiter at Mcat! *Meat!! MEAT!!!*, he smiled widely at me over the top of her head, winked conspiratorially, and indicated with a nod that I should continue with my conversation.

"If I name him Attila, see," I elucidated, stumbling a bit at first as I was still stunned at Brad-Christopher, "the chances of his getting beat up at school are greatly minimized. People just don't go around beating up people named Attila. In fact, the only problem I see would be if he turned out to be very effeminate of feature, in which case some knobhead might think it funny to nickname him Tilly."

"And Balthasar?" Choking incident averted, I watched Christopher go as she took a big gulp of water. "You can't think of anything objectionable, like with Attila, that might keep you from doing *that*?"

"God, no. What's wrong with Balthasar?"

"Everything?"

"But Balthasar was one of the three wise men. You

know, the guys who brought all that stuff to Jesus. You *are* always saying that you'd like to see me become more religious."

"Wouldn't it be easier to just attend church every now and then?"

"I don't see why you're getting so upset about Balthasar. It's not like I wanted to name him Melchior or anything, which was the name of one of the other two wise men, in case you've forgotten." Elbow on the table, I waved my fork around in the air and squinted as though deep in thought. "Now, as for the last wise man, I can never quite remember his name…."

"Me, either."

"Anyway, it doesn't matter. I'm almost certain it's going to be a girl."

"Oh?"

"Yes. And if it is, I'm going to name her Angharad. After one of the characters in those Lloyd Alexander books I used to love so much as a child."

"I told your father it wasn't wise, teaching you to read."

"But if it does turn out to be a boy after all, I have one other name I've been kicking around." I leaned over, laughing, distracted by the fiction I was creating even as I spoke. "You know, I met one woman who said that her doctor swore to her that she was going to have a boy and that he was sure because the boy, based on the pictures, was going to have a really big—" I looked around at the other diners, lowered my voice still further and whispered knowingly "—a really big *you know*. Turned out in the end, though, that what the doctor thought was a boy with a big—" meaningful pause again "—*you know*, was in reality a girl and a big shadow."

"The name, Jane? You were going to tell me about this other name?"

"Oh, right. Here. Let me write this one down for you." I rummaged in my purse until I found a pen and a crumpled sheet of paper.

"I don't know why you have to be so secretive," my mother said as I scribbled.

I looked up at her, cagily, going a little bit Nancy from *Oliver Twist*. "Don't want anyone else to steal it, do I? Don't believe anyone else has got one of these." Then, like a hardened businessman, I shoved the folded slip of paper across the table toward her.

She carefully unfolded it, giving it the ticking-bomb treatment. When she saw what I'd written, she gasped again. "You can't be serious, Jane! Surely even you can't be intending to call your own baby…Satan?"

"Oh, Mother," I half whined, as though she might be the most drearily stupid woman in the world. "That's just the way it's spelled. When you pronounce it, however, the accent is on the second *a,* like the name of that old diet guru Martin Katahn, except that this is pronounced Satahn and spelled Satan. Have you got it straight now?"

Okay, so maybe the Satan thing was a bit cruel. But she had called me a butterball, hadn't she? And it hadn't been the first time. Now, then, I ask you: what girl wants to be called a butterball, with fair regularity, by her *own* mother?

Tit for tat; Satan for butterball. The way I figure it, it's all a wash in the end.

So Mother went back to gulping wine, while I continued to wonder just what the hell Christopher had been doing there.

"Jane, I can explain everything."

Well, this was certainly a first in my life, someone directing those words at me. Usually it was the other way round.

"Yes, I'm sure you can, David. Like why, after years of telling me that the only meat gay people go for is filet mignon, you should choose to open a cattle emporium."

"There's no need to be so hard on him." This from Christopher who'd come knocking on my door with David following the late-night closing of the restaurant.

In my fuzzy bathrobe, I felt at a slight disadvantage to their well-groomed splendor.

"It's really all my fault," Christopher continued, moving into the room and making himself quite at home. "*He* wanted to open a vegetarian place, perhaps with a heavy Middle Eastern influence, but *I* told him, 'No, no, no, no, no. Covent Garden's got way too much of that granola stuff going on as it is. Really, the Retro Nouveau Hippie movement—or whatever the hell you want to call it—should be going out the fashion window just about any second now—'"

"Which was when *I* said, 'How about fish?' " cut in David.

"Which explains how hilarious we got when I spelled out Fish! *Fish!! FISH!!!* that time we all went to that greasy tandoori place, because of course I explained to David that it would be worse than useless to open an all-fish place in the middle of England, as if people would come there for the crab cakes or sushi or something—"

"But then afterward, after we dropped you off that night, Christopher said, 'But you know, having a one-note restaurant might not be a bad idea, and I really do think that meat is on its way back in. As a matter of fact, we're just about due, calendar-wise, for a Retro Yuppie movement, and they were always big on steaks as big as a plate—'"

"Hence, Meat! *Meat!! MEAT!!!* was born."

I glared at them both. "That still doesn't explain why all of a sudden you're interested in meat other than filet mignon *or why you didn't invite me to the opening!*"

"David doesn't have to eat it," Christopher answered the first. "He just has to cook it."

"I was scared to," shrugged David, answering the second.

"But why?" I asked.

"Because he's the chef," said Christopher.

"I didn't mean you!"

"Because of, well, the way you are now, for example," said David. "You know, you really have been quite a volatile little girl ever since Trevor left."

Which was true. Despite my euphoria at having met Tolkien, I was so used to playing the part of the Pregnant Woman Whose Man Has Left Her at work, that the role had permeated the rest of my life. Plus, I was in love, and being in love produces just as many volatile emotions as being jilted does, so it was sort of like I was having a double dose of PMS at every waking moment. Then, too, even though I *was* in love, Tolkien hadn't called me yet.

David continued. "I didn't want to push you over the edge in a situation where there would be, quite naturally, a lot of steak knives involved."

Since what he said made a warped kind of sense, at least within the context of our bizarre world, I chose to ignore it, rounding on Christopher once more. "And what about you? How did *you* wind up getting to be Butcher Brad? Hmm?"

"Oh, that. Well, I quit my day job as an architect, didn't I? After all, good help is always hard to find, David needed good help, and I love David."

This was really the limit. I flopped down on the sofa, completely deflated. "Oh, why can't *I* be a gay man?" I asked the ceiling, reflecting on how much these two loved one another and how, well, uncomplicated their love seemed.

It was a good thing that I was the only one in the room who knew I was occupying the moral low ground here, for I had neglected to tell my best friend David about my discussion with Alice and the book I was writing in the early hours of the morning.

Why? you may well ask.

Because while it was perfectly acceptable for me to have my best friend think that I would do such an insane thing because I'm, well, insane, it would be quite another for him to learn that there was now a profit motive involved. What can I say in my defense? I have a weird morality and I didn't want David, who had always loved me in spite of my worst self, to think ill of me.

Determined to be unreasonable to the bitter end, figuring that what they didn't know about my own omissions wouldn't hurt me, I rolled over onto my stomach and glanced sullenly at David over the top of a pillow. "And when were you going to tell me about all of this?"

"When I was a success?" he asked more than answered.

"Well," Christopher put in helpfully, "at least you got the better of your mother for one brief shining moment today."

Oh my God. OhmyGod. Omigod*omigodo*MYGOD!

It was Tolkien, on the phone, calling me at last!

Oh, I thought frantically, if only I could place him on hold for a moment and put in an emergency call to David. Surely *he'd* know the right things to say.

But I couldn't do that. I mean, I knew that I couldn't do that. That would be insane. What I had to do was, I had to still the wild beating of my heart just long enough to hear him say—

"—pick you up at eight on Saturday night, then?"

"Yes," I just barely managed to reply.

"Glad to hear that you can talk." I was sure I heard him smile through the phone. "This is the first thing you've said since you said 'hello.'"

I closed my eyes with the sheer joy of it, holding the phone tight against my ear. "Yes."

"Okay," he said, "that's great then. You can talk and we have a date."

"Yes."

"Yes."

From the thrill of triumph with Mother to the agonizing pain of defeat with Sophie: with her baby's due date just around the corner, yes, dear reader, it was time once again to be showered to death. What with all of the wedding-baby showers of friends, acquaintances and near strangers that I'd been to in the last few years—a fate that I am certain is shared by all other UUs of my age—there were times when I felt as though I'd been a well-wisher at the happy events of every woman in the European Union.

I suppose that, as her only sister, I should have been more instrumental in planning Sophie's first baby shower. But I'd been rather busy lately, hadn't I? Anyway, the upshot was that I'd forgotten all about it and so the arrival in my mail slot of an invitation to her shower had come as a bit of a shock. Oh, I'm sure she must have told me about it at some point, probably rather frequently, but whoever listens to Sophie if they can help it?

I did know that, unlike with bridal showers, baby showers were rarely a surprise. True, if you made a bridal shower a surprise and the bride happened to be a fairly big drinker, you then ran the risk of her not showing up for whatever fake event you'd told her you'd planned on the given day. But if you tried to make a baby shower a surprise, you ran the added risk, not just of the honoree not showing up, but that when she did so, she'd be so shocked and overwhelmed by the outpouring of emotion that she'd go into premature labor and then whoever'd thrown the party would have the burden of a baby spending the first few months of its life in an incubator on their conscience.

All of which made me glad that I wasn't the one who was hostessing Sophie's shower. The problem was the person who was.

"No, Mother, for the last time. I'd love to be able to help you transform the living room into a faux nursery for Saturday, but as I've already said I think a few thousand times, we're rather swamped here at work these days. You know, even though it's still summer, the fall lists will be coming out soon and then it will be Christmas…."

"She is your sister, Jane."

"Yes. I'm sure you've mentioned that a few times. In spite of that, though, I'm sorry. I'll just have to be a guest this time." Which was good because then I'd just have to phony smile at everyone when I first met them and not through the entire day as a co-hostess might. "Anyway, I thought that Sophie'd made a lot of new friends during those parentcraft classes that she and Tony have been taking. Can't you put the touch on one of them to help you hang silicone bottle nipples as decorations?"

"Well, I suppose…"

The day of Sophie's shower finally dawned, one of those airless days you get sometimes. As I walked up the path, I reflected that my personal forecast read: "should be anywhere else but here."

The living room had been transformed into a nightmare of baby cuteness, too awful to live through again via my own powers of description. Suffice it to say that, since Sophie and Tony had been adamant about not learning the sex of the baby ahead of time, there was every yellow, blue and pink permutation of baby-themed items on display, not to mention the bunting and balloons. When I tried to go into the kitchen, just off the living room, to see what kind of food and beverages would be on offer for the afternoon—some wine, maybe?—I was struck in the face by a low-flying decoration that had been attached to the ceiling: a yellow cloth nappy with "Welcome Loved Baby" stitched in alternating letters of pink and blue across the place where the baby's bottom would one day be. I was beginning to feel that I'd stumbled into a Hieronymus Bosch painting in which H.B. himself had stumbled onto the wrong color palette.

"Are you sure you should be drinking wine, Jane? I thought that pregnant women these days didn't."

"Oh. That?" I laughed nervously at Mother's words, pointing to the wineglass on the counter as if someone else might have put it there. In reality, having not seen any wine bottles set out along with the inevitable fruit punch and slimlime cola, I'd fished in the back of the upper shelf of her fridge until I came up with what I'd known I'd find there: an industrial-size bottle of cheap Italian red. "Oh, I just put that out in case some of your other guests might want a glass but were too shy to ask. You know, I'm sure that not everybody you've invited today can all be pregnant."

"Actually…"

But I was saved by the doorbell, telling my mother to get it as my hands were completely tied up—couldn't she see?—with the task of finding a place in the fridge for that huge jug. While she was gone ushering guests in I took the opportunity to down the entire contents of the large glass of wine. It was going to be a long afternoon and, if I wasn't fortified well, I'd die.

Research, I reminded myself.

Sucking down the last of the dregs, I reflected on how I might best utilize what would undoubtedly be an awful day. I'd knocked off the first third of the book, which represented the first trimester of pregnancy, effortlessly. This annoying shower business, I decided, would find its place in the last third somewhere. As for the middle of the book? That I'd write last. Middles of books, as everyone knew, were always the most tedious. It was beginnings and endings that were fun. So, in a way, I was here on business. Bloody hell, if I were already a published author, I could probably deduct my present to Sophie as a business expense.

Research.

"Jane, this is one of Sophie's new best friends, Peg. They met in parentcraft class. Peg's offered to help me co-hostess the festivities today."

The woman before me would have been scary even if she wasn't pregnant but, with a belly bulging under her bow-tied maternity blouse that looked like it was set to go off at any second, she looked like a battleship with its very own individualistic destroyer missile.

"You must be the sister," Peg said, shifting the very large and prettily wrapped package she was carrying onto one hip so that she could offer me her hand in a stiff shake. "I've heard of you."

From the skeptical look on her face, apparently none of it was good.

"Charmed," I replied.

"Oh!" my mother cried, remembering her hostess manners. "I should have taken that big package from you right away. Is it heavy? Here, let me show you where the table is that I've set up to lay out the presents. Oh, and you come too, Jane. I'm sure you'll want to see it as well. Since you just came straight to the kitchen when you got here, you didn't get a chance to put your present for Sophie down, either."

When we got to the present table—more pink, more yellow, more blue—Peg put her present down and both women turned to look at me: me, who was clearly carrying nothing larger and nothing more than a fashionable handbag, barely bigger than a cigarette case. I opened it up and pulled out the folded-over sheet of paper. They looked at me like I was daft.

"It's a gift certificate," I explained.

"For your sister?" they both asked as one.

"Well, it's not just any gift certificate," I explained. "It's to one of those super-duper mother-baby shops. You know the places? Mother Mayhem, Diaper Dream, one of those." I looked at the gift certificate to see what it said. "Oops." I laughed a hollow laugh. "It's called Mother and Baby. Now how could I forget something as simple as that?"

"Do you know you have a red stain on your blouse?" Peg asked. "It looks oddly like cheap Italian wine."

From there, the day only worked its way firmly toward worse.

I wound up getting as drunk as repeated trips to the kitchen when no one else was there would allow. This meant that I focused my alcoholic efforts on the period of time when my mother had seen to it that everyone else had overfull plates, finally sitting down for ten minutes to eat herself, and the period of time when everyone was firmly focused on Sophie unwrapping her presents, as though spare disposable diapers and bottom wipes were the most fascinating things in the world. This further meant, having downed two glasses in rapid succession on each of the two occasions I had escaped to the kitchen, that the shower passed like an alternately blissful and hellish blur with Sophie's friends impressing me as no more than a massive amoebalike blob of pregnancy as they seemed to move in a group, the presents streaming by my consciousness with me looking a little bit silly when I screamed when a giant stuffed purple animal—I think people said his name was Barney something—got too close. Other than that, nothing much bothered me until my mother accused me hissingly, in the kitchen, of being drunk.

"Am not," I hiccupped.

"Are so," she said, adding, "and you pregnant."

"Am not," I maintained.

"Oh, yeah? Then what's that red stain doing on your shirt?"

"I told you before—I poured a couple of glasses in case there were any unpregnant guests who wanted any."

"Before the stain was the size of a spot. Now it looks more like Australia."

"Well, I didn't *try* to turn it into a whole continent. I was merely trying to remove the stain that was already there."

"Well," my mother pointed out, "you didn't do a very good job."

And so it went.

Not long after being accused of being a drunken pregnant woman, I pleaded hormonal fatigue to explain away the wooziness, congratulated Sophie on helping to make the world a more overly populated place, and hailed a taxi, worried that I was too drunk to take the tube and might somehow get myself into trouble.

Of course, had I been in usual top form that day, I might have thought to point out to dear old preachy Mum that family legend had it that she'd spent both of her own pregnancies bombed to the gills. Or, alternatively, I might have pointed out that she herself was not exactly a font of maternal sentiment, having repeatedly heard her recall her decision to have a second child so quickly after the first as: "Jane? Oh, yes. Well, we didn't think it would be good for Sophie to be an only child. You know how people so often get a second cat so that the first won't be lonely? Well, that's why we had Jane. Jane was our second cat." As it was, the opportunity had eluded me.

The last thing I would ever want, I thought to myself as I bounced along in the back seat of a shiny black cab, would be to become like any of those women I had just been with.

Whom I couldn't remember very well at all.

For our first formal date, Tolkien took me to a private club where they had a retro band competition going on and they had this foursome of mop tops on stage who were seriously into their Beatles thing. Yawn. As if any Englishman ever needed to hear "Hey Jude" *just one more time.* On the plus side though, since it was a private club and one had to be accompanied by a member to get in, and since no one I knew would be caught dead there, the chances of my running into anyone who knew me as five-months-pregnant Jane were zippo. On the downside, I did have to listen to what was probably one of the worst renditions ever of "Yesterday." Yes, we all know that it's the world's all-time favorite song, but it really is a lot like the whole "Stairway to Heaven" thing: once you've heard the same song eighty million times, it's kind of tough to feel the same sentimental charge (unless of course one keeps on smoking dope heavily well into one's later years). I mean, come on, it's like having a multiple orgasm that's gone on one too many times; after a while, it gets to be like, "Uh, honey? Do you think we might go out for some chips now?" Back on the plus side, however, when the band did a fairly credible version of "I Want to Hold Your Hand" and Tolkien shyly asked if he could hold mine, something that used to be just a little bit too hard in me began to melt and I found myself grinning widely.

Naturally, given my extraordinary situation—I certainly didn't want him to think that I was pregnant, while I definitely didn't want anyone else to suspect that I was not—I had to take extra precautions about everything. Take him picking me up, for instance.

Tolkien, being the gentleman that he was, had insisted upon picking me up at my place, despite my protestations that it was completely unnecessary and that I could easily get anywhere on my own steam to meet him at any time he'd like.

"Besides," he'd said, "you can never begin a relationship from a place of trust if you start out by always meeting at neutral locations. I've got to see your place and you've got to see mine. Otherwise, how will each of us ever know that the other isn't leading some kind of double life?"

"Oh? Forgive me for saying this, but isn't that a little extreme? After all, how can we begin a relationship from a place of trust when we begin it from a place of mistrust?"

"I suppose I should make a confession up front. I'm an undercover cop for Scotland Yard. Remember that mustache on the first night we met? I'd been working a case earlier."

Good God! Scotland Yard, C.I.D.! If I'd had any sense, I would have pulled out right there, before running the risk of being caught out by a real professional.

But I didn't have any sense. Or at least apparently not where Tolkien Donald was concerned. I agreed to see him again, and I even agreed to let him pick me up.

Of course that in itself required its own peculiar machinations.

Ever since I'd moved to Knightsbridge, I'd been cursed with the kind of nosy neighbors that I'd previously thought existed solely within the realm of television. In my case, the Marcuses had always seemed to have their hands right in Trevor's and my soup, even though they lived on the floor below. So naturally, when Trevor and I had broken up, they'd been right there with their front-and-center seats, on hand to hear whatever they could with their water glasses peeled to the walls but most notably the word *baby* getting bandied about like a neon-green Spaulding at Wimbledon. Now that they thought I was pregnant, it was important to maintain that fiction, particularly in case either my mother or Sophie should stop by and get snared in a conversation with them. This meant that they needed to see me in the same loose-flowing nondescript outfits that I'd been wearing to work in order to maintain the illusion that some growing might be going on beneath my clothes. This also meant that when Tolkien came to pick me up, *in July,* over the funky and tight-fitting outfit I'd selected (I was going for sexy but not trampish and was sure I'd succeeded), I'd donned a long shantung-silk dark coat of the tentish variety that I'd found in a secondhand shop, the kind of coat formerly worn by politicians' wives in the fifties who'd wanted to downplay their pregnant conditions by admitting to no body shape at all.

"You won't be too hot in that?" Tolkien'd asked, his brow furrowed in concern as I locked the door behind me.

"Not at all," I'd responded, passing the Marcuses' open

door as we'd crossed the second-floor landing on our way down. I gave Mr. and Mrs. Marcus a friendly smile while mouthing the words "just a friend," all the while thinking, "you silly old cows. If not for you, I wouldn't be sweltering in this ugly thing."

"Really, Tolkien," I'd assured him, "I'm fine. It's just that, in the summer, I find that some places turn on the air-conditioning *so* high that I need to wear something warm until I've had the chance to acclimate my body temperature. I'm sure that once we get to where we're going, and I've taken my usual minute, I'll be ready to shed this thing in no time at all."

Oddly enough, considering his C.I.D. experience, he didn't appear to take my oddness for anything more suspicious than the unabashed display of oddness that it was.

Of course the elderly Marcuses—her with her floral aprons over housedresses and he with his suspenders that served no business-world purpose whatsoever—were also the reason that I, later on that same evening, having decided that I liked the Beatles again just fine if they gave me an excuse to hold any part at all of Tolkien, when he asked if I wanted to go back to my place, was forced to reply, chirpily, "Oh, can't we just go to yours?"

The way I figured it, with me being pregnant, I couldn't very well let the neighbors start thinking I was some kind of tramp, now, could I?

Tolkien looked embarrassed for the first time since I'd met him. "But your place looked so comfortable, Jane, while mine is, well, so bachelory."

"Now, now," I wagged my finger coyly, "weren't you the one saying earlier that you'd show me yours if I showed you mine?"

And so he did.

It turned out that by "bachelory," what Tolkien had really meant was lacking in personality. Oh, sure, there were tables and chairs and assorted other furniture, as well as the prerequisite male perfect sound system and trillion-strong collection of tapes and CDs. But there was nothing meaningful on the walls and, except for the testosterone temple to music, everything had a transient feel as if it could poof up in smoke in a minute and the owner wouldn't mind.

"Well," he said, pouring me a glass of wine, after I'd as politely as possible commented on the neuter decor, "a person never knows when he might have to up and move."

"Oh." That explained everything. "Your job must have you moving about frequently, all that undercover work and stuff."

"No, not really. So long as I have effective disguises, it's not really essential for me to move from safe house to safe house."

"Well, then, did you just move here recently?"

"No. Been here about two years."

"Ah."

"See, the way I figure it, sometimes a person goes through periods in his or her life when they just know that they're in transit, like one of those caterpillar things on the way to something better." He looked at me meaningfully then. "The way I figure it, the last couple of years of my life have just been a holding pattern."

In the event, it didn't matter that all of Tolkien's furniture, even that in his bedroom, was no more than utilitarian. In the event, all that mattered was that he treated me to the kind of orgasm that made my toes curl, my eyes snapping open with both disbelief and belief, and that I was able to be there to see the same thing happen for him.

God knows, it wasn't going to be easy, keeping my pregnant and nonpregnant worlds running well and simultaneously, but I was newly determined to try.

"Gee, your baby doesn't move very much, does he? Are you sure he's okay in there?"

"What the hell do you think you're doing?"

Stan from Accounting had snuck up on me noiselessly while I'd been going over the quarterly sales figures on the latest Colin Smythe. He'd put his arms around me from behind, determinedly rubbing my abdomen.

"I'm checking for early fetal movement," he said, still rubbing.

Oh, the things we pregnant women had to endure. "Well, *my* baby's the silent, refined type."

"But I thought all you skinny bitches had babies that you could feel moving real early."

"How would you know a thing like that?"

"Because my sister's a skinny bitch and her baby started moving right before the end of month four, just like clockwork."

"I can't believe they allow members of your family to breed, Stan. There ought to be a law." Damn! When I'd read about early fetal movement in the pregnancy books, I'd known that this was going to be one of those niggling little picayune details that was going to rear up and bite me on the arse; I just hadn't imagined it doing so in such a tactilely odious way. "And cut that out!" I said, finally batting his rubbing hands away. "Go find some numbers to crunch or something."

In spite of how much Stan from Accounting annoyed me, I knew that he kind of had something there. In the absence of the more typical evidence of a fetal presence, like kicks that others could feel, it would be nice if I had something tangible to offer. Hoping to get some bright ideas, I phoned Dodo and told her I wouldn't be in to work that morning, claiming a nosebleed that just wouldn't quit, graphically adding a thoroughly ruined white silk blouse for good measure. Then, instead of going into the office, I hightailed it over to a prenatal clinic I'd noticed one day. I figured it was as good a place as any to go trawling for ideas.

Okay, so maybe I was on some kind of blind scavenger hunt in which I had no idea what I was scavenging for, because, truthfully, I wasn't even sure what I expected or hoped to find. All I knew was that Stan from Accounting might one day demand proof of my baby's existence and a prenatal clinic seemed like the right spot to learn what— other than big, fat bellies—other women used as proof that there was legitimate life growing within.

"Can I help you?" asked the nurse behind the glass partition as I entered the crowded waiting room. At Sophie's baby shower I'd absorbed the lesson that, while two might still be considered company, one pregnant lady often constituted a crowd.

"Oh no," I said, looking around in hopes of spotting a vacant seat.

"You're not here to see a doctor?"

"God, no."

Ah! Found one!

"Then you're here for…?" She left the question open-ended, I suspect in hopes that I would finish it up. When I failed to do so, however, she must have figured the entire conversation was now up to her. "To pick someone else up perhaps?"

I stabbed the air with my forefinger. "That's it exactly."

I began riffling through the remaining magazines on the cheap wooden table—God! Why did Reese Witherspoon have to be on everything this month?—until I remembered that I was supposed to be there doing my research, not reading magazines for free.

"Hello," I said brightly to the very pregnant lady sitting right next to me. "Been coming here long, have you?"

She tried not to look at me as though I were the oddest creature on earth. "Er, well, I have been coming here for as long as I've been pregnant."

"Ah. I see." Not very forthcoming, was she? I could see that I was going to have to work hard at this one. "Do you find that—being far along as you obviously are—that people ever expect you to offer them some kind of surefire proof that you're really carrying a baby in there and that it's not just some kind of a hoax you've cooked up?"

Without bothering to answer me, she struggled out of her chair and over to the nurses' station, demanding to see the doctor right away.

Oh, well, I thought to myself as I watched the bewildered nurse allow her to pass through, there were still plenty of other pregos out here for me to question.

I leaned across the cheap wooden table in order to whisper to the moderately pregnant woman who was just on the other side. "How about you? If other people can't feel your baby kick, do they just accuse you of making it up?"

Another one who wouldn't answer the simplest of questions. Rather than engaging in the fun of talking to me, she too went up to the nurse, saying she was ready to pee in the cup now and that when she was done, she'd gladly freeze her butt off in whatever cold room wasn't being used at present.

After she'd also passed through, the nurse addressed me, a suspicious expression on her face. "Excuse me, who did you say you were here to pick up?"

"Umm...Julie?"

She shook her head.

"Sharon?"

She shook it again.

"Marianne? Siobhan? Lily?"

She began to rise from her chair, all starch and authority.

"Well, who have you got on your appointment list there?" I asked, getting desperate. "I'm sure it must be one of them."

"You're going to have to leave," she said, forcing me to my feet as she gripped me under the arm and marched me toward the door. "You obviously have no business being here and you're disturbing the other patients."

"But it's a free country."

"Actually, it's a constitutional monarchy, which is not necessarily synonymous." Then she slammed the door in my face.

I sat on the edge of the curb, trying to keep my feet out of the way of passing traffic as it whizzed on by. Well, that hadn't done any good. I'd wasted the morning with a bunch of pregos and I still didn't have the answer to the question of what proof I had to offer suspicious minds like Stan's from Accounting.

I was just beginning to debate the idea of hunting down some Greek food, when the very pregnant lady, the first one I'd spoken to while still inside, exited the clinic door. She was holding some papers in her hand that she was excitedly looking at as she moved down the street.

Hopping to my feet, I brushed off the bottom of my shorts and hurried to catch her up. "Excuse me?"

"Oh, God, it's you again," she accused, pressing the pages to her breast.

"Please don't run off," I begged. "You looked so happy when you came out of there." I indicated the clinic door. "I wouldn't want to do anything to change that, and I can assure you that I'm absolutely harmless. I only wanted to ask someone, someone who would obviously know the answers to a few innocent questions about pregnancy."

She still looked skeptical.

"Look," I pointed, "there's a bobby right there on the corner. If I upset you too much, you can always have him arrest me."

She folded her arms. "So what did you want to know?"

"Well, mostly, what I want to know is what you offer people as proof that you're really pregnant? I mean, *I'm* content to take you at your word, but say if other people couldn't feel your baby kick, even though you told them it did, do you have anything you could show them that would make them sit back and say, 'Ah, there really is a life growing in there'?"

When I'd posed the question, I worried that she might call the bobby but, oddly enough, her expression softened into a smile.

"Well, today I've got these, haven't I?" She showed me the pages she'd been clutching, peering over my shoulder as I studied them. They were blurry black-and-white photos with swirly shapes on them that were kind of like the Milky Way but rounder.

"What are these?" I asked.

"Why, they're my baby."

"These?"

"I had an ultrasound done today. These are the sonogram pictures. This is my baby's head," she pointed, "and this is his bottom."

I didn't tell her, because I thought it might be rude, but her baby's head and bottom looked exactly the same to me.

She must have read my expression because she shrugged, unconcerned. "Well, that's what the technician said anyway."

"You're kind of late in your pregnancy to be having one of these, aren't you?"

"Not necessarily. They can do them from the fifth week right on through."

"Nothing's wrong, I hope."

"Oh, no." She looked slightly embarrassed. "It's silly, really. But, well, the first time they did an ultrasound, the genital organs weren't distinguishable yet and, well, I did so want to decorate the baby's nursery before he came. It is a he, by the way, you can tell by that thing over there. Anyway, I figured that by having another ultrasound done in my seventh month—" God! I'd thought she was nearly done! Good thing I hadn't said anything "—they could tell with reasonable certainty, even though it's never hundred percent."

"They're really great pictures," I lied. "You can really see a lot in them." My mind, however, was turning toward other things. "Now, say a person was only supposed to be in her fourth month of pregnancy. If that person had a sonogram, would it look similar to yours?"

"Well, for starters, no two are alike, I wouldn't imagine. Then, too, I'm not an expert, but I would think that someone who'd had some experience with these things *might* be able to detect a difference."

Rats! Stan from Accounting had relatives who bred like rabbits, apparently. If he'd been reading this lady's sonogram instead of that idiot of a technician they had in the clinic, she'd probably have been able to do up the nursery in little toy boats and blue, blue, blue months ago. In other words, Stan would probably be able to tell that these sonogram pictures showed a pregnancy that was far more advanced than mine was supposed to be at this point.

I felt dejected. "I guess then that it wouldn't matter how much I offered you to sell me your sonogram pictures. They wouldn't do me any good anyway."

"You were going to try to offer me money so that you could have these pictures of my baby?"

Glumly, I nodded.

She snatched the pages back out of my hand. "You're a sick, sick woman," she hissed and, before I even knew what I was about, she was off, moving down the street as quickly as her varicose-veined legs would allow.

Great! Now what was I going to do?

For the remainder of the day I—there's no other word for it—*stalked* women as they came out of the clinic. Still worried about Stan from Accounting's baby sophistication, I made sure to only target women who looked like their own pregnancies were within range of where mine was supposed to be at this stage. I know it wasn't particularly the nice thing to do but I just thought that if I could only get my hands on one of those pictures, I'd be made at work.

But, no matter how much money I offered those women—and I was willing to pay a lot—none of them were willing to part with those precious pictures of theirs. God! What was wrong with them? You'd think I was trying to buy their actual babies or something instead of some silly pictures. They could keep the babies, as far as I was concerned; pictures were much less fuss.

Yes—yes—yes, I *know* what that sounds like. And, believe me, I'm not sooo insensitive that it's beyond me to understand why these women might want to retain this early evidence of life growing within. But I didn't want to think about that right then. After all, they *were* going to eventually get babies to replace those pictures, while I, on the other hand, *needed* those pictures.

Still, by the end of the day I felt somewhat haggard. I knew I was lucky that none of them had tried to have me arrested, particularly since I had that same uneasy feeling I'd always had at university whenever I'd been in the process of purchasing illegal drugs. I envisioned myself stealing some pictures, possibly going through the clinic's trash after they'd closed for the day or whipping them out of the hands of some unsuspecting prego before sprinting off down the street, hoping the bobby wouldn't catch me before I managed to hail a cab, but I knew that wasn't on.

So there I was, in the middle of London, hot, tired, and I hadn't even gotten to have my Greek lunch. I was no closer to having tangible proof of my pregnancy and I now had a whole slew of pregos mad at me. Life as a writer-researcher pretty much well sucked.

At the end of the month, Dodo invited me to come with her for a long country weekend. It was curious how she'd come by the loan of the estate, which happened to be Duck's End, Colin Smythe's place. He'd offered it to her in a fit of gratitude over her ingenious saving of the American version of *Surf the Wind*. Somehow, she'd gotten another bestselling author to write a scathing letter to the *New York Times* concerning their reviewer's scathing review of Colin's book and the *Times,* in a most democratic fashion, had duly printed it.

Apparently, reviewers, contrary to their own inflated self-beliefs, don't matter very much. Oh, sure, books have to be reviewed, if only to have an alternative to advertising, but it just doesn't matter very much what gets said. "Attention must be paid," said Willie Loman, referring to something else entirely, and he was right but that was as far as it went.

If we were going to be weekending at Colin's place, then he was going to be weekending in the South of France, but before leaving for the airport, he'd been kind enough to take us on a little tour of the estate's more notable features.

The country estate proved to be everything one could want from such a place, even if it did have that unfortunate name. There were all kinds of lovely stone and brick-colored roofing on the outside that made it look more like it should be on a hillside on the outskirts of Florence than thirty miles outside of London. On the inside, the halls had Middle Eastern runners rather than carpets, a great hall with a fireplace that stretched up half of one barn-size wall, and there was even a genuine suit of armor, an unusually small one that Colin said was rumored to have belonged to Rizzio, the little Italian who had hung out with Mary Queen of Scots, that association leading to his untimely demise at the hands of her jealous husband's men.

Of course, when I, who have always been fascinated by the life of Mary, expressed undue interest in this detail, Colin quickly conceded that it might just as easily have belonged to a dwarfish distant cousin of a distant cousin of Henry VIII. He hastily added that he'd acquired the estate itself for a song from an MP who'd had to step down from his post and then rapidly sell his home in both disgrace and financial disarray following the disclosure that not only had he been caught out in the usual acts of buggery and/or marital infidelity, but that he'd compounded his crimes against the Crown with further acts of misuse of public funds, expense account fraud, acceptance of campaign monies from known criminals and just plain all-around bad judgment.

"I hate to have my fortune grow on top of someone else's misfortune—" Colin shrugged "—but sometimes circumstances can't be helped and, anyway, he did need the cash from the sale fairly quickly if he wanted to escape out of the country in time to avoid that awful prosecution."

He led us out onto the terraced back patio where, much to my delight, there was an Olympic-size swimming pool with water the color of sapphires. The midsummer temperatures had recently soared to all-time highs in London and, even with all of that cool stone, the house itself had been like an airless oven. Of course, I couldn't risk swimming alone in front of Dodo, lest she notice by my unswollen belly that there was nothing procreative going on, but I might be able to sneak dips in when she was off showering or reading some of the manuscripts she'd been obsessive enough to lug along or even if she retired early at night. And if I could manage to steal a moment of luxury for myself, how nice it would be to take a dip in this sparkling pool of refreshment, surrounded by cool tile which was in turn surrounded by lushly colored flowering bushes that were at peak bloom. How nice it would be were it not for the added presence of the bikini-clad duo who were lounging in lounge chairs at water's edge.

"Oh, I'm sorry, Dodo, Jane, I forgot to mention that I'd also invited Darius Lynch and his wife, Pamela," said Colin.

The bikini-clad duo looked to be in their early thirties and, even from across the far side of the pool, as they waved their highball glasses at us, I could see that they were impossibly tanned, impossibly spoiled—witness the gold chains on both—and impossibly yuppified. Sotto voce, Colin added, "I'm sorry, but it couldn't be helped. Darius is my investment counselor and if I hadn't done something to thank him for all the money he's saved me this past year, well, it just would have seemed churlish. Still, I don't suppose you'd expected to have to share your weekend in the country with perfect strangers."

No, I for one certainly hadn't, but as Colin left for the airport himself shortly afterward, it would have seemed churlish on our parts to issue complaints at this late date. Besides, what could we do? Drive back to the city in the beastly heat? Kick the Glitter Twins out?

As it was, we decided to make the best of a bad job.

Dodo approached the bronzed couple, hand out for a firm shake, determined to begin as she meant to go on. The problem, from my point of view, was how she began.

"Hello, I'm Lana Lane, Colin's editor, but people often insist on calling me Dodo, so you might as well, too, and this is my assistant, Jane, who's four months' pregnant."

And that was all it took to ruin the entire weekend.

Turned out that, in spite of having everything else that money could buy, Pamela Lynch hadn't as yet been able to buy herself a pregnancy and that was what she desperately wanted most. Even trying the fertility treatments that had yielded positive litters for women over in the States had resulted in *nada* for Pam, as she familiarly insisted on me addressing her, conversely insisting on calling me J.T. no matter how I tried to discourage her. This meant that the entire weekend was spent with me playing Mary to her little lamb. If I took an early morning walk in the gardens, there she was, regaling me with stories of those sexual encounters she'd had that involved thermometers. If I snuck down to the massive kitchen in the middle of the night to see if there was any pudding left over from dinner, there came Pam, scaring the shit out of me by sneaking up behind me at the fridge, ready with her turkey baster stories, the likes of which were enough to keep me from falling asleep again.

Of course, the bottom line in all of this was that she desperately wanted to know where I, J.T., had managed to succeed where she had somehow failed. It was patently inexplicable to her that lowly J.T.—"an *assist*ant editor and not even a real editor," as I couldn't help but overhear her complaining to D.L., her husband, over their cocktails—should succeed at anything she had failed at, particularly since I wasn't even married, an addendum that I failed to see the significance of.

She really, really made me hope that the world never got the chance to learn what she'd be like as a mother.

And Dodo, was she any font of sympathy?

Hardly.

"Oh, Jane," she said, not even bothering to glance up from the manuscript she was reading, a village comedy of manners that she was seriously thinking of acquiring, "don't you think it's part of your duty? I mean, isn't that part of the pregnancy package—the sharing of information among pregnant ladies as well as those unfortunates who would merely like to be?"

"All right!" I finally shouted later that same night. Having been practically accosted in the kitchen, I was hoping that a little exasperation would buy me some breathing space. "I'll tell you how I did it—I had sex, okay? I had sex, one time, missionary style, no bells or whistles or bows, *and I got pregnant!*"

But even that wasn't enough. Pam wanted to know things like how long the man'd kept it in for and what meal I'd last eaten and how long before.

God! The way the woman just went on and on and on about it, why, you'd think she was doing research for her own book!

Still, I suppose that even I would have been inclined to feel sorry for her, what with her seemingly endless desperate attempts to conceive, were it not for a conversation I heard between her and Dodo early on. Dodo, who may not have been a font of sympathy for me, was positively oozing it for Pam. As she covered Pam's bronzed and bejeweled hand with her own beautiful one, she soothingly half asked, half suggested, "Have you and Darius considered adoption? Surely, there must be an endless supply of simply marvelous children who need—"

"God, no!" Pam had shrieked, practically tearing her hand out from under Dodo's. "Do you really think that I would ever be caught dead raising someone else's whiny brat? My God, if a baby doesn't come out of your own body, if it doesn't share your own blood, then what in hell would be the point in taking care of it?"

And still she came after me for procreation tips.

Of course, the worst thing about all of this me-and-my-shadow stuff with Pam was that I wasn't even able to enjoy the one thing I'd really been attracted to by Colin's place: the pool.

After all, I was in my fourth month. If I put on a bathing suit—a one-piecer, a bikini, really anything involving latex—people would see in an instant that I was still skinny. And if I tried to stuff my suit? Well… What would happen if some of the stuffing leaked or, worse, I actually got the suit wet and people could see the outlines of something very unbabyish? I just couldn't take the chance.

Thus I spent the weekend by the pool fully clothed: baggy pants, artistic oversize man's shirt, sunglasses, big hat. Very Katharine Hepburn, the only problem being that it wasn't the soignée Katharine of *The Philadelphia Story,* but rather it was the entire-body-covered beekeeperish Kate from *On Golden Pond.*

"Aren't you sweltering in that?" Dodo asked, coming poolside in a bikini so small and of such a clingy material even when not wet that I could have counted the tiny bumps around her nipples if I hadn't been too embarrassed to continue staring.

"Course not." I tried to sound as if I meant it. I couldn't remember the last cloudlessly sunny July day when temperatures had risen over ninety, but I would certainly remember this one. If only I hadn't promised Alice that I'd write that blasted book…

Not for the first time, I wished that I could confide in Dodo about the book contract. Dodo truly was a great editor and I'd been having some problems with building sufficiently credible character motivation into the story. I knew that Dodo would somehow magically be able to spot the solution that I was too close to the project to see, but if I told Dodo about the book contract, then I'd have to tell her about the fake pregnancy, too, and if I started telling people about the fake pregnancy then the raw material for the book would disappear. Not to mention that they'd all go back to treating me as Unimportant and Unpregnant Jane again. Well, except for Tolkien, of course. And David. And Christopher.

"Aren't you going to put on your suit to go swimming?" Dodo asked.

"God, no! It's horrible for the baby!"

Dodo looked at me as though I were daft. "What are you—daft? Pregnant women swim all the time. I'm almost certain they do. It's supposed to be the perfect nonstressfully gentle exercise…." She paused, seeking a higher authority. "Why, look at all of those Jane Fonda women. I'm sure they—"

I cut her off. "Oh. Well. If you want to talk about Jane Fonda…"

"What does that mean?"

"Nothing." I exhaled, studying my nails. "Just that her books came out in the early eighties. For God sakes, Dodo, you're in publishing—you *must* know *that*."

"But what's that got to do with anything? I just don't see—"

"No, of course you don't, dear—" I could afford to be patronizing here "—but that's because *you've* never been pregnant."

"So?"

"*So,* as every pregnant woman knows, the technology

and knowledge is changing all the time, faster than the Internet. Oh, sure they say now that smoking can be harmful, but a couple of years from now? Some doctor in Singapore'll prove that low birth weight is a product of eating carrots. It's just a matter of time. Same thing with swimming. Used to be, people thought that swimming was the perfect thing for us pregnant ladies, just like you thought, Dodo. But that was the early *eighties,* when people were still listening to U2 for the first time and it actually seemed as though they had legitimate things to whinge about. This, however, is, oh, *about two decades later,* and now anyone who knows anything about pregnancy knows that swimming pools are strictly taboo for pregnant ladies."

Well, I didn't actually say, "So there," but I might as well have done.

And Dodo, to give her credit, did not say, "Well, I still think you're out of your fucking mind, Jane," as she might have done. After all, she didn't know anything, not really, and these nonpregnant friends of Colin Smythe certainly didn't know anything, so who was there left to argue with all of my quantum leaps of illogic?

From where I was sitting, we were even.

Of course, nothing ever lasts for very long, certainly not in any ongoing relationship. As we loaded up the boot of the car for the return trip back to London late Sunday afternoon, Dodo looked at me critically over the top of her sunglasses. "Are you planning to hit the maternity shops at any time soon? I'm afraid the Kay Hepburn look doesn't suit you at all and, anyway, I doubt any of our authors would find it comforting. Might make them all start free-associating to *The Lion in Winter* and who knows what could happen then."

The fetus was now four inches, receiving its nourishment from the placenta. It was developing reflexes, like sucking and swallowing. The rate of body growth was now faster than that of the head, making it more balanced looking than it had been. There were little teeth buds, and fingers and toes had become well defined. Now that it was more human looking, it might look complete on paper or in a sonogram, but at this point, it could not survive outside of my uterus.

Somehow, in just four months' time, the idea of the baby had become as dependent upon me as I had become upon the idea of my pregnancy.

the fifth month

Well, Dodo did have a point, bitchy though it might be. It was time I started looking at maternity clothes, although God knows with what I was going to stuff them. I'd been so determined to prove to everyone I was interested in impressing—read: everyone—that I could be better than anyone else in the world at not allowing pregnancy to ruin my perfect figure, that for a moment there I'd actually forgotten that at one point the time would come when I would have to either put up or shut up. After the baby was born, I planned to be equally superwomanish. I would show the world, and Sarah Jessica Parker, how quickly a real woman could bounce back to bikini perfection following the birth of a child. After all, I couldn't very well go through an entire nine-month pregnancy without ever gaining a visible pound. Could I?

To procrastinate the problem of what to fill my maternity clothes with, I decided to put the cart before the horse by going shopping first. At Harrod's. I figured that if I was a little depressed about my situation, finding out if Vera Wang did any *I Love Lucy*ish maternity numbers with big polka dots and little Peter Pan collars—even though I'd never be able to afford them—might cheer me up.

As a child and young adult, Harrod's had never been a part of my existence, save as a name on other people's shopping bags and a place to which tourists on the streets occasionally asked me directions.

It was my mother who'd been the anti-Harrod's Taylor, as I seem to vaguely remember my father traipsing me through there on a spree one Christmas season, pre his early demise. I also seem to remember a cloud of alcohol that surrounded him and thus me, the careful-not-to-look-stunned yet still stunned looks of shopgirls, and a spectacular train set that my mother complained about when we got it home even though it had a conductor who looked just like Will Shakespeare. When the conductor pulled the whistle, out came the tune from the song that The Fool sings to the mad king in *King Lear;* at least, it was the tune most commonly used in modern theatrical productions, the unnotated originals having been lost to history. For my mother's part, of Harrod's she said, "If I needed a store where I could get a silver satin bumbershoot with matching sequined trim for two hundred pounds I would go there, but since I don't..."

Well, of course she had a point. But, as I learned from Dodo upon being hired by Churchill & Stewart and being taken to Harrod's by her on our lunch hour on my very first day, a person didn't need to buy a two-hundred-pound silver satin and sequin bumbershoot in order to have fun looking at one. From then on, I was a confirmed Harrod'soholic, but I always obeyed what I perceived as the unwritten dress code to a tee, which brings us to the undeniable fact that:

There are two distinct types of Harrod's shoppers, definable by what they wear when they go shopping.

Type One is the modern wealthy woman, the woman who doesn't have to care about what she looks like when she sets out to spend a fortune on nonessentials, since the raised letters on her platinum credit card say something to the effect of HRH The Princess of Wales, or near enough. If she's going out to purchase a ball gown, it's fine to wear jeans, trainers and a navy blazer, provided it's the *right* jeans, trainers and navy blazer. Type One is also a catchall for everybody who thinks that Harrod's is Disney World with clothes, not even wearing the *wrong* jeans, trainers and blazer, but rather, anything that their McDonald's-stained hands happen to grab on their way out the hotel room door.

Type Two comprises just about everybody else. Type Twos dress to shop, often having entire outfits in their wardrobes that are never used for anything *but* shopping. Type Twos are blue-haired ladies for whom Harrod's will always be their father's England; are young women who *wish* they had credit cards that read HRH The Princess of Wales; are foreigners who have sense enough to know when they're entering the most elite department store in the world; are ladies who wear suits with matching bags and shoes, frequently pink, the shoes always having a heel. When Royal Ascot Week is in season, they have been known to wear hats. In short, Type Twos look like an army of women dressed just like the late HRH The Princess of Wales, except that no one has seemed to bother to tell them that if you are a real princess, you wear jeans to go shopping.

Even though I knew the two types—one could say I had been the anthropologist to first isolate them in the wild—I still was a committed Type Two, despite the fact that I was fully aware of the inherent pitfalls of allowing oneself to be classed thus.

On the day in question, then, I had my pink suit on, with its miniskirt, but not too mini, and fairly low-cut jacket with the three cloth-covered buttons. I had my height-enhancing near stilettos on, whether they killed me or not, and even though Ascot was long gone, I had my retro pillbox with half veil pinned on, if only to cover the incriminating dye line on my scalp that could clearly be seen by anyone snobbish enough to look closely which, given the fact that the place I was in sold strappy sandals at the cost of a good week's salary, was probably everybody within sight. My matching handbag was of a cute little box shape that hopefully said Paris.

I would have dearly loved to have tried on a half-dozen pairs of those strappy sandals in various colors, but I was a woman with a mission and so made straight for Maternity.

The Amerasian woman who tried to wait on me when I got there was so beautiful that I was glad I was just looking, determined to deny her the opportunity of a sale.

"Can I help you?" she asked coolly.

"Just looking today." I breezed by her, sorely tempted to tell her to go retie her navy-and-maroon striped tie or something.

She tugged on the lapels of her navy jacket to straighten it to perfection and returned to arranging a display of scarves on the counter as I began to move from rack to rack.

Hey! Some of this stuff wasn't half-bad. If a person had to be pregnant in this day and age, at least there were plenty of fashion opportunities for not looking hideous. It wasn't all polka dots, tents and bows anymore. Instead, there were cute little jumpers—well, maybe not so little— and funky jeans overalls for bumming around on weekends. There was smart officewear and there were even some stunning ball gowns, should one be lucky enough to be invited to Buckingham Palace before term.

"Hey!" I said aloud. "Some of this stuff is super. May I try a few of these on?"

The salesgirl looked up. "I thought you were just looking today."

In my hands I held one of the pairs of overalls and a shiny ball gown that was of a dark-pink hue shot with gold; in other words, it was a color that had only been scientifically identified in nature within the confines of a nail polish bottle. "Well, I was just looking. Before," I added with a tight smile. "Now, I'm just trying."

"Very well, madam," she said, taking the things from me and putting them in a vacant stall. "If there's anything else I can do for you today—perhaps the same garments in a different size?—please do not hesitate to call."

"Please do not hesitate to call," I singsonged imitatively under my breath as I shut the stall door behind me. I hung the garments on the hook provided and went about the business of stripping down to my undies.

First I tried on the overalls. My God! What a joke, I thought, studying my figure from all angles. Sure, it made me look different than my usual self, but it certainly didn't make me look pregnant. Instead, what I looked like was one of those parsimonious people who has lost a tremendous amount of weight but who hasn't bothered to replace the elephantine garments still left in one's wardrobe. The ball gown fared no better, although I still loved the color, tacky or no.

Well, this wasn't doing me any good. I could buy an entire closet full of new clothes and I'd still be no closer to looking pregnant than I did any other day. I'd just look silly.

Then my eyes fixed more firmly on something hanging from another hook.

When I'd first entered, I'd dismissively taken the hanging item to be a fanny pack left by some tourist rushing off to catch a bus, but now I saw that it wasn't that at all. True, the tastefully navy-blue item had adjustable straps to go around the waist, but instead of having a pouch for carrying money and passport and hotel keys, there was a perfectly rounded half-moon of some firm yet soft padded material attached to the straps. *What was this?* I wondered. But as I removed it from the hook and studied it more closely, it didn't take me long to figure it out.

My God! It was a pretend baby! This bundle of cloth must be what women who were like me—in other words, skinny women, only in their cases skinny women who had good reason to expect not to be so for long—put on themselves when they wanted to try on clothing in Maternity departments before their bodies had caught up with their need to shop. What fun!

I lost no time in unzipping the back of the ball gown just enough to squeeze the belly enhancer in, adjusting the straps around my waist. Then I rezipped the back. Hey! This was sensational, I thought, studying myself once again from all sides. Now I looked like Napoleon's Josephine, only instead of having my protruding belly be the result of an Empire waist, it looked as though it was because I'd been slack about entering into my period of confinement. My God! With this thing on, I really did look pregnant and, oddly enough, it wasn't the off-putting sight I'd imagined it would be. Rather, it looked kind of, well, cool.

As I stared at myself, I wondered what it would be like if this weren't just a pretend baby, if it were in fact the real thing. Would I suddenly feel differently about the future? Would I ever be able to live up to whatever expectations he or she might have of me?

I was still positively entranced by my own reflection when it occurred to me that I'd been in that stall for a long time. Shrugging off my momentary bout with sentimentality, it further occurred to me that soon the salesgirl would begin wondering if I was trying to steal the ball gown by forcing it into my hat. I began reluctantly removing the gown, thinking all the while.

Well, I really didn't need the ball gown for anything, and I was sure I'd never wear the overalls no matter how trendy, but this cloth baby…now, this was something I could use.

If I had one of these, why, I could instantly begin show-ing at work. I'd have to suffer no more snide remarks from Stan from Accounting and I'd be able to begin shopping for maternity clothes to my heart's content. Only I cer-tainly wouldn't do it here, I thought, gasping as I caught a glimpse of the price tag on the ball gown, not unless I wanted to take on a second job.

But where could I go to purchase one of these handy cloth babies, I wondered, putting my own clothes back on. I studied the navy-blue item I wanted so desperately, searching for a manufacturer's name and address, but found nothing. Blast!

Then a thought occurred to me: a perfectly wonderful, wonderfully awful thought. What if I were to just, oh, take this little baby home with me? Would Harrod's be any the wiser if I were to slip it under my jacket and rebutton it— ugh! that was tight!—like so? After all, the salesgirl very well knew that I'd only brought the two garments in the dress-ing stall with me, so even if she noticed that I was bulging a little bit more than when I'd come in, she'd just attribute it to the eyestrain brought on by viewing an endless stream of women in varying stages of pregnancy day after day; she'd assume I must have been bigger before, with the ill taste to wear a pink suit that was too small for my condition, and that she'd simply failed to notice. Surely, even if she did notice a size discrepancy, provided I handed both security-tagged garments over to her in person, she'd be too well mannered to say anything. And since no one would ever security-tag something that was just a dressing-stall prop, I'd be able to sail right on out of the store without setting off any alarms.

I'd just hand her the garments—like I was doing right now—holding my pillbox hat and bag over my bulging belly. I'd just smile—again like I was doing right now— and thank her for her time, assure her that I'd be back just as soon as I was further along in my pregnancy for some-thing other than looking and trying, and—

Snagged!

"Excuse me, madam," she said, smiling oh-so-politely as she took me firmly by the elbow, "but if you'd just come with me…"

She got another girl to cover the department for her and then waltzed me down to Security. It had never been my ambition in life to find out what the interior of Harrod's Security looked like, but who could guess at the turns one's life would take?

And who could have guessed that anything within the walls of Harrod's could ever look so utilitarian, I thought, squirming in my metal chair as the jacketed guard with the walkie-talkie paced before me, being both good cop and bad cop all at once since there was only one of him. He looked intelligent enough to be doing just about anything else for a living and when he spoke, his Scottish accent was all Sean Connery with its brushy *sh* sounds for every *s*. I almost felt sorry for him. I mean, I could tell that he would have liked nothing better than to reach inside my overstuffed pink jacket and yank out whatever it was I had hiding there, but he couldn't very well do that, now, could he? He had to wait for his female counterpart so that she would handle my body if need be, and she was on her break.

"You know," he said, exasperated, "you'd make it a lot easier on everybody concerned if you'd just hand over whatever you've got concealed under there."

Suddenly, tired myself, I could see the wisdom in what he was saying. After all, by not handing it over now, all I was really doing was delaying the inevitable.

I reached up under the back of my jacket, undoing the strap. "Oh, here," I said, exasperated as well, slamming the cloth baby down on his metal desk and folding my arms across my once-again flat front. "Do with me what you will."

"What the hell's that thing?" he asked, picking it up and studying it as I had done earlier.

"What does it look like? It's a cloth baby," I said, not really sure that this was the technical term for it. "You keep them in the dressing stalls of the Maternity department here. They're for women to use when they're trying on clothes early on in their pregnancy and want to know what the clothes will look like when they fill them out."

"Jesus Christ! Now I've seen everything!" He looked at me like I was some kind of an idiot. "Why the hell didn't you just ask for one? If we keep them as a courtesy to our customers, then it's probably the equivalent of something like a paper shopping bag with our logo on it. God knows why anyone would want to take one of these home with them, but I'm sure if you'd asked Sally nicely," he went on, referring to my Amerasian friend, "she'd probably've gladly let you take it. Chances are, some clothing manufacturer sends them to the store for free as part of a promotional gimmick."

He tossed the cloth baby back and I caught it, clutching it to me. "Here," he said, "take it, if you want it so badly, only—" and here he disappeared into a storage room off to the side, emerging with a legitimate bag "—at least put it in here."

I hastily obeyed.

"Now, then. Off with you. And don't come back here for a while. Just because I didn't catch you stealing anything worth stealing, it doesn't mean that I'm going to want to see your face on my security camera any time soon."

He didn't have to tell me and my baby to go twice.

"It's all your fault," I said to David, not long after I'd arrived home from the Harrod's debacle and he popped down with Christopher for a visit.

"*My* fault? Just because you take it into your insane head to commit petty theft in the house that Fayed built, how can you possibly say that it's my fault?"

Of course, it *wasn't* his fault, not completely, not since

I'd made a pact with that devil Alice to write a book that would make me rich and famous. Okay, so maybe it wasn't a pact in the strictly Hawthorne sense, since there was in fact a very concrete, nonsupernatural contract, a copy of which was tucked away in my filing cabinet. But it certainly felt like a pact.

Yes, I was still keeping that teeny tiny little secret from my best friend. Not given much to self-examination over the emotional motives for why I do what I do, I would have been hard-pressed to explain why I was still keeping it from him. Was it really for the reason I was always telling myself it was, that I preferred he think I kept up the charade because I was insane as opposed to finance-conscious? Or did it have something to do with the fact that what he had with Christopher appeared to be real, and that while what I had with Tolkien was stupendous, the fact that I couldn't tell him everything about me kept the relationship from feeling real? Therefore, it sometimes felt as though the book was the only real thing I could call my own...if that makes any sense at all...which it doesn't necessarily, not even to me. But there are times when my life has made almost no sense at all, and I suppose that this was just one of them. I just knew—instinctively, perhaps—that while David thought no less of me now, he would think less of me if he knew about the contract.

Anyway, while I was (pretty) sure that it was the only secret I'd ever kept from David, I wasn't ready to fess up, which meant that I still had to plow ahead with saying unreasonable things to him like:

"Well, if it weren't for you and your harebrained scheme—"

"What harebrained scheme?"

"You know, the one you came up with two months ago, the one whereby I fake being pregnant—"

"That was *my* harebrained scheme?"

"You two can't possibly still be arguing about this, can you?" yawned Christopher, picking up a magazine from the coffee table, flopping down on the sofa, putting his long legs up on the table while leaning back and...

"*Yeow!*"

"What the *hell* was that?" Christopher cried, jumping forward as the white-and-gray puffball that he'd nearly sat on went whizzing past.

"Kick the Cat," I said, racing after him.

"I'm not going to kick your cat," Christopher yelled after me with some asperity. "You know, Jane, you really are a sick, sick woman."

Why were people always saying that to me?

"I wasn't telling you to kick my cat," I said, returning to the living room with the kitten now in my arms. He'd burrowed underneath the bed in my bedroom, but I'd managed to coax him out. "I was merely telling you his name—Kick the Cat."

"*You* got a cat, Jane?" asked David.

"Of course. I love cats."

"But you hated Punch the Cat."

"Well, that was different. Punch the Cat was a cat who deserved to be hated. Kick the Cat, on the other hand," I said, nuzzling the kitten's nose with my own, "is a pussy with balls."

"Oh, dear God," said David, "now I've heard everything."

The next morning found me sitting at my desk with my new cloth baby in place, situated beneath the loose clothing I'd picked up at a discount shop on my way home the day before, following my near arrest at Harrod's. As I sorted through the manuscripts Constance'd dumped on my desk on Dodo's behalf, I thought I looked pretty smart in my new jumper with its Baby Roo sign, downturned arrow, and pouch. Still, looking darned cute and pregnant at the same time wasn't enough of a positive to mitigate the negative of having to wade through novel proposals that began, "With the cold war at an end, Russian spy Vassily

Andropov is having trouble adjusting..." Derivative. Yawn. Or "When some silver spoons are found missing at Windsor Castle, the Queen's favorite Welsh corgi, Toto, who also has the power of speech, helps Elizabeth II solve..." Libelous. Yawn. Or, from a desperate American unable to achieve publication Stateside, "On a plantation in the Deep South, around the time that the Civil War breaks out..." I'll send *that* rejection letter out tomorrow, Scarlett. Yawn.

And then of course there were the gadzillions upon gadzillions of coming-of-age stories that kept streaming in like so many lemmings headed for the cliffs; I mean, didn't any of these people realize that everyone who mattered had come of age by now? Who cared that they had childhoods that needed getting over? Sometimes I just wanted to shout: Just get over it, for chrissakes!

Good God. Wasn't there anything new being written under the writing sun anymore? And why was Dodo, my new best girlfriend Dodo, still dumping her manuscripts on me when she knew that I was suffering from...now, what was that new symptomatic complaint I'd come up with for the fifth month? I quickly consulted *What to Expect*. Ah, yes. Lower abdominal achiness brought about from the stretching of the ligaments that support the uterus. I had to find a way to remember that better somehow. Perhaps a mnemonic might help?

Anyway, didn't Dodo realize that I had my own unsolicited manuscripts to contend with? After all, people without talent did write to me directly sometimes. These were usually the sorts who felt they could improve on their chances by setting their sights a little lower. Having gone to one of the public reference libraries in order to scrutinize *The Writers' and Artists' Yearbook,* published by A and B Black, so that they could swallow every possible detail of how to approach publishers, the hopefuls had consulted the lists of agents and editors. Seeing that Dodo, aka Lana

Lane, was Editor for Churchill & Stewart, they would have similarly noted my name as Assistant Editor. Deducing that everyone and his brother would be writing to Dodo in the hopes of getting her to buy their book, the lower-sights setters would make the further deduction that I, being merely an *Assist*ant, would be still looking to make a name for myself, that I would be eager to discover the next Martin Amis, and that I would have a lot less for them to compete with in terms of what was on my plate since everyone and his brother was not writing to me.

Hah! The idiots should see my desk! That, coupled with the fact that, unlike Dodo, I did not have a me to palm work off on, meant that they had even less chance when they wrote directly to me than when their manuscripts were channeled to me through Dodo. True, sometimes publishing gold could be mined from the slush pile, but still…

I was just wondering whether an offer to Constance of a free lunch in exchange for her taking a half-dozen of the hated manuscripts off my hands would work, when the free-association thought occurred to me to go online for a little electronic entertainment. It was always fun seeing what e-mail had come in overnight: reactions from Alice to the bits and pieces I was regularly sending her from the manuscript that I had tentatively titled *The Cloth Baby;* tales of horror stories at author appearances as told by acquaintances at other publishing houses; panicky missives from Colin Smythe, who was now riding the superhighway with everyone else; solicitations for sex photos.

I tapped in my password, Odette, the more-exotic-than-Jane name that I'd secretly wished had been mine all through my youth. I waited to connect, which always seemed to take too long, just like fast-food restaurants never seeming to be fast enough—I mean, you actually had to wait *some*—and then I was in.

There was that satisfying little yellow envelope, the one that popped into my computer's iconic mailbox as it intoned the three most current orgasm-producing words in the English language: "You've got mail." In my eagerness to get at it, I put my hands under the desk and pulled in order to propel my swivel chair closer, only to be stopped when the expanded belly that was my cloth baby bounced me back off the wood. Well, that was going to take some getting used to. Not willing to make the same mistake twice, I pulled myself closer to the screen more gently.

Now, then. Who was writing to me today?

When I double-clicked my mouse on the yellow letter, I saw that there were four new messages.

No, I wasn't interested in "*Tits*illating (sic) Teens." And they could keep "Boffo Boys in the Buff" as well. I hit the delete button twice. The third item was a vacation offer to Disney World in Orlando, Florida. Now this intrigued me.

Just the other day, I'd e-mailed an acquaintance at Bloomsbury about a movie adaptation of Virginia Woolf's *Orlando* that I'd rented on videotape. Was it possible that the Mouse had somehow seen what was in the contents of that letter? After all, another time, having e-mailed my Bloomsbury acquaintance about Norman Mailer under the slug line "The Naked and the Dead," I'd received a solicitation from a firm advertising one-night courses in necrophilia.

I punched the delete button on the Mouse as well.

Let's see. Even though these things only worked with the number three in fairy tales, would the fourth letter be the charm?

The sender appeared as mshakespeare@aol.com and the slug line read, "S.O.S.!!!"

Hmm. Well, now. This was curious. AOL stood for America Online, but I didn't know any Shakespeares in the U.S., either *m* or otherwise. As for the S.O.S., I'd heard sometime back that, given the advances that technology had made, the old system of Morse code was going to finally be retired, all of the knowledge concerning those dots and dashes just becoming another thing of the past. Not

long after I'd heard that, however, another item had appeared on the news concerning a group of people who'd
somehow managed to get themselves locked in a church.
For a while there, it'd looked as though they were going
to be stuck there for the night and miss their seven o'clock
dinner reservation, when one member of the locked-in
group, who happened to know Morse code, went up into
the bell tower and rang out the ancient naval distress sig-
nal. It might not have saved the *Titanic,* but in this instance,
a passerby recognized the call, summoned help and the entire group was able to sit down to dinner on time. In light
of this, some thought that maybe people shouldn't be so
hasty to dispense with the old ways. Of course, there were
others who thought that everyone should just carry a cell
phone in case of disaster—no one locked in the church
had one—and then there were the Americans who
thought that everyone should carry a gun as well.

But back to mshakespeare@aol.com who, apparently,
had not heard that S.O.S. was going out of business and
still believed that someone would hear if he or she just
shouted loud enough:

Dear Ms. Taylor,
  Help!
  I am a thirty-six-year-old novelist who has just
written a brilliant first novel—my seventh—but no
one here will buy it. (Please don't hit the delete button; I know that EVERY writer says their book is
brilliant, but mine really is.) It's a satire, and every ed-
itor-agent here says the same thing: that it's pee-your-
pants-funny AND intelligent, but that they can't take
it on or represent it because—get this—Americans
don't like funny books. I in turn told them, "But what
about Nick Hornby? What about Helen Fielding?"
To which they said, "Oh. Those. Well, those writers
only sold in America because they were Brits." This

is where you come in. The way I figure it, at this point I could either impersonate an English author—(which just seemed too hard) or approach an English publisher (you). Anyway, in a nutshell, my novel takes the whole prototypical single-girl Britcom thing and kicks it up a notch to the next level. This time around, she's not just looking for a steady date or maybe someone to settle down with; this time, she wants to have a baby. Anyway, I hope you'll agree to at least look at it, because I really am desperate and would hate to have to start selling my late mother's antiques.

Yours in hope and desperation,
Mona Shakespeare
New York, NY

P.S.: I don't know why all the agents and editors think that Americans don't like to laugh. I mean, I know that we haven't realized yet that sex is funny or that fucking is funny while saying *fuck* isn't, but I like to laugh whenever I can and I think I'm still an American. Oh well. M.

P.P.S.: Please don't get offended that I use *British, English, Brits* and *English persons* interchangeably. We Colonists can be slow and no one over here's been able to figure it out yet. And please don't get me started on Scottish, Scotch and Scots. M.

Good God! The woman was a loon! Still, there were some good things about her query letter, like the fact that she addressed me with respect, that her last name was the same as my all-time favorite author, and that she wanted to make people laugh. And I certainly could relate to desperation. Plus, she said her book was about an English girl who wanted to have a baby. I figured I should at least look at the thing; for all I knew, it might be competition for *The Cloth Baby,* although it was hard to feature that there could be another human being out there in the universe who was faking a pregnancy for nine months so that they could write a bestseller about someone who was faking a pregnancy for nine months. Figuring to make Mona Shakespeare's day, I tapped out my reply:

Dear Ms. Shakespeare,
    Please send complete manuscript to the address which follows. I make no promises, but looking at anything has never completely killed me.

And it wouldn't. There, I thought, hitting the send button. It was nice to make someone else's day for a change. And it might prove instructive to get a peek at Mona Shakespeare's manuscript.

I can't wait to see you again, the card attached to the flowers said.
    Okay, so maybe it was a corny cliché, flowers with the old *I can't wait to see you again* card attached, but no man I'd ever been with had sent me flowers at work before, much less remembered that my favorite flowers were peonies—giant, pink, slightly-out-of-season, who-knew-where-the-hell-he'd-got-them peonies. If my life was doomed to be a cliché, I'd just as soon it be the flowers-at-work cliché as opposed to the trying-to-trap-man-by-becoming-pregnant cliché that it had formerly been. In a nutshell, I was of a mindset to be charmed by romantic clichés.
    I buried my nose in the bouquet and inhaled.
    "Who sent you those?" Louise did a double take as she passed my open door.
    "Nobody," I said, trying to palm the card before she could read it.

Louise stood before my desk, arms crossed. "You're *embarrassed*," she observed with obvious delight. "C'mon, who sent them? Was it Trevor, trying to get back in your good graces?"

"God, no!"

"Then who?" Before I could stop her, she snatched the card from my hand and read what it said, mouthing the words with a puzzled frown: *"Can't wait to see you again."*

Good thing Tolkien hadn't signed it, I thought. I don't know why, but it would have felt unseemly, wearing a Baby Roo jumper while receiving flowers from the man I wanted to have sex with again so badly. I figured that Tolkien hadn't signed his name, assuming that I would know from whom the flowers came, there being a) no unnamed stalkers in my life and b) no other men I was sleeping with that I might mistake as the sender. Either way, the man was an optimist and I decided there and then that I *liked* optimism in a man.

I was also relieved that he hadn't signed it, because I had no desire to have my pregnant and unpregnant worlds collide, and females get so nosy whenever there's a new man on the scene.

"Who then?" Louise pressed. "If not Trevor, then who sent you these flowers?"

"Um...er...um..."

"Yes?"

"It was *David!*" I finally answered her. His was the only name I could think of given that I needed the name of a person who might conceivably send me flowers.

"David?"

"Yes, David. You know—my friend, David. You've met him with me before here and there."

"True, he's the gorgeous one. But isn't he gay?"

"Of course."

"Then why would he send you flowers at work with a note attached that reads—" she studied the card once more "'—*Can't wait to see you again*'?"

"Oh. That." I pooh-poohed her with my hand.

"Yes." She still looked suspicious. "That."

"That's just David being a good friend. He knows how low I've felt lately, being pregnant with no man on the horizon and all. This is just his way of cheering me up. He's trying to make me feel as though there's still a high level of masculine interest in me, even if it is gay interest."

"God," she said, eyeing me with mild hostility as she dropped the card in my trash.

"What?"

"You are *so* much more lucky than you deserve."

I waited until she was safely out of sight before retrieving the card from the trash and reading it one more time: *Can't wait to see you again.*

Louise was right, I thought, holding the card tight in my hand. I was much more lucky than I deserved.

I slammed my door, so as to receive no more surprise intruders, and punched in the familiar number on my mobile.

"David!" I whispered a shout when he answered.

"Yes, Jane. I know who I am. Is there anything urgent?"

"Tolkien sent me flowers!" My whispered shout was even more gleeful this time.

"That's wonderful, Jane. Do you realize, by the way, that I am working here sometimes?"

I had decided to have an amniocentesis.

Oh, not the kind involving a long, hollow needle getting inserted into the uterus by first going through the abdominal wall. Good God, no, certainly nothing as painful as that.

No, what I was going to do was have what I thought of as a more figurative procedure. True, I wasn't over age thirty-five, the single most common reason why amnios are ever performed. Then, too, there were no tubal defects or chromosomal abnormalities that I could point to in either Trevor's or my backgrounds and I didn't think I'd be able to convince people that *both* of us were carriers of autosomal recessive inherited disorders such as Tay–Sachs disease or sickle-cell anemia. I'd decided then that Madame Zora was going to recommend that I have one done because, according to her, it had become necessary to assess the maturity of the fetus's lungs and, despite her most feverish extrasensory efforts, the tarot cards weren't saying. Anyway, since amnios were typically performed between the sixteenth and eighteenth week, my timing couldn't have been more perfect.

I had realized that in my case, because I hadn't been able to get any mothers to give or sell me the pictures from their sonograms and because I'd then told everyone at the office that Madame Zora was staunchly against expectant mothers seeing the pictures from their sonograms, I'd need to have some other kind of diagnostic test to determine the sex. I hadn't bothered to explain why Madame Zora took this singular view, not really having to since everyone thought she was barmy anyway. The bottom line was that by having an amnio now, not only would I know my baby's sex in advance, but I could actually pick it. How many people could do that? (Well, soon, probably loads; but I was definitely a baby step ahead of my time.)

I'd decided that I would have a girl. Girl babies were easier to care for and besides, later on, what with the absent Trevor factor, I wouldn't have to worry about people lecturing me about the need to find a husband, since they might claim that a boy should have a father figure if at all possible. Of course, I still had the problem of where I was going to find an infant when the nine months were up and I was forced to deliver, rather than admit that I had been lying to everyone all along, but I could worry about that later. Who knew? Maybe Alice was right: maybe once I was rich and famous, no one would care about how I'd deceived them. Funny, but I'd originally started out on this weird journey by believing I *was* pregnant, then I'd tried to get pregnant so that Trevor and I could have a baby together and so that I could experience that "rosy world" thing, then I'd wanted to continue *pretending* to be pregnant because life seemed so much nicer that way, then I'd met Tolkien (which had absolutely nothing to do with pregnancy at all, save that it was preferable that I *not* be), then Alice had offered me a contract to write a book about a woman who impersonates being pregnant for nine months, and now…and now…

God, my life was just one confusing mess. Who knew where it all might end?

"It was me," were the first words out of Tolkien's mouth when I answered the phone.

"Yes, I did know that," I replied, certain I was responding correctly.

"How did you know that?"

"Well, you are an optimist, aren't you?"

"Yes."

"Yes."

Now that I was officially showing, there were a lot of perks that came along with my expandable abdomen: like being allowed, nay encouraged, to take extra breaks at work and to palm off any authors that I didn't feel up to dealing with onto anyone else in the office who wasn't already occupied; like my mother actually being nicer to me than to Sophie because, even though Sophie's baby had just been born something like a minute ago, Mother now knew that *that* baby was healthy. With my baby still in transit, as it were, she couldn't be too careful and so poor old Soph was left sucking hind tit.

But showing had its decided downside, too; witness all the unsolicited advice I was getting on a pretty much hourly basis. My mother and Sophie? Well, we already know about that. Even laid up in hospital following a forty-six-hour labor, Sophie'd had the presence of mind to ring me so that she could point out just one last time, shouting down the line, "And whatever you do, Jane, don't let anyone talk you into an epidural!" As if I would be foolish enough to ever have a painful birth. As if.

Then there were the ladies in the supermarket, neighbors I'd never spoken one word to before, the ticket taker at the Cineplex, and even the postal worker who made deliveries to our office building. (Him: "My sister says that eating sweets when you're pregnant instead of eating proper organic whole foods is like playing Russian roulette with your unborn child's metabolism." Me—throwing the rest of my Smarties packet into the trash bin: "Just leave the fucking packages, why don't you?")

Finally—or most recently, I should say—there was Stan from Accounting who, at the monthly meeting, looked pointedly at my breasts before pointing out, "I hope you're planning to breast-feed. You do realize, don't you, that if you don't you will be depriving your child of what is literally his genetic right?"

This from a man who, not five minutes before, had been telling us that once we'd edited all of our books down to the point where we didn't think there was one more word that we could spare, if we would just then shave off another ten pages, the company would be saving hundreds of thousands of pounds a year.

I looked at this man who would have gleefully shorn 350 pages off of each of Tolstoy's books—I'd often heard Stan say that no modern novel had any business running any longer than 223 pages—and said quite eloquently, "Stuff it, Stan."

"Oh, come on, now. There's nothing to be getting all hot and bothered about. After all, you are among friends here. We accept the fact that your hormones are raging at an elephant-stampede level now, but still, someone's got to tell you that breast-feeding your son—"

Notice how Stan was the only person in my acquaintance who was convinced I was having a boy? Specifically, that the being who would be sucking on my breasts would undoubtedly be a boy?

"How are you so sure that I'm having a boy?"

"Well, you are carrying the baby low—"

Something else to worry about. Perhaps my padding was in danger of falling down around my hips. "Yes, I know. But what if I were to tell you that the amnio said it's going to be a girl?"

"*You* had an amnio? You who are so determined not to have your baby come into the world, and I quote—" and here he did a disturbingly credible imitation of me "'—via the historical roughness of the testosterone-centered medical establishment,' unquote, you had a risk-taking amnio?"

"Yes," I said, chin high, making the whole thing up as I went along, forgetting all about my party line concerning Madame Zora, fetal lungs and inconclusive tarot readings. "I had a cousin who delivered a Down's syndrome baby. It doesn't do to take any chances under those circumstances."

Stan reddened. "I'm sorry to hear about your cousin's baby, Jane."

I forgave him much more quickly than I normally would have done, possibly due to that niggling guilt feeling that was gnawing on my gut. I didn't mind accepting sympathy that wasn't really due me for a pregnancy that wasn't real, not when it came in the form of longer lunch hours and a cushioned stool under my desk; but blithely accepting sympathy on behalf of a nonexistent medical condition, when that medical condition was a very serious thing to all of those affected and the people who loved them, well, that was just too much even for me.

"It's okay, Stan," I said. "You couldn't have possibly known." I recovered my old self fairly quickly, however. "And my baby is definitely a girl."

Well? Why couldn't I have whatever baby I wanted if I was the one calling the shots? Hell, I might have twins yet. Or better still, if the Yanks kept topping themselves, having litters of more than seven or eight where really just one would do for most people, why couldn't I break some kind of record here? All it would take probably would be enough foam rubber padding. Besides, once the nine months were up and no baby to show for it, I'd probably have to hightail it out of town anyway. Why not go for broke?

Nah. Too much bother having a multiple.

"Anyway," Stan said, no longer red, having gotten over his embarrassment as quickly as I'd gotten over my guilt, "I've never before seen a pregnant woman whose breasts didn't enlarge any. Usually a pregnant woman's breasts grow larger. And swollen. And tender." How the fuck did Stan know these things? Surely his sisters weren't talking to him about *that*. "Are you sure you're getting enough calcium and taking your prenatal vitamins? After all, you don't want to starve the little bugger, even if it is a girl."

I looked down at my breasts which were still, distressingly, the same 34B they'd been since I was twelve. Oh God, I groaned inwardly, another thing I'd overlooked. Before too much longer went by, I'd definitely have to find something reliable to stuff a bigger bra size with, something that wouldn't float away on its own if I were to be accidentally pushed into the Thames.

"Thanks for pointing out my possible calcium deficiency, Stan," I said with a saccharine smile. "Now, in the meantime, stuff it."

"Ahem." This rather unoriginal sound came from Dexter Schlager, the hair-disadvantaged Editor-in-Chief of Churchill & Stewart, who was seated all the way at the other end of the table and who always touched his egg-like dome as though there might be something there other than smooth skin. "Excuse me, ladies and gentlemen, but if we've devoted a sufficient amount of time to Taylor's breasts, perhaps we can return to the matter of cutting ten pages each from every book on next spring's lineup...."

I know I already cited Stan as being the "finally" as far as unsolicited advice went, but actually there was one last straw yet to come, this camel's backbreaker coming from Rock, the purple-mohawked punk from Wavy Do who, despite her own perfectly dreadful looks and poor choice for a name change, was one of London's best kept secrets being the kind of *par excellence* colorist who could make Rod Stewart's hair color look natural.

After Stan'd managed to turn our monthly into a meeting that would go down in the annals of Churchill & Stewart as "The Breast Meeting," I'd taken a detour to the Ladies' on my way back to my desk, there to see if my normal-size breasts really did look radically disproportional to the beginnings of a swollen belly I'd allowed myself to acquire.

Yep, I saw in the mirror, turning sideways, that rat bastard Stan was right: I didn't look a thing like that sweet lady with the sensible flat shoes and the feeding-ready breasts on the cover of *What to Expect.* I'd have to begin remedying this situation, and fast, with a little judicious stuffing—perhaps a mere padded bra would do the trick? After all, what was needed here was comforting-looking breasts, rather than the intimidation style that nature had blessed me with—but I also couldn't do it too fast or Stan might get suspicious, say if I went up three cup sizes over a single weekend.

In fact, it was while I was reviewing the many options available to me for nonsurgical breast enhancement, scrutinizing my appearance in great detail, that I first noticed how desperately in need of a touch-up was the true medium-brown hair color that was at the root of my greatly improved shade of raven. A few weeks back, I'd worried that the snobbiest of Harrod's shoppers would critically notice my dye line, but then I'd quickly forgotten all about it, what with the near arrest and all. Now I realized that it had gotten out of hand. It occurred to me that I had been so busy of late, what with the baby and all, that I'd let longer than the usual five-week interim pass since my last appointment with Rock.

Dodo walked in just then and caught me spreading the hair around my part in an effort to discover just how damning the view was from the vantage point of anyone who was taller than me. Dodo, being taller than me, glanced down at my scalp and said, "Good God, Jane, by all means take extra time for lunch if you need to, but be sure to have Rock do something about that. This is no time to be letting your looks go."

Dodo, whose Carole Lombard hair was completely natural, also went to Rock, who merely styled it in a modified pageboy each week. By going to Rock, it was Dodo's hope that people would think that she was naturally a dark-haired woman who had her hair dyed like everybody else, the primary hope being that she wouldn't be tarred with the same dumb brush as the rest of the natural blondes. As evidenced by the fact that one hundred percent of the people she worked with called her Dodo and ninety-five percent of those in her personal life—those who had become aware of her work nickname—also called her Dodo, there were times when I thought to warn her that her efforts just weren't working. She might as well have her hair done by someone more normal-looking and easier to get along with for all the good the Rock subterfuge was doing her. Better yet, and cheaper, she could probably just set it herself every night with large Velcro rollers.

Still, Dodo's advice about my looks was sound and so I rang up Rock right away, only to have to resort to bribery in order to get my way.

Me: "It's an emergency. I look like shit."

Rock—sound of her drawing heavily on cigarette not quite drowned out by even louder sound of blow-dryer in background—"It doesn't matter, luv, does it? I've only got the two hands, don't I, and they're both booked up for the next three weeks."

Rock considered herself having passed elocution lessons by seeing every movie that Brenda Blethyn had ever made.

Me: "I'll pay you double."

Rock: "Great. Won't help me grow another hand though, will it?"

Me: "I promise to know exactly what I want, to tell you in a clear and concise fashion, and not to make you go through all of the stylists' magazines with me before deciding on the same style that I've worn for the last five years."

Rock: "Closer."

Me: "Fine. I give. I promise not to even once—not once—ask you why you can't do something with your own hair that remotely resembles the nice things you do to everyone else's. I promise not to ask you what's so fucking great about the color purple."

Rock: "Done. See you in a half hour. I can take you sooner if you can get here faster."

Twenty minutes later, I was standing at the reception desk of Wavy Do; the same twenty minutes later, there was a purple-haired woman whose nose and ears were like a walking jewelry box shrieking practically right into my face.

"What the hell's the matter with you? Are you daft?" shrieked the woman who you may have already guessed to be Rock. "I can't dye your hair for you when you're bleedin' pregnant! Didn't you ever bother to read *What to Expect When You're Expecting?*"

"Er...I...er." I was flustered. "Er...yes."

"And?" Rock prompted, as though this were some kind of quiz.

I tried desperately to remember what the book had said on the subject. "And...and..." All of a sudden it came to me in one big rush, like some kind of LSD flashback except that this was a fetus-care flashback. "Nobody's sure if hair coloring does any harm but just to be on the safe side, if an expectant mother is going to color at all and is concerned, she should stick to vegetable dyes." I breathed as if I'd just run a marathon. "Did I get it all?"

"Near enough," conceded Rock grudgingly. "You left out perms."

"But I never get perms."

"True."

"Well?"

"I don't keep vegetable dyes in the shop, you know? It just seems too weird to me. I mean, like, I know that vegetables are supposed to be good for the baby and all, but if they enter the mother's body in any way other than through her mouth—like through her scalp, say—the idea just weirds me out. I mean, it's not very natural, is it? Havin' your mother eatin' through her head?"

"No, I guess not," I had to admit. It did seem weird when she put it like that.

But then, all of a sudden, Rock looked like she was getting angry about something, which was a pretty scary thing. "Hey, now! If you're startin' to show already, by my calculations—" and here she began counting on her fingers "—I've done your hair with regular full-chemical dye at least two times since your baby's conception. Why didn't you tell me before?"

"Don't hit me," was all I could think of to say.

Forty minutes later, I was back at my desk with a fairly presentable trim but with the medium-brown roots still coming in strong.

"What happened?" Dodo wanted to know when she got back from her own lunch.

Wordlessly, I handed her my by now well-thumbed copy of *What to Expect,* open to the section on "Hair Dyes and Permanents." Apparently, she hadn't read that part before, either.

After a few moments, she said optimistically, "Well, it does say that the risks are only theoretical."

"Yeah," I said, resigned. "But you know Rock."

"It's not really such a bad shade of medium-brown," she tried again.

"Not if your name's Mickey and you love cheese."

"I think it looks beautiful," said Tolkien Donald. He was studying my two-toned hair. "There aren't many women who could pull it off like you do. I seem to remember, back in the seventies, there was an American export of a television show I used to watch, *The Rookies.*"

"I don't remember that one."

"No? It was about these three cops, rookies, working under this curmudgeonly lieutenant. One guy was black and cool, one naive and white, and one straight and married. You know how the Americans can be—they probably thought they had every demographic in the world covered with that one. And I never could figure out how they could get away with keeping on calling the show *The Rookies* after the first season. I mean, it's not like a cop can go on being a rookie forever. But I'm getting away from the point, which is that the straight and married cop was married to a woman who was played by the actress Kate Jackson, who at the time had two-toned hair just like yours. It was black on the top and then switched to auburn in the middle. I used to wonder how a person could be born with hair that was so odd and that looked so great. And you know what the really strange thing was?"

I shook my head, mesmerized that he was so mesmerized by what I thought of as my hideous hair.

"Well, the really strange thing was that on *The Rookies,* Kate played a character named Jill. But then, later in the same decade? She pops up on another show, *Charlie's Angels,* only now she's got shorter hair that's all the same shade and her character's name is Sabrina while there's this other actress on the show, Farrah Fawcett-Majors, who's got all kinds of different shades going on in her hair and now *her* character's name is Jill."

"So what's she doing now? Kate Jackson?"

"I don't know, do I? I started growing up after the seventies." Then he was back to hair. "Of course, on *The Rookies,* Kate's hair wasn't exactly like yours. It being the seventies and all, her hair was razor straight and always looked like she ironed it before she left the house each day. Your hair, on the other hand, is twenty-first century hair. It's trendy and spiky and fun, and the two-toned effect is much more interesting on your short hair than it ever was on Kate's."

So this was what my life had boiled down to: I'd met the most perfect man, a man who would spend a half hour talking about some old program just to make me feel better about the fact that the entire world now knew that I dyed my hair, and I couldn't tell anybody about it, now, could I? Well, except for David, of course; and, by extension, Christopher. I could just hear my mother: "Oh, Tolkien. What a wonderfully tolerant man you must be. In my day, very few men would have willingly taken on a woman with another man's baby on the way." Or better still, Tolkien to me: "Is there a reason you'd like to share with me, Jane, for why you wear an inflated object underneath your clothes whenever we do something with your sister and Tony?"

No, it wouldn't do. Despite the inherent frustration of having finally met a man that I could point to and say,

"Look, he's decent and he likes me," and yet not be able to tell anyone about him, I knew that if I wanted to continue dating Tolkien Donald, and I did, then I was going to have to do it under the shroud of the utmost secrecy.

"I have a low-lying placenta."

What it really was, was that I had a pile of work on my desk that I didn't feel like attending to, not when there was a perfectly gorgeous day going on outside.

"What?" Dodo still hadn't looked up from the galleys that had just been delivered.

"*I said,* Madame Zora says I have a low-lying placenta."

The increased volume of my voice, coupled with the information contained therein, finally caught her attention.

She whipped off her reading glasses. "Good God, Jane, that can't be good. Still, if I recall correctly, isn't it a bit early to be worrying about that?"

Dodo had a mind like a steel trap and a near photographic memory which was one of the reasons she'd risen so high in the business so quickly. When she wanted to, she could quote whole passages from any of our authors' books better than the authors themselves, and that after only one reading. She pulled her parlor trick on me now.

"As a matter of fact, if I recall—" she squinted up at the ceiling and I suddenly recollected with a sinking feeling that she had her own copy of *What to Expect* and was probably better versed in it than I was "—an estimated twenty to thirty percent of placentas are low-lying in the second trimester, but most of them move up to the upper segment in time. When this doesn't happen, a diagnosis of placenta previa is made, but that's relatively rare. In fact, it only occurs in one percent or less of full-term pregnancies and, of those, only one out of every four is ever located low enough to cause any serious complications. So you see, Jane, it really is too early—"

I cut her off. "Madame Zora says that it's not too early to be worried in my case."

"But the question here of course, Jane, the one that keeps arising, is, does Madame Zombie know what the bloody hell she's talking about?"

"She's not a witch doctor." I assumed a wounded expression. "I really wish you wouldn't talk about her that way. She happens to be the woman who's going to deliver my baby."

"I'm sorry, Jane, but—"

"And *she* says that she's never seen such a low-lying placenta in all of her career. Why, *she* says, if it were any lower, it'd be hitting the tops of my shoes. So, you see, it *isn't* too early to worry, because it's been my experience that, in any given situation, if there's only a one out of four in every one percent chance of a thing happening—" and here I let the hormones rip — *"IT'LL HAPPEN TO ME!"*

"I'm sorry, Jane, I didn't mean to imply…" Dodo came around the desk to hug me.

"No, of course you didn't. No one ever does."

"But you have to admit, even though I've never met her, your Madame Zomba can impress as being eccentric."

"Well, *she* says that my low-lying placenta—"

Dodo cut me off before I could begin screaming again. "Yes, I know, dear. And it really was wrong of me to sound the least bit resistant to what is obviously a legitimate problem." She grabbed my shoulders and held me at arm's length, smile bright, encouraging. "I know. Why don't you take the rest of the day off and go give that low-lying placenta of yours a break?"

As I feigned reluctance to accept her generous offer, I felt a twinge of guilt even as I thought about what fun it would be to spend the day window-shopping or listening to a midday concert outside Saint Martin's in the Fields rather than being cooped up in here. It was getting to the point where it felt as though I was inventing complications on a regular basis. And here was Dodo being so very understanding once again. Was it possible that I was beginning to develop Munchausen's syndrome? No, I told myself, not possible because in my case I knew that I was making the symptoms up.

"You're so brave, Jane," Dodo said now, a beautiful liquid crystal of a tear caught in the corner of her eye. "I don't think I could ever be as brave as you've been."

I demurely looked down at my Joan & David feet, at least what I could still see of them over my mound of fake stomach, portrait of Madonna and Child only without. I fell just shy of actually shuffling my feet and saying, "Aw shucks, twarn't nuthin', ma'am," in imitation of Colin Smythe's beloved John Wayne. Instead, I kept the "Aw" part, simply making the addendum "anyone would do the same in my shoes."

Hardly. However, if I played my cards right, no one would ever be the wiser.

But just where in hell was I going to come up with a baby?

My baby was now an eight- to ten-inch fetus and, if he or she had been real rather than imaginary, strong enough to be felt by me. Its body was covered with soft downy lanugo, and hair had begun to grow on its head. Brows and white eyelashes were making an appearance and there was something called a protective vernix coating which covered the fetus.

I couldn't say that I'd noticed any decrease in mood swings, which was supposed to be characteristic of the fifth month, but Mother had always said I was a late bloomer. The irritability that was supposed to still occur occasionally was still a more than occasional thing. The absentmindedness was new but at least, thank God, I hadn't experienced any swelling in my ankles, feet, hands or face and I had yet to develop hemorrhoids. All in all, mother and fetus were doing just great.

the sixth month

Men like to play at sports. Women compete at everything else.

We were all gathered around the kitchen of Tony and Soph's tiny apartment, talking about whether or not their baby'd one day kick arse for Manchester United and cooing over its ten fingers and toes. The "we" I refer to were the proud parents and Baby Jack, along with our mother and a six-pack of ready-to-pop women—all of whom reminded me of cast members from *The Crucible*, save for the fact that none of them wore white bonnets—and their various spouses and significant or insignificant others from Soph and Tony's parentcraft classes.

"Smart not to've had the epidural," said smug Peg, whom I remembered from Sophie's shower and whom I was tempted to call Goodwife Peg, or Goodie.

"Easy for you to talk," said huffy Trudy. "When I had my first, I was in labor for nearly three days." She held up her fingers to count, drawing out the syllables. "*Three days.*

I threw up on my own feet while standing up in the hospital shower more times'n I can count. If they hadn't given me the bloody epidural on the third day, I'd've murdered someone."

I sniffed. "I'm not having an epidural *or* going to the hospital."

"Well, you're fucking nuts, you are," said Trudy.

"Shh. The baby," shushed Goodie Peg.

"I'm having a midwife named Madame Zora who's delivering my baby for me at home." I rubbed my tummy. "I'm not even going to have to put my feet up in stirrups. She's going to let me do it the natural way, the old-fashioned way—I'm going to squat and squeeze it out."

"Trudy's right," said Goodie Peg sotto voce so as not to have the baby hear. She leaned closer to my ear. "You are fucking nuts."

Double, double, boil and bubble, you stupid bitch, I thought, even if I was spoiling my own literary allusions.

"I think it's important to stay home with the baby at least the first two weeks," said Helena, who worked for a multinational corporation.

Dora, who was a legal assistant, snorted. "Two weeks? Try two months."

"Two years for me," said Elizabeth, a cosmetics salesgirl.

Goodie Peg smiled beatifically. "I'm planning on staying home until my little girl gets married."

"I'm going to start a day care center in my home," piped up Patty, who looked about sixteen. "I want to be around as many babies as I can. And," she added assertively, "I don't care how much birthing babies hurts. I'm not taking the chance of my baby coming into the world already hooked on drugs, not even if the labor hurts so much that it feels as though someone took a long glass tube and slowly shoved it straight through my eye."

"Do you think Manchester'll go all the way then this

year?" asked Tony, a rhetorical question if any of the men'd ever heard one.

As if in proof of this, amid the sound of a chorus of popping beer cans, they all answered almost simultaneously, "I don't see why the hell not."

Sophie, the tableau's Madonna, who had been silent up to this juncture, picked a very interesting moment to point out to one and all, "You know, everybody, I don't believe Jane's ever changed a diaper in her life."

"It's true," my mother chortled, the chortling part really surprising me since, previously, I had only ever believed that this was something people did in books. "Jane's never changed a nappy in her life. And why should she have? After all, she was the youngest and it certainly wasn't as though anyone was ever going to encourage her to sit for anyone else's kids."

"Here's your golden opportunity, sis," Sophie said, moving to hand off Baby Jack to me, Jack whose diaper was filled with the stuff that had started Sophie down this scatological path in the first place.

Instinctively, I moved in the other direction, toward the door and the staircase down and out. "Gotta run," I said, backing up as though Baby Jack were a gun set to go off at any moment. "I just remembered an urgent appointment that I forgot."

"You're not fooling anyone, you know," the voices from above mocked me as I took the flights of stairs two steps at a time, the potential risk of damaging my baby by falling be damned. "You'll find out soon enough. You can't avoid it forever, you know."

I had just finished reading the first three chapters plus synopsis that Mona Shakespeare had sent me. Actually, she'd attached the file to her next e-mail following my response to her desperate query and I'd only just got a chance to look at it. Weird times we were living in, when an ed-

itor could only make tactile contact with a manuscript sub-
mission if she was willing to first download it into her
computer and then print it out.

Still, I supposed that it was time efficient and cost effective on her part.

Of course, as luck would have it, I'd been completely
preoccupied with this and that for the past month and so
had forgotten all about her book almost as soon as I'd
downloaded it and printed it out. I'd only just rediscov-
ered it when I'd accidentally bumped a stack of month-
old correspondence off the corner of my desk that I'd also
not found time to get around to in the past month.

Sometimes it felt as though you could no longer turn
around in a bookshop or at an editorial meeting without
being confronted with yet another pink-covered book
whose pages told about the wacky adventures of yet another twentysomething Londoner who labored in publishing—I don't know why they all have to be in
publishing, but they always are—and who will do anything
in her power to find Mr. Right. Even though I was under
thirty myself, just barely, I could still not quite grasp the
entertainment industry's skewed vision of a world in which
important characters could *only* be under thirty as if, upon
hitting thirty, they might magically go up in smoke.

Still, it was refreshing at least to see one person attempting to make her publishing doll move in a different
direction, and this bizarre American woman who had sub-
mitted to me a portion of her bizarre manuscript had
done just that.

And the best part of all?

Her book about modern pregnancy was *nothing* like *my*
book about modern pregnancy.

Pregnancy was funny, there were no two ways about it,
and Mona Shakespeare had succeeded in hitting the thing
squarely on the head. She'd deftly satirized the silliness of
a world that briefly canonized women, for a nine-month

period of time, just for proving themselves able to procreate, just for proving themselves capable of having something come out of their sex lives other than orgasms. Her heroine was called Stacy—like working in publishing, all these heroines have girlish names—and her problem wasn't that she couldn't get a man to marry her. Rather, because she'd been sleeping with anyone that she could get her hands on—always using brightly colored condoms, of course, color-coded according to which partner she was with at the moment, though one had obviously sprung a leak—in her massive manhunt for a regular date, once she'd turned up pregnant she hadn't a clue as to who the father might be. Hers was definitely not your mother's Cinderella story. With so many candidates to choose from, then, she'd taken each aside to tell them what had happened in the hopes that just one out of the bunch would have the decency to stand by her. What she hadn't counted on, however, was the Madonna factor.

Ten years ago, a man faced with the unwanted pregnancy of some girl he'd slept with might simply say, "Prove it." Now, the world had become so baby-besotted—all you had to do was note how much attention had been paid to the singing Madonna's pregnancies in order to prove *that* was true—that Mona Shakespeare somehow managed to make it seem plausible that ten men would not only *not* turn their backs on the product of a one-night stand, but would embrace the shot at fatherhood! Even though they didn't really know the mother at all and, in some cases, didn't like what little they knew.

Apparently, both men and women were so busy these days making a solid go of their careers first that they were having trouble fitting in the necessary time to meet the kind of persons a person could seriously consider procreating with. When the time clock ticked them over to the other side of thirty—and most of the men Stacy slept with in Mona Shakespeare's book had made the Humpty

Dumpty fall over to the other side—rather than self-destructing in sixty seconds, they were desperately casting about for suitable partners with whom to try to recast their image upon the face of a child. What Mona Shakespeare's book turned on then—which, by the way, was titled *The Rubber Slipper*—was the idea that Stacy was trying each of these men on as her pregnancy progressed in order to see which one would make the best dad. I was impressed enough with the first three chapters I'd read to e-mail Mona Shakespeare right away to send more.

I was also sufficiently impressed to shout out, "Dodo! Come quickly! I think I've got us a winner here!"

Dodo, however, was preoccupied enough with her own work to shout back, "Can't you come to me, Jane? I am pretty busy at the moment."

I immediately put on my tired-pregnant-woman's voice, lowering my tone just enough so that she'd have to strain to hear me. "I suppose so. Although I have been feeling somewhat knackered lately. What with the baby making me feel beastly and all."

She was in my doorway in an instant. "I'm sorry, Jane. How rude of me." She tried not to look like she wanted desperately to get back to her own work. "There was something you wanted to share with me?"

"Just this!" I crowed triumphantly, rising from my desk with more bounce than any knackered pregnant lady had a right to have and waving the pages of Mona Shakespeare's manuscript in my fist. "I think I've found us our next bestseller!"

"Oh, Jane." Clearly Dodo was experiencing one of her jaded days. "They're *all* bestsellers. I have a stack of submissions to go through on my desk—" and here she gave me an accusing look because I'd been pulling hormones lately to avoid having to help her do her job "—and they *all* come with letters from their authors saying that they're bestsellers."

"I know all that, Dodo, but this one really is. This is one that'll make none of us here at Churchill & Stewart care anymore if Colin Smythe's next Regency-style novel is set in Japan with the main character being a gay sumo wrestler who longs to one day ski in the Swiss Alps! I'm telling you, Dodo—sit! Sit! Sit! Sit!"

And right then and there, I made her sit down at my desk and read every last word of the printed-out pages from *The Rubber Slipper.* All the while, I alternated pacing up and down in front of the desk with sneaking around to peek over her shoulder and see where she was at whenever she broke into laughter, which was often.

"I particularly liked the one American that Stacy dates," she chuckled, putting down the last of the pages, "the one who, even though he's returned home to Idaho following his vacation fling with her, upon hearing of her pregnancy, comes rushing back to London with a baby-size pair of six-shooters for his *son* to wear in the crib."

"Which is when Stacy says, 'How do you know the baby's going to be a boy? I'm almost positive I feel a girl coming on and if I'm right, I know she'd much rather have a set of knives,' before sending him packing to America and moving on to Suitor Number 4, Mitch, the frustrated walking tour guide from the West Country who hates all tourists and who we'll meet just as soon as Ms. Shakespeare sends us chapters four and up."

"God, Jane, I really think you might be right about this one. It really does feel...so...right. And that name! Do you think she's having us on—Mona *Shakespeare?*"

"Well," I said defensively, "it's not like she's trying to convince us that her parents named her *Gladys.* Now, Gladys Shakespeare would be a bit of a stretch. Anyway, think of the marketing possibilities. Helen Fielding trades on Henry. Joanna Trollope trades on Anthony. If any publisher could find someone with the last name of Brontë who could string more than two words together successfully, they'd slap a pen in their hands so quickly Bramwell would do another spin in his grave."

"Yes, I know that, but this Mona person's an American."

"And you think the Americans are more averse than we are to capitalizing on famous names? Look at the Hemingway legacy. Why, I'll wager you that there are more Hemingway offspring and subrelatives currently writing than Papa had cats."

"Yes, but Mona's American, while Shakespeare's—"

"Oh, stop being so elitist, Dodo. We'll cross that marketing bridge when we get to it and I'm sure we'll manage to use good old Billy S. to our best advantage. Why couldn't he have had an illegitimate offspring from some fan who'd come to see him with her father, whose own offspring several generations down the road in turn eventually became slave owners in Virginia and decided to adopt the use of the last name of the man who'd shagged their grandmother or great-grandmother or whatever upon completion of *The Taming of the Shrew?* Nearly four hundred years in the ground, and people are discovering new things about Shakespeare all the time, new plays even, so why not this?"

I noted the pale expression on Dodo's face and went on before she could voice her objections to the notion of desecrating the Bard's memory, even in the name of greater sales. "But we can worry about that later. The important thing now is that we get Mona to send us the rest of that book before some American publisher gets smart enough to snap it up first. I want that *Rubber Slipper.*"

"And if the rest isn't as good as the beginning?"

"It will be. And, if it's not, we'll work on it with her until it is. *Bridget Jones* sold something like 900,000 copies before it even hit the States. When's the last time Churchill & Stewart had a debut novelist who could sell a million copies out of the gate?"

"I see your point."

"First we find out what Mitch is up to in chapter four."

"Oh!" She was suddenly like a little girl. "I *do* want to find out more about what the frustrated walking tour guide is like."

"Then we check out chapter five."

She consulted the synopsis. "Edward Mumford? The podiatrist who ends up getting arrested for molesting his patients?"

"Yes."

"Oh, this is a fun book."

"Yes, it is. And we're going to take this thing one step at a time and do it right."

"I suppose there really isn't any reason why Shakespeare *couldn't* have some American descendants."

"No reason at all."

"Virginia, you said?"

I shrugged. "It could just as easily be South Carolina. Just so long as it's somewhere that they have cotton."

"But Mona's in New York."

"Well, people do have a tendency to move around a bit after a couple of hundred years. Still, if the details bother you, we can always make the female ancestor of Mona's who slept with Shakespeare Dutch. She could be a Dutch woman whose family had temporarily escaped to Strat-ford-upon-Avon in order to avoid some kind of windmill crisis or something."

"I think you're right after all, Jane. I think maybe we should leave those details for later."

"Fine."

"Of course, I'll help you in any way I can with this one and I'd really love to be hands-on about it, but I do real-ize that Mona wrote to you. You know, this could be the making of your career."

"Actually, I'm starting to count on it."

"Could you feed Kick the Cat for me, David?" I asked. "He's really been quite peckish lately and I'm worried that if I don't keep his bowl topped up, he'll eat the first mouse he sees."

"That is what cats do," he said, but he retrieved one of Kick the Cat's beloved cans of Fishy Fiesta from the cabinet over the kitchen sink nonetheless. I thought that the stuff was just about as noxious as a substance could possibly be and still be called "food," but he loved it. The cat, that is; not David.

"Yes, well…" My voice trailed off, distracted by the task at hand, as I removed the back from a crystal picture frame that I'd bought cheap.

"How are things going with Tolkien?" asked David, as he did every time I saw him.

"Fine," I said. "We have great fun, great sex, I have more real talks with him than with anyone I've met since I met you, I see who he is and I love that, I let him see who I am and he still manages to love that—"

"The only problem," David said, "is that you have this pregnancy charade going on with most everybody in your life and you can't tell him about it, because then he would think you are dishonest plus a stark-raving loon."

"Well, there is that."

"You should really bring him round to meet us sometime," said Christopher, who had recently moved in upstairs with David, their relationship progressing at an alarmingly quick, and healthy, rate.

"Yes, you really should," enthused David, putting his arm lightly around Christopher's shoulders. "Perhaps we would rub off on the two of you, he would ask you to marry him, and you would say yes and abandon your ridiculous scheme."

Never able to do anything by halves, it was just my luck: instead of one fairy godmother, I'd somehow managed to wind up with two.

"I thought we had already agreed that this was all your fault," I said to David. "After all, it was you who turned this fake pregnancy into some kind of bet between us."

"I—"

"Could you pass me those scissors?" I asked Christopher, who had just seated himself perpendicular to me at the table, bottle of ale in hand.

"What are you doing with those underexposed photos?" he asked idly, as he did what I'd asked.

"Making my own sonogram pictures," I said, snipping away.

"You're doing *what?*"

"Making my own sonogram pictures," I answered again, holding the photos up to the light so that I could trim the edges more neatly.

When my repeating the same exact words failed to illuminate things sufficiently for them, I explained how, ever since my day at the clinic two months ago, I'd been wanting to get my hands on some sonogram pictures to show the people at work.

"But no one would sell me theirs, even I'm not mean enough to tackle a prego in the street in order to steal hers, and the idea of diving into the oversize refuse bin in the alley behind the clinic in hopes of finding something there just made me go all queasy."

"You do realize, Jane," pointed out Christopher, "that these underexposed shots of yours don't look a thing like a real baby."

"Yes, I know. But, then, neither do real sonogram pictures, so you could say that science and I are even."

"Yes, but sonogram pictures are more than just dark gray pictures with a few squiggly specks of light in them."

"Well, not by much."

"Yes, but they do usually have data all over them," Christopher went on.

"Data?"

"Yes. You know, things like the patient's name, the date and time of the procedure, the office where it was done…"

As he carried on with further information involving measurements in centimeters, I wondered if he were somehow related to Stan from Accounting with his fast-breeding sisters. Now that he mentioned it, though, I supposed that I did remember registering, on some subconscious level, some of this *data* when I'd looked at the sonogram pictures of that prego outside of the clinic, but it certainly hadn't concerned me at the time. As for the exact details of what he was talking about now, it was all too complex for my purposes.

"If people ask," I said, studying my handiwork, "I'll just tell them that Madame Zora took these with a new machine she got in acknowledgement of the technological revolution, but that she doesn't like to do her pictures like just everybody else. I'll say that instead of all of that printing and those centimeters you mentioned, she prefers to mark the back of her snaps with hex signs individualized to fit the patient at hand."

"You're a sick, sick woman, Jane," David said.

I met his eyes briefly over the top of my completed arts-and-crafts project, and smiled, feeling the gleam in my own eyes as I reflected on how wonderful this was going to look in my office. "Yes, I do know that."

Maybe it was because I still hadn't gotten quite used to the difference that the cloth baby made in my center of balance because, like real pregnant women, I was experiencing a problem in terms of increased clumsiness. If I were really pregnant, the reason why I couldn't seem to keep from dropping things to save my life would have to do with the loosening of joints and retention of water, both of which could make a person's physical ability to grasp things something less than perfect. Another thing the pregnancy guides attributed clumsiness to was lack of concentration brought on by the "scatterbrain syndrome" that seemed to be part and parcel of bringing new human life into the world. In my case I'd found that the scatterbrain syndrome was part and parcel of keeping all of my deceptive balls in the air at once and I accepted the attendant clumsiness as the natural byproduct.

But my family members and the people at work were less inclined to blithely accept my advanced case of the "dropsies" as a charming result of my current condition. Sophie no longer encouraged me to pick up Baby Jack; no hardship, that. Mother would not allow me to drink tea out of a china beaker and, even when we were in public, insisted that fine restaurants put my beverages into unbreakable paper cups. And as for the people at work, not only had they laid in a supply of paper goods in the kitchen area, but they'd also forbidden me to open any jiffy packages, even if they were addressed directly to me, because, as Stan from Accounting so succinctly put it, "God knows what the butterball would do if she happened to come into contact with a staple," to which Louise had added, "Besides, we can't very well have her accidentally shredding the pages of the only copy to the next bestselling Harry Potter clone, now, can we?"

Of course, if Dumbo-like clumsiness weren't enough, not to mention the insults that seemed to go along with it, the cloth baby had impacted my physical life in another negative way: just like with travelers who carry too much weight on one shoulder, the additional weight I was carrying in front, faux or no, was causing me to have the kind of back distress that was also common to carriers of real babies.

Naturally, I tried all the advice concerning backaches that I found in the pregnancy guides, at least the advice that didn't seem completely asinine to me. Keeping my weight gain within the recommended parameters was easy since I still weighed competitively less than any other pregnant lady in her sixth month. I gave up wearing high heels and flat heels in favor of the doctor-recommended two-inch heels necessary for keeping the body properly aligned. I never lifted anything abruptly, always bending at the knees rather than at the waist and lifting with my arms and legs rather than with my back. I carried grocery bags balanced one on each side, milkmaid fashion, rather than in one big bag at the front. I tried not to stand for long periods and, if I absolutely had to, kept one foot on a short stool with the knee bent to prevent strain on my lower back. Since my job did require a fair amount of sitting, I learned to "sit smart," using a chair that afforded adequate support and refraining from crossing my legs, no matter how deep the desire to show off the fact that, two-thirds of the way into my pregnancy, my gams still looked great; I also kept my feet elevated on the little stool hidden under my desk and never sat more than an hour without getting up to stretch. I purchased a firmer mattress, used a heating pad at night that would have been forbidden to me if I were really pregnant, and tried to learn how to relax.

And my back *still* hurt.

"Here, goddammit," Dodo groused, dragging two rolled-up exercise mats into my office and unrolling them on the floor in front of my desk. She heaved the guest chairs farther out of the way.

"What's this?" I asked.

"Down," she instructed, already having lain down on one of the mats herself. She was flat on her back, arms straight at her side, knees bent with feet flat on the floor and a comfortable distance apart.

"But what are we doing?" I tried again, lying down on the mat next to hers and imitating her form.

"Oh, shit," she said, getting up quickly and nearly yanking me to my feet. "I nearly forgot. You're past your fourth month and shouldn't lie on your back. Here, stand beside me over here with your back against the wall. Now, exhale as you press the small of your back against the wall. Then inhale and relax your spine."

She made me do this twenty-five times before she told me we were doing something called the pelvic tilt.

"But *why* are we doing this?" I pressed. "Why, when we both have a ton of work to do?"

"Because obviously that stupid Madame Zenobia of yours didn't bother showing you how to do the exercises that will help alleviate the pain in your back—and help alleviate the pain that the rest of us are beginning to feel at hearing you continually whinge about the pain in your back."

"*Well.* If I'd known you felt—"

"No time for that now. We've got to do twenty-five repetitions of the dromedary droop before I go to my three o'clock meeting."

"The dromedary *what?*"

But there was no time for that either, apparently. Before I even knew what I was about, my well-heeled and elegant boss had dropped down on all fours on her exercise mat, indicating with an impatiently equine toss of her head that I should do the same. "Come *on,* Jane."

"But isn't a dromedary a camel?" I asked as I obeyed her, but she ignored me, barking out orders that evinced a heretofore unseen military side to her personality.

"Keep your back in a naturally relaxed position! Don't let that spine sag! Head straight, neck aligned with spine! Now, hump your back, tighten your abdomen and buttocks, allow your head to drop all the way down! Slowly release your back! Raise your head to the original position! Aaannnddd REPEAT!"

Dodo'd been in such a hurry to get me on an antibackache program when she'd first stormed my office that she'd clean forgotten to close my door behind her. And so it was that, somewhere between the fourteenth and fifteenth dromedary droop, with our buttocks in the air and our backs humped, we heard the most odious sound imaginable, causing us to snap our heads toward its source as one, as if we were two puppets dancing to the rhythm of a single puppeteer.

"Well, that's a sight I'd've paid good money to see," oozed Stan from Accounting as he slouched in my doorway. "But, then, why pay for the camel, when you can watch it hump for free?"

"*Get out!*" we shouted.

Once Stan was no longer darkening my doorway, I collapsed on my side, oddly tired after the mild exertions.

"Gosh, I'm tired," I breathed. "Can we stop now?"

"Well, we haven't finished yet but, ohhh," she relented, "all right. However—" she held up a cautionary finger "—I will be back tomorrow and the day after that and the day after that. I intend to have the rest of your pregnancy be backache-free whether you like it or not. Now, here—" she extended her hand, "let me give you a hand up."

I gratefully accepted her offer, grabbing on tightly. But as I rose, something in my new unbalanced state caused the forward momentum to carry me too far and, once I was up, I just kept going until I bumped smack into Dodo, the cloth baby bouncing me back off of her.

"Oh my God!" she cried, wonder filling her eyes. "I just felt the baby kick!"

"That's not possible," I replied hurriedly, honestly, not thinking.

"Why, whatever do you mean?"

Now I was forced to backpedal. "Oh, it's just that, well," and here I affectionately rubbed my belly, "she's not much of a soccer player, that's all. Some babies aren't, you know, and this one's one of those. Hardly ever does the kicking thing and, when it does, it's usually only me that can feel it on the inside, never anyone else on the outside."

"But how strange! I know what I just felt, Jane, and it was definitely a kick."

"Don't you have that meeting to go to?"

But she was already on me, one hand rubbing my belly to see if she could get it to do it again.

As I sighed, I realized that I might as well submit. She was going to do it anyway, so I might as well sit back and try not to hate it. Still, like any real pregnant woman at my stage of the game, there was a part of me that sometimes grew tired of this pregnancy. Really. Pregnancy, pregnancy, pregnancy:

Couldn't anyone ever think of anything else?

Tolkien idly stroked the back of my arm, as I lay curled up naked beside him, my two-toned hair against his gorgeous chest. It was a constant revelation, the notion that despite the same body parts and the same basic actions being involved every time, that sex with the right person could be a source of continual amazement as new facets of the other person were discovered with each encounter, each touch.

"Mmm," I purred.

"Mmm," he echoed.

"I love being here with you like this," I purred some more, for once not frightened that if I told a man what I was really feeling, I'd scare him off.

"Me, too," he said, and I knew he meant it. Then he pulled back a bit, lifting his cheek from where it had been resting against the top of my head, and looking down at me. "And do you know what else I'd love?"

I looked up. "Mmm…what?"

"To meet your family."

I was immediately startled back out of purr mode. "What?"

"Your family, Jane, I'd like to meet them." He smiled. "You know, it is the normal thing that people usually do when they meet each other and wind up feeling as we do."

"I guess I hadn't thought about that."

"You seem hesitant."

"Yes, well, if you knew my mother and sister, you'd be hesitant about wanting to meet them."

"Is it that you're embarrassed by them? If so, I can certainly understand about familial embarrassments. Believe me, having had parents who refashioned themselves Elrond and Galadriel and having been renamed Tolkien myself, I can safely say that I do know how bad it can be."

"Oh—" I smiled ruefully "—it can be worse."

"You know, the few times they've come up in conversation, you've alluded to the fact that your relationships with your mother and Sophie are somehow lacking. Don't you think they'd be happy for your happiness? Even Elrond and Galadriel, weird as they can be, are always happy whenever I'm happy."

I thought seriously about what he was asking me: would Mother and Sophie be happy for my happiness? I shook my head. I didn't know. And that was perhaps the saddest part of all, that I couldn't say with any degree of certainty that my own family would be happy for me.

"I don't know." I smiled a little sadly. "I don't know how they'd be."

Not to mention, a voice in my head kept reminding me, that this was no time to have my pregnant and my nonpregnant worlds collide.

"How about the people you work with then?" he suggested.

"No," I said, thinking of that worlds-colliding problem again. "They're not much fun, either."

"Oh." He looked so dejected.

"Hey!" I brightened. "I know!"

"Yes?"

"Yes. There *are* some people I'd like you to meet."

To claim that I'm no different than anybody else might present a bit of a credibility stretch, I know, but there is at least one thing I have in common with the rest of the world: having found myself to be hopelessly in love, and having found that feeling to be returned in kind, I wanted to shout that fact to the world. The only problem was that in my case, my current life was built on such a mountain of mendacity that there was almost no one I could share the good news with.

If I were living a different kind of life, if I were a member of a different kind of family, I would have brought Tolkien home to meet everyone in an instant. As it was, I made do with the one person who knew more truths about my life than anyone else and the man that *he* loved. In other words, I took Tolkien home to meet...

"Tolkien, this is David. David, Tolkien. Oh, and that man over there is David's Christopher."

In honor of the occasion, David had offered the use of their apartment, figuring that he'd be more comfortable cooking in his own kitchen than in mine, and figuring further that it would be good to have the floor that I lived on function as a buffering zone between where we were and where the nosy Marcuses were two floors below.

I suppose that when I'd told Tolkien that we were going on a double date with my best friend, I might have mentioned that my best friend was a gay Israeli ex-fighter pilot and that his date would naturally be his male lover, but I hadn't done that, figuring it wouldn't matter to Tolkien. And it didn't. What mattered most to Tolkien was that I obviously held David in a higher regard than anyone else that I knew; the rest of David's CV was just so many details.

"David's *great*," Tolkien enthused, leaning across the table to whisper his enthusiastic pronouncement to me while Christopher helped Tolkien replace the appetizers with entrées.

"What do you like best about him?" I asked, curious. I wasn't used to a boyfriend loving my best friend, Trevor having hated him, and I really did want to know.

"Well—" he thought about it, then rolled his eyes, shrugging, "—he can cook."

"Yes, he is marvelous that way."

"Oh, and there's also the small fact that he absolutely adores you."

I beamed, I was that happy.

After dinner, after a dessert that made me glad I was at least smart enough to know that men always prefer a woman who will share dessert with them than one who claims to be keeping to her diet even on an important occasion like this, I left Tolkien to help Christopher stare at the CD collection, while I went off to the kitchen to corner David, using the pretext that I needed more wine.

"Well," I asked, feeling a bit breathless in the midst of my anxiousness to hear the verdict, "what do you think?"

"You really want to know, Jane?"

I was feeling a bit cautious, but: "Yes."

"You really want to know what I think of your Tolkien?"

Now I was impatient. "Yes!"

The sleeves of his white oxford shirt were rolled to the elbows, revealing black hair on strong arms that he crossed as he leaned against the closed refrigerator door.

"What I think is…"

"Yes?"

"What I think is that if I had not already found the love of my life, *and* you were not my best friend, I'd go for him myself."

"But he's not gay," I objected.

He smiled, shrugged. "Details."

"Really?" I squealed, trying to contain myself and failing miserably. What I really felt like doing was jumping up and down like the girls in the office did, but I'd tried that enthusiastic-schoolgirls-on-a-trampoline routine with David once before and his lack of enthusiasm for it had proved disappointing. "You *really* like Tolkien that much?"

"Yes, really."

"But why," I asked, all seriousness again now, "why do you like him so much?"

"Because he is so—um, how can I put this delicately so as not to offend?—" and here he smiled devilishly "—because he is sooo *not* Trevor."

Dodo had Mona Shakespeare's bookcases.

No, I don't mean that she *stole* them, or anything else criminal like *that*. Dodo isn't me, after all.

No, what I mean is that the bookcases I always envisioned in Mona's New York flat—crammed with the works of every important dead writer and every living writer who might be important once they were dead or who were currently important for one pop culture reason or another—existed in reality, and they existed in grand style in the flat of Dodo, my boss, who had invited me to see where she lived for the very first time since I'd worked with her.

I perched anxiously on the edge of her moss velvet couch, trying not to let my fake baby frontage over-topple me onto the ecru chenille carpeted floor as I waited for her to bring drinks in.

Drinks were brought in on a small round tray that looked to be solid silver.

"Are you really sure you just want water?" she asked, depositing a crystal glass in front of me.

"Yes, that's fine," I said, watching covetously as she removed a tall expensive-looking bottle of red from the tray and a large goblet.

She poured herself a shimmering glass and then seated herself on the other side of the coffee table, positioning herself in what used to be safely called "Indian-style" but what people now preferred to call "tailor-sitting," which I did not, because there really are no more tailors in the world, save on Savile Row, except for me, who spelled my name different and didn't like to sit like that anyway. So there.

First glass.

"I've always wished we were closer, Jane, which is why I invited you here this evening."

Enquiringly: "Mmm?"

"Since you've had this baby thing going on, I've felt that I *was* closer to you than to anyone else at the office."

Reflectively: "Mmm."

"You see, I've never had many—and during some dry periods in my life, not any—girlfriends."

Empathetically: "Mmm."

"And I never had a sister."

Wistfully: "Mmm."

Second glass.

"Do you know how hard it is to meet men when you have the kind of high-level job that I have?"

Trying for sympathy, but missing entirely: "Mmm."

"Or to have meaningful relationships with anybody when one's good looks get in the way?"

Again missing the sympathy thing: "Mmm."

Third glass.

"Why are people so threatened by me?"

This was a question requiring more than an "mmm" answer. "Mmm, I don't know."

Dodo set her glass down fast, nearly cracking the delicate crystal. "You mean that you're not?"

I examined my mind, since she seemed to be looking for deep thought here. "No," I shook my head slowly, "quite honestly, I'm not."

"Why ever not?"

I thought some more, about the smashing good looks and the top-of-her-game career she had that I did not. And then I thought about how otherwise empty her life was, if for gal-pal talk like this she had to resort to, well, *me.* But I couldn't very well say, "Because your life seems so empty to me," now, could I? So, instead, I said, "I don't know. I guess I'm just too big of a person to be bothered by petty jealousies and envy."

Yes, I know: it was a good thing I wasn't the one drinking the wine, because otherwise I'd have had to choke on it.

But, apparently, Dodo didn't detect anything false in what I'd said. Reaching out, she impulsively squeezed one of my just-your-basic hands in one of her exquisite ones. "Yes, I know, Jane, you are a big person."

"Well, there's no call for making pregnant-woman jokes."

"No, I mean it. And you're wise too."

Okay, now this was where I became certain that she was dead drunk and that if she remembered this conversation at all in the morning, she'd remember it cringingly.

I inched the bottle far enough down the table that it was out of any convenient reach, but she was already too far gone.

"Tell me, honestly, Jane, what do you think?"

"About...?"

"About women and careers and romance and babies—do you think it's possible to have it all?"

I thought about the career we'd both chosen, publishing, and how what with the quantity of egos constantly pinging through the publishing stratum—authors, agents, editors, all of whom had smashing big egos—it was a wonder that at the end of the day any of us had anything left over for anything. But, yes, in answer to Dodo's question, I did believe that a woman could have success at both career and romance—not necessarily easy, but she could—the only really sadly discouraging thing being that in Dodo's specific case, she seemed to want it all so desperately and yet it eluded her.

"Yes, I do," I said. And then, trying to be encouraging, I added, "I guess sometimes it just takes time."

"But I haven't got all that much time," Dodo objected, "at least not for having babies, since I just seem to keep getting...older."

This time, it was me covering her hand with mine, not knowing anymore what to say.

"Well," she brightened, "at least I have your baby to look forward to."

"Elrond, Jane. Galadriel, Jane."

Apparently, in addition to the home they still kept in Barcelona, Tolkien's successful parents also had a lovely estate just outside London as well.

When they were out of the room, I leaned over and whisper hissed to Tolkien, "But I thought they went by Ron and Claire now."

"Oh, they do," he said. "But if your parents had named you Tolkien, you'd go on teasing them at every opportunity life presented you with, too. Anyway—" he shrugged as we watched them reenter the mahogany study, bearing a tea trolley laden with teacups and triangular sandwiches "—they expect it from me. Wouldn't have it any other way."

"What were you saying, my boy?" Elrond-Ron patted combed-back white hair that needed no patting.

"I was saying how lovely things have been around here since you and Mother decided to stop being hippies and start making money instead."

"Yes," agreed Galadriel-Claire, who seemed just as interested as her husband in adjusting hair that didn't need adjusting, in her case a believable henna chignon. "Although I notice you haven't caught the money-making bug yet."

"Yes, well," Tolkien said, "I suppose one of us has to remain an antiestablishment holdout."

"Yes," said Elrond-Ron, "but you're a copper."

"I don't know," I defended, taking Tolkien's hand in

both of mine and smiling at him. "Maybe he's just one of those antiestablishment coppers everyone's always hoping to find."

"They have those, dear?" Galadriel-Claire queried, shocked.

"I'm certain they didn't have those when we were hippies," said Elrond-Ron.

"Yes, well," I said, "I guess things have improved since then, haven't they?"

Galadriel-Claire, perhaps thinking that one of the greatest improvements entailed having manicured toenails rather than filthy ones, gave a hearty laugh. "Yes, they really have."

"Tolkien says you're in publishing," said Elrond-Ron.

"That's right."

"A lot of money to be had in that, is there?"

I thought about the contract I had with Alice. "Yes, there can be."

"Excellent."

"Dad?"

"Yes, Tolkien."

"If you don't mind my saying, you and Mother have become even more money-oriented since the last time you were in town. Don't you ever miss your—um, how to say this—ideals?"

Elrond-Ron waved a hand. "Ideals. They're a fine thing to have, but then the world keeps changing, often in ways you can do nothing about and, well, bonds become a safe place to be."

Galadriel-Claire leaned forward with enthusiasm. "The way we see it, we'll make lots of money now and enjoy it. Then, when we die, we'll leave everything to our favorite charities." She looked straight at Tolkien, a frown of dismay furrowing her prettily tweezed brow. "You won't mind, will you, darling, if we leave everything to charity rather than to you?"

"God, no," he said, and clearly meant it.

"How about you, Jane?" Elrond-Ron focused his gaze on me. "Will you mind—" he gestured at the moneyed life around him "—if Tolkien's parents leave everything to charity?"

"God, no," I echoed Tolkien.

Elrond-Ron looked at Tolkien with approval. "God, I love this girl," he said, taking out a cigar and using the end of the cigar to indicate me before lighting it.

"Me, too," said Galadriel-Claire, taking the cigar from his fingers and drawing on it.

"Anyway," I shrugged, "why should I mind?"

"Will you marry me?"

"Will I do *what?*"

"Will you marry me, Jane? I know that we've only been dating for a short while, but I feel as though I know you better than any other woman I've ever been with in my life."

Obviously, those other women couldn't have been very open. "If I convince you that you're insane," I responded, "would that induce you to shelve this crazy idea for a while?"

"No. Even if you do think it's crazy, I don't care. I've always thought it was foolish for people to waste what time they have on this planet on foolishness—there's little enough time as it is. I suppose that sometimes people waste time because they're confused, but I've always thought that, once a person knows what they want, they should make their intentions known at the first opportunity. What I want is you, Jane."

So here it was, the moment I'd waited for all my life, it seemed: someone that I wanted, who wanted me just as badly and was willing to say so.

"What's it going to be, Jane? If you tell me no, that it's too soon, I'll know that what it really means is that you'll never be ready. Because I don't think it's possible for me to feel this way without you feeling the same way back. And if you can feel the same way back, and still say no…"

I was torn.

If I married him, I'd have to give up my baby, tell everyone that something had gone drastically wrong. I thought about the little extras at work, the nice way that Sophie and my mother had treated me of late—not like a criminal who was trying to purloin someone else's joy, but as a worthy woman in my own right—and even of the impending shower, still some weeks down the line. And it wasn't just all of that, merely all the selfish things; it was that, somehow, over these several months, I'd grown attached to this insane project of mine as I'd never been attached to anything in my life.

And then there was the book I was writing, of course. How could I give up on that dream now, when I was so close to realizing it?

Devil Alice's words now came back to taunt me, singsonging in my head: "Well, you did always say you wished you were a paid storyteller," she'd pointed out.

And then there came my mother's voice, with her ever unoriginal maternal wisdom: "Be careful what you ask for."

To which my own voice in my head, my own voice that was now thoroughly annoyed with Devil Alice and my mother's voice, responded, *"Blah—blah—blah."*

Then the startling thought occurred to me: I *could* give all of that up—the familial attention, the perks at work, the within-my-grasp success of the book—if it meant that I could have Tolkien in exchange. It was that simple.

Right on the heels of that startling revelation, however, was the thudding realization that it *wasn't* that simple. To draw back from my plan now would mean that I would have to come clean, and I *wasn't* yet ready to do *that*. After all, I could hardly get people to believe that it had all been a hysterical pregnancy, not this late in the game, and certainly not since I'd been brilliant enough early on to name Dr. Shelton as my obstetrician—even if I'd had the foresight to fire him since—brilliant Dr. Shelton who could surely be depended upon to detect if a woman were really pregnant or just merely crazy.

And here was the biggest thing: it was the "something had gone drastically wrong" part that was really the chief problem. For, if I wasn't willing to yet admit to lying all this time, and no one would ever believe it had all been some misunderstanding, then the only alternative would be to tell people that I had *lost* the baby; not lost it in a "can't quite remember where I put it" sort of way, but lost it as in "the baby died."

I just couldn't bring myself to do that, and not merely because of all the pain it would cause to people like Dodo, people who had invested care, concern and, yes, even love into my pregnancy. No, it wasn't merely that. It was that it would be *wrong,* wrong for the same reasons that I'd felt uncomfortable earlier when I'd accepted sympathy from Stan from Accounting after telling him I needed an amnio because of the threat of Down's syndrome.

There was my weird hairsplitting morality kicking in again: it was perfectly okay for me to accept unearned attention for a positive thing, a pregnancy that wasn't real; but it was wrong for me to accept it for something that was a true tragedy to too many people.

I just couldn't bring myself to do it. Tolkien, the man of my dreams, would have to go. There just wasn't any other way around it.

Besides, it probably wasn't such a bad outcome after all, I would tell myself later, after he had gone and after I had cried. If I were to marry Tolkien Donald and if my mother were then to talk him into going back to his original name, Donald John, which she would probably do, and if I then were to adopt his last name, I would become Jane John which, when you say it fast, sounds sort of like what you might wind up with if you were to ask a Chinese person to imitate a ding-dong-ing doorbell. Anyway, that was the way I rationalized it to myself.

Too bad that I loved him.

Originally, I'd had a financial motive for continuing with my scheme; now, there was a lopsided moral one. Did it really matter which motivation was stronger?

True, I still didn't know how I was going to get out of this mess when the nine months were up; but then, I'd never known that, had I? All I could do was what I'd always done, really: cross my fingers and leap into the unknown.

Lately, in part perhaps to sublimate my feelings over losing Tolkien, I'd been overcome by a nearly uncontrollable urge to tidy up my surroundings, engaging in a syndrome of behaviors that I'd read was not uncommon in women during their second trimester, particularly the latter part.

It's part of the whole nesting thing and, apparently, the body's pretty good at knowing how long it'll be up for such exertions. It's as if there's a clock inside that knows that in just a few short weeks, things'll have progressed into the third trimester, when the body begins to become unwieldy and symptoms can mirror the first in terms of fatigue.

I found myself in precleaning mode then on, of all things, an early Saturday morning in late September. I had my hair babushkaed, I'd found an old shirt of Trevor's that I'd initially worn when we'd painted the apartment salmon pink together, and I was sipping coffee while looking at the selection of paint chips I'd picked up at the store. It may have taken me nearly three months to realize it, but it'd suddenly occurred to me that I no longer needed to be surrounded by a color I'd come to abhor. I was determined to redo every room in the apartment and equally determined that this time I'd paint each room a different color. This way, if I suddenly developed a hatred for one of the colors I'd committed the walls to—something difficult to change, like red or navy or black, for instance—there'd always be other rooms that I could escape to. Of course, not being either an idiot or a twelve-year-old Eminem devotee, I'd put aside red, navy and black in favor of the more decoratively pliant shades of peach (close to salmon but not nauseating in small doses), leaf green and mauve.

Having put off for as long as possible what I'd have liked to put off forever—I could tell this when I started to swallow actual dregs of coffee, a sure sign that procrastination has gone on far too long—I realized that if I wanted to beautify my nest by painting, I should really engage in the nesting act that involved more obsessive cleaning of it as well. Good God! Sometimes this pregnancy stuff seemed as much of an act of penance as saying Hail Marys for masturbation.

I decided to begin in the bedroom. Even if it wasn't one of the public rooms where my few visitors could appreciate my alterations, it was the room that was the first thing I saw in the morning and the last upon retiring at night. I began with the easy stuff: the bed making, the putting of week-old discards into the clothing hamper, the hour-long pause to flip through a magazine that I'd bought and then forgotten about.

Well, there was no need to take this nesting thing too far too quickly; after all, it wasn't like I had anything but myself to put in the nest.

From linens, dirty socks and "How to Keep Your Man From Leaving" (too late!), I made the natural and inevitable progression to the most hated job of all, dusting, which would be followed in as short an order as I could make it by vacuuming. Of course, if I was going to be painting the room mauve soon—the kitchen was going to be peach, the living-dining area leaf green, while the bathroom was going to remain pristine white for those occasions, now rare, when I drank too much and could only deal with the cleanest of slates—I had better do a more thorough than usual job of it. Instead of just taking the feather duster, then, and waving it in the general direction of my knickknack-strewn dresser, I supposed I'd actually have to make contact with the furniture. As a matter of fact, if I wanted my paint job to come out looking as good as possible, and I did, then I really should move the furniture away from the walls and dust the baseboards as well. That way no unsightly dust would bubble up the paint job, marring the smooth effect I'd hope to achieve. And, besides, I'd only have to move the furniture to the center of the room when I painted anyway.

The dresser turned out to be not much of a problem and the cabinet that discreetly housed the TV still less so. The bed, however, when I got to it—the heavy queen-size sleigh bed—made me wish that I'd been less ambitious about the amount of space I'd felt was required by Trevor's and my energetic lovemaking. Really, I thought, straining as I alternately tried the tugging and shoving approaches, if I'd known I was going to one day be required to move it myself, I'd have settled for oral sex on a tatami mat.

"Ugh!" I grunted, making a sound not unlike those that Trevor had once made in that very bed, as I finally succeeded in forcing the back legs of the bed over the ridge of the Turkey carpet, an area piece that didn't come quite to the wall and which had caused the bulk of the moving problem.

I collapsed against the space of wall closest to where the bed had been, exhausted. As I rested my elbows on my bent knees, formerly neat hair now coming out of my babushka at all angles, the thought occurred to me that life would be a whole lot easier if one could just push everyone out of the nest early, say early enough to obviate the need of making a nest in the first place. Of course, the inevitable next thought was to think that it was silly of me to have had that last thought when, after all, and as I increasingly had to keep reminding myself, there wasn't anyone destined for this nest but me. I never got the chance to fully think that thought through, however. Instead, my eyes, ignoring the dust Harveys that had grown up behind the bed, had alighted upon a slim file folder which the humidity of the damp air was keeping smashed up against the wall where, presumably, the bed had previously kept it. The folder was situated behind the side of the bed where Trevor had slept for two years.

This was odd, I thought, crawling over to it. In his zest to get away from me as quickly as possible, he'd obviously, unwittingly, left a part of himself behind. I wondered what it was. I flipped open the folder, began studying papers.

By the time I was finished, I had a whole new picture of the Trevor Rhys-Davies I'd thought I'd known so well. Gone was the picture of him as a paragon of virtue, at sharp counterpoint to what he had clearly described as my own devious machinations. Here to stay was a picture of him being, if not quite another Nick Leeson, then at least the kind of stockbroker who wasn't averse to using insider information to feather his own nest. No wonder he was able to afford such an astonishing array of suspenders.

It all came down to a company called Thames Waterways. And, if my eyes were not deceiving me, what I was holding in my hands was the kind of information that Trevor's employer, not to mention the Inland Revenue, would dearly love to have; the first, because no one likes to be made a fool of by a subordinate at work (Constance immediately sprang to mind); the latter, because they would probably appreciate the opportunity to collect all of the back taxes he owed on the funds he'd illegally acquired. If they wanted to put the screws to him, they could fine him *and* send him to jail.

What in the world had come over Trevor? What could

have possibly possessed him to take up such a risky scheme? He'd never shown any inclination to want for more than what his job provided him. Was it the true par-simonious colors of the fifty percent of his nature that was Welsh shining through, the Rhys part finally rearing its head? Was it an aberration, a one-time thing, or were there secret files elsewhere in his life, with other Thames Water-ways tucked away in them? You'd think that the generous salary he was paid would be enough to keep anyone happy. It may not have been princely, but it was enough for Knightsbridge and that was plenty. Still, you did always hear that enough was never enough for anybody and maybe, being around all of those inviting numbers every day, the temptation had finally proven too great.

Oh, well, I thought, rising stiffly from the floor and going to put the folder underneath the socks in my bot-tom drawer. The Inland Revenue might be very interested in all of this, but I certainly wasn't going to be the one to tell them. After all, Trevor had thus far kept my secret for me and so it wouldn't be fair of me to turn him over to the thumbscrew boys at Inland Revenue and the Crown Prosecution. Okay, so maybe he'd only kept it because he'd been sent out of the country by the home office, but still...

Besides, I thought, returning to the chore of dusting the baseboards, I had more important things to do. I still had a whole flat to paint.

Ye gads! (I've never said that before in my life; I certainly hope it's spelled right.) My fetus was now a whopping thir-teen inches long—my, how it had grown!—and weighed about one-and-three-quarter pounds, so less than the com-bined weight of two "I'm very depressed"-size bags of M&Ms. The fetus had thin skin, like its mother, and the skin was shiny as well and had no underlying fat. It had little finger and toe prints which were visible. (Sigh!) The eyelids were beginning to part and the eyes to open. If born now, it would need intensive care in order to survive, but survival was possible.

If someone were to come along and administer intensive care to me right now, would I survive this crazy stunt I was pulling?

the third trimester

the seventh month

It was hard to believe that my mother—let me repeat, ladies and gentlemen: *my mother*—had deigned to throw me a baby shower in her *own home,* and she even seemed to care mildly whether I had a good time or not.

She had the garden room positively festooned with all kinds of pink things and, for a guest list, she'd invited Sophie's six-pack of parentcraft class friends, all of whom now had tiny babies of their own, which meant that there was an endless stream of diaper changing going on throughout the party that was supposed to be in my honor, making it more of a poop party really. Mother had also invited Sophie, of course, and Dodo, whom she'd met. She'd tried to get Dodo to give her the names and numbers of my friends at work, but Dodo, knowing that I would never want to face Minerva or Constance or Louise or, heaven forbid, Stan from Accounting, across a pile of rubber nipples and throw-up pads, told my mother that they were all on vacation that month.

As they gently helped me get seated, as if I really were

seven months pregnant, I looked around the room at Sophie's friends. All of them—Goodie Peg, sour Trudy, offi-
cious Dora, mascaraed Elizabeth, sweet Patty, and Helena,
who'd already returned to work part-time—were trailing
those little portable baby seats with them wherever they
went. When everyone was finally seated around the huge
mahogany table Mother'd had Tony drag into the garden
room for the occasion, it was like the meeting of the Five
Families in Mario Puzo's *The Godfather,* save that none of
us were technically gangsters and that, instead of *consiglieri,*
each woman had a baby seated slightly behind her and to
the right.

Before I knew what I was about, I found myself opening packages of things, and well, frankly, I didn't know what
most of the stuff was for. Sure, I'd been to plenty of other
people's baby showers before, but I'd never actually paid
any attention when the women were opening the presents. I mean, who does? Certainly not people like me.
Whenever I had to go to other people's showers in the past,
I just bought the expectant mothers gift certificates to
what I hoped were appropriate shops, daydreamed while
they unwrapped everyone else's presents, ate the pasta salad
if it wasn't too vinegary, ate the store-bought cake no matter what kind it was because it always seemed churlish not
to, drank however many glasses of wine that I could lay
my hands on if they were liberal enough to put any out,
and went on to the nearest pub to get completely sloshed
at the earliest possible moment that etiquette would allow.

And, as for any opportunities I might have had when
reading the pregnancy books I'd bought to glean information on what commercial items a newborn baby might
need, well, I hadn't bothered with any of those chapters,
had I? After all, it wasn't like I was going to need to know
anything about what a baby might need after delivery, since
delivery was the end of the line in my plan, and particularly since there was no baby. So, as I sat there opening

prettily wrapped present after present, I tried my best not to look completely perplexed by some of the items, or the names that the others were insistent on attaching to them.

Receiving blankets? Yes, but what exactly did that mean? Right after I had the baby, if I ever had a baby, is this what I was supposed to receive my baby with for the first time? If so, I hoped that someone would at least have the decency to clean him or her up first; the blankets really were too nice to get all messed up with placentas and all of that other icky stuff that newborns might be trailing behind.

"Ooh!" I said, confident that I'd finally recognized something. Actually, I'd been oohing a lot at this shower. I'd seen other people doing it all the time at other showers and figured that if I did it enough, people might not notice how mystified I was. "Ooh! Look at the pretty design! What beautiful cloth diapers! Actually," I added, confidingly, "I hadn't decided yet between the merits of disposable and—"

"They're not diapers," interrupted Goodie Peg. "They're meant to go over your shoulder when you burp the baby after feeding, so she has something other than you to spit up on."

"Oh. Sorry." I laughed, hoping I didn't look as embarrassed as I felt. "What's the difference, though? Same baby, different secretions, right?"

Nobody else seemed to think so, and I quickly moved on to the larger packages, figuring that playpens and strollers were things I could usually puzzle out on my own; it was just the smaller items of baby care that always seemed to throw me.

I was about to get all excited about a high chair that the baby could use a little farther down the road in its life, maybe once it got past the stage where it needed its head to be supported all the time lest it fall off like the man's wife in the story about the woman who always wore a yellow ribbon around her neck, when I heard a discordant sound, just barely discernible above the oohing of the other ladies. My hearing had always been extraordinarily good, the better to torment me when the refrigerator made that humming sound I hated or whenever my mother talked.

"Shh!" I shushed the other ladies, sensing it might be important. "Quick! Patty!" I shouted, when I'd located the source of the sound, unable to rise from my own seat quickly enough what with the cumbersomeness of my fake baby weighing me down. "It's little Herbert! I think he's choking!"

And it was true. Sweet Patty's baby Herbert, who himself was no bigger than a minute it seemed, was choking on something he'd managed to get into his mouth, his face beginning to turn colors.

Dodo, who knew how to administer the Heimlich to any breathing being, man or beast, immediately moved into action. Before Patty even had a chance to think about panicking, Dodo was doing her thing, a tag projectiling its way out of the baby's mouth in another few seconds, following which Herbert, quite understandably, began to cry.

Babies were such small things really that, in spite of all their messiness, they certainly did bear close watching. In that instant it made sense to me, what some first-time parents said, that when they brought their babies home from hospital they were scared to sleep themselves for fear that something might happen to this tiny person who was now completely dependent on them. Sometimes babies did need someone to take care of them, didn't they?

It suddenly felt like such a close call, that I felt curiously like crying myself. As for Patty, she already was, her trembling voice carrying the scolding note of fear as she addressed Herbert, all the while holding him as though she'd never let him out of her sight again.

"Oh, Jane," Patty gushed after first extracting the non-speaking Herbert's solemn promise that he would never frighten Mummy to death like that again, "however did you hear him over all of our racket? You saved my baby's life."

Somehow it didn't feel right accepting credit where it wasn't due. "It wasn't me, really. It was Dodo who saved the day, knowing all of the emergency medical care stuff like she does."

"Don't be modest," said Dodo, modestly. "I just did the technical part. No one would have even known Herbert was in trouble if you hadn't heard him."

"It was nothing," I actually got to say for the first time in my life.

"Oh, please," said Elizabeth, the heavy mascara making raccoon eyes on her since she'd started to cry in sympathy for Patty's worry and, more especially, at the thought of such a thing befalling her own little Jemma, "you mustn't pretend it was nothing, Jane. You saved a baby's life."

I was starting to feel just a wee bit cynical again. I was tempted to point out that it *was* a baby's life and not Albert Schweitzer's; that for all we knew, rather than growing up to be another Albert Schweitzer, little Herbert might grow up to be Attila the Hun. But I said nothing of the sort. I knew the crowd I was working well by now, and I wasn't about to fall into that trap of saying the true thing again.

"Well, anyone might have done it," sniffed Trudy.

The group glared at her as one.

"Well, okay, maybe not *anyone*," she conceded quickly in order to avoid being tarred with Desitin and feathered with cotton swabs. "But anyone with really good hearing could have done as well. I remember reading once, a scientific study that said that each year a child grows older, his or her power of hearing decreases markedly. You've got to admit, Jane is young, the youngest in the room, so it's easy for her."

"Don't be absurd," Dora tut-tutted. "Jane's not young anymore—she's practically thirty."

"Besides," put in Helena, "you're speaking utter nonsense, Trudy. Patty's the youngest here. Everyone knows she's only about as old as Prince Harry."

By now, all of the mothers had their babies in their arms, no longer content to have the most important part of themselves playing where they couldn't be seen.

"Well," pronounced Goodie Peg, who had the tendency to act as policy maker for the group, as she placed her baby, who had also been named Peg, to her breast in order to feed. *God, I wished she wouldn't do that in front of me; I might be getting a shade better at some of this baby stuff, but I still wasn't ready for suckling.* "Well," she said, "I think it just goes to show what I've suspected all along. Jane is a natural mother. She's got the instincts and, you know, not all women do, even though the romantics would have you think otherwise."

My, this was a different tune from the one she'd been singing at Sophie's shower, when she'd practically accused me of being an alcoholic. Still, the others nodded their assent. I'm not sure if it was that they agreed or if they were just scared of her.

"What was it anyway," Sophie asked, "the thing that little Herbert was choking on?"

"You mean this?" asked Dodo, holding up a half-chewed tag that had formerly been attached to a stuffed animal, a large pink octopus that Trudy had bought. Apparently, in our absentminded heaping-up of the presents as I unwrapped them, the overflowing stacks had gotten near the babies and thus within perfect reach of little Herbert's grasping little hand.

"Oh! Those things are *death!*" Goodie Peg nearly shouted, pointing an accusing finger at the offending object. I think she probably would have burned the guilty tag at the stake were it not for the fact that open fires probably posed some kind of risk to babies as well.

There ensued a very animated discussion on the subject of leaving tags attached to items because, for whatever the reason, babies were always tempted to eat them and could wind up choking; obviously, any thinking person— and here they all glared at Trudy again which was really unfair since she was nowhere near little Herbert and had not been one of the ladies who were haphazardly stacking opened presents—would have removed all dangerous tags before giving the gift, rather than leaving it up to the possibly busy recipient to think to do it right away herself.

They moved from there onto the ever popular topic of baby-proofing one's home, with special emphasis placed on cords of all kinds, electrical outlets, and the optimum storage height for chemical products. This soon escalated into a full-blown natter on the popular wisdom that it was best not to put any bedding, like comforters and such, in the crib with baby because baby might suffocate. ("And what am I supposed to do in the middle of winter," demanded Trudy, "let my baby bloody freeze?"—"You're supposed to pay your heating bill on time and put the heat up high enough so that he doesn't," said Peg.)

As I watched and listened to the swirl of women's talk around me, I realized that everything had changed after I got Dodo's attention in time to stop Herbert choking. Now, oddly enough, despite the fact that I still hadn't a clue as to what any of this baby stuff was for, a curious thing was happening. People had begun to say to me, first Goodie Peg and then the others, in ways that indicated that they sincerely meant it, that they thought I was going to make a terrific mother.

Later, when I tried to put on the Snugli that Goodie Peg had given me, getting it all wrong somehow by trying to step into it instead of putting it on over my head, Goodie Peg didn't even laugh at me like you'd think she would. She just smiled openly and said, "Oh, don't worry about it, Jane. You'll get the hang of it. These are just the little details that everyone has trouble with in the beginning. But I know—I know it in my heart—that you're going to be a terrific mother."

"Oh, I know!" gushed Elizabeth. "Isn't she just? I knew it from the minute I realized she wasn't dyeing her hair anymore." The cosmetics salesgirl looked around the room knowingly. "*All* the best future mothers refuse to dye their hair or wear nail polish."

"Well," Dodo chimed in, obviously wanting to be a part of this group that she so clearly was not a part of, a group I'd only been allowed entrée into because I was wearing a fake foam tummy that I'd "acquired" from Harrod's, "*I've* known that Jane was going to make the absolutely best mother there ever was, ever since we were at a weekend house party together and Jane refused to go into the pool because of all of those new studies they have out now about it not being good for the baby." The others were looking at Dodo like she was starkers. She desperately looked to me for corroboration. "Do you remember that, Jane?"

But I was too preoccupied with the thoughts I was having to save her this time. What, I wondered, in the whole bloody world did these women see in me that I didn't see in myself? After all, I would never dream of saying to another woman that I thought she would make a good mother. Hell, most of the time when I saw a pregnant lady, I found myself tempted to reach out and grab the woman by the arms, perhaps say, "Good God, after you have it, you're not going to drop it on its head ever, are you?" or "Don't you think it might be better if you gave it up for adoption?" I never thought that anyone looked like they'd be a good enough mother. What I mostly thought was that there ought to be a law against most people even trying. Yet here were all of these women, gathered in one place, and they all thought...

"Oh, Jane," shy Patty sighed as she embraced me, little

Herbert, still in her arms, only getting slightly in our way. "If only I could believe that I'd be half as good a mother to little Herbert as I know you're going to be to your little girl."

See what I mean? These women were all fucking nuts.

Still, I was beginning to get odd, fuzzy feelings in my tummy when I looked at some of the things they'd brought me: the tiny matched outfits; the mobile with Pooh and Piglet and Tigger and Eeyore on it; the socks that looked like no human being's feet would ever be small enough to fit them, despite the evidence of the live babies in front of me.

Stuff and nonsense. It was still all smelly diapers and spit-up to me.

That same evening, I had the most wonderful dream, which was odd since its chief component was the source of my scariest waking nightmare: a baby.

In my dream, there were three figures: myself; a man who had one of those cloud things in place of where his face should be, like what they use on TV when they're trying to protect the identity of some squealer; and, at the center of both of our attentions, but in a nice way, a baby of indeterminate gender. (Was the man with the cloud thing for a face Tolkien perhaps? I liked to think so. I liked to think that if there were somehow a baby in my future, that Tolkien would somehow manage to wind up being the father.) We weren't really doing anything special, not really, just doing the kinds of things that you see families who aren't Tolstoy families doing in books and on the screen. We were doing the eating thing, the playing thing, and the caregiving thing. And, it wasn't as though me and the male figure looked like a pair of grinningly mindless village idiots, either, so much as that we looked capable of doing whatever we were doing and glad to do it.

When I was awakened by my own bladder at around

2:00 a.m., as I made my way to the bathroom I had the peculiar feeling that my dream had been a part of some kind of bonding ritual, not exactly Stonehenge maybe but definitely something age-old. I felt as though I'd just completed a practice run and been found not wanting.

I endeavored to return to that bucolic place, crawling back under the covers a few moments later. Once sleep came, however, I was unable to find it. The same three figures from before were there, only this time, it really was Tolstoy territory. Oh, I don't mean that there were revolutions going on or people throwing themselves under trains, nothing so dramatic as that, but we were out of the territory of boringly happy families and into the norm.

And the worst part of it all was me.

The male figure and the baby figure were still performing their roles just fine, while there I was, the unprepared and incompetent one. If I wasn't forgetting to do things, like feed the baby, I was losing things; at one point I even lost the breast with which to feed the baby with, which might not sound possible, but there you have it. There I was in my nightmare, searching around for it until I finally located it buried in an overflowing basket of dirty laundry. Of course, by the time I found the breast, the baby was nowhere to be seen, search as I might.

I woke up screaming about a quarter to four, just loud enough to cause the Marcuses below to bang on their ceiling with a broomstick, just like they'd done in the old days whenever the sex that I was having with Trevor began to sound as though we were having too good of a time. Anyway, I couldn't get back to sleep at that point if I'd tried, nor did I want to; I was too frightened of what awaited me. Instead, I sat up drinking cup after cup of tea until my nerves were jangling so much from all of the caffeine that I was ready to go airborne, at which point I deemed it an acceptable time for me to call Sophie without disturbing her family.

I don't know why I turned to her, really; sometimes, I guess only a sister will do and, if you've got one, you hope that the one that you've got will be up to it.

I didn't give her the opportunity to groggily complain to me about the impossibility of ever getting enough sleep when one is the mother of an infant or about the rudeness of people who telephone at hours when only a true emergency should be calling.

"Oh, Soph, I had the worst nightmare!"

And I proceeded to tell her about the hungry baby, the missing breast, the laundry basket and the missing baby.

"And that's not even the worst part! The worst part is that, not two hours before, I'd been having the most marvelous dream about a happy family. How could I have such opposite dreams in the same night? Am I going nuts?"

"No, you're not going nuts, Jane," she yawned in my ear. "You're just pregnant."

"I am?"

"Well, aren't you?"

"Yes, of course I am. What I meant was—" But she didn't let me finish.

"All pregnant women have these sorts of dreams."

"They do?"

"Of course they do. It's all tied up with all of those mixed feelings of anticipation and anxiety that the woman is feeling. Just ask me—I had them all. You name it—the one where I was trapped in a car wash, which represented my fear that the baby would deprive me of my freedom. The one where I ate twelve servings of plum pudding with brandied hard sauce and washed it all down with a fifth of Scotch, which was a manifestation of my frustration at having kept myself to such a puritanically restrictive diet. The one where my baby was born already being a twenty-five-year-old football player, which represented my fear of being able to handle a little baby. I'm telling you, Jane, all pregnant women go through this."

"Then why don't you ever hear them talking about it?"

"Well, you wouldn't exactly go around crowing about it, either, if you were having screaming nightmares about being attacked by burglars and wild animals. And, if I were you, I wouldn't be too eager myself to go around telling people about that one involving the missing breast and the laundry basket." She yawned again, much more forcefully. "Now, may I go back to sleep, Jane? Somehow, your crisis has managed *not* to wake up Baby Jack and I'd like to keep it that way."

"But just one last time, for comfort's sake—you're saying that I'm not psychotic and that these kinds of dreams and nightmares are natural?"

"Yes, Jane," she said before hanging up on me, "that's what I've been saying. It's perfectly natural for a pregnant woman to be having these kinds of dreams."

Which, I thought as I stared at the phone after I'd replaced the receiver, didn't explain why I was having them.

The remainder of Mona Shakespeare's book had come in and it was every bit as brilliant as the first part had been.

"Do you mean brilliant in the way that I hate?" Dodo asked. "You know how I can't stand it when you turn on the television and the man on the street's overusing the word *brilliant* to describe everything from a new fish-and-chips shop to the way Tony Blair's hair blows in the wind. There was a time when *brilliant* referred to a person or thing being very bright, glittering, striking or distinctive. You wouldn't say that a new fish-and-chips shop was glittering, would you? Or that the way Tony Blair's hair blows was very bright?" For someone who spent her life in a literary world, Dodo sometimes had a lot of trouble coming to terms with the elasticity of language, wanting it to be more a science than an art. And when she got worked up about a word, things could get pretty heated. "There was a time when Rachmaninoff—"

I couldn't take it anymore. To shut her up, I grabbed her by the shoulders and gave her a little shake. "It is Rachmaninoff, Dodo. The bloody Mona Shakespeare is a Rachmaninoff."

"Really?"

"Yes. It's *Rhapsody on a Theme of Paganini*. It's *Vesper Mass*. It's the goddamned *Prelude in C-Sharp Minor* if you want it to be."

"Really?"

"Well, if you can call a biting satire that has more facets than Elizabeth Taylor's diamonds the same as a piano concerto, if you can call a comic novel that scathingly deals with the plight of the modern childbearing woman in very modern times the same as chamber music..." I was exasperated. "No, of course it's not the same! But it *is* brilliant. I only threw in the stuff about the Rachmaninoff because I know how much you like him. They're really not the same at all, but they *are* both brilliant."

"Brilliant?" Dodo was beginning to soften, a wistful look overcoming her features, a look that was arguably known to editors the world over. "It would be nice, for a change, to publish something that was brilliant."

"Oh, yes, Dodo, it is, it really is, and it's all here this time." I waved the sheaf of pages in front of her. "It's everything we'd hoped it would be—the part about Mitch the frustrated walking tour guide..."

"Ooh. I wanted to read about him."

"...and the horny podiatrist..."

"My mother had a dentist who fancied hers."

"...plus, there's also the gynecologist who loves his job, the pizza delivery guy who wants to be an astronaut, the guy responsible for routing mail at the office where she works, the other guy from where she works—the senior editor—who claims to have such a low sperm count that he sees this as his one big chance even though he and Stacy have always hated each other and the only reason they ever slept together was that they both had too much wassail at the company Christmas party, and, finally, the one who Stacy's mother actually likes. They're all here this time and it's every bit as good as the first three chapters we read."

Dodo eagerly grabbed the pages I held out to her. "Oh, Jane, this really is it, isn't it? The kind of thing we live for?"

"Yes, I think it is."

"Well, if it's as good as you say…"

"It—"

She held up a hand to forestall my indignation. "…and I'm sure that it is, then I think we'll have to get Ms. Shakespeare to come over here to meet with us. You know, no matter how perfect a novel is, there are always one or two things that need to be tweaked and, anyway, with all the money I envision us making off Ms. Shakespeare's career, I think Churchill and Stewart can afford to foot the bill for her for a week in London."

As Dodo nattered on, I pictured Mona Shakespeare, in her New York apartment, receiving the e-mail that would change her life. I pictured her sitting before her computer, which was set up on a card table next to a wall whose single window either looked out on a brick wall or a flashing neon sign that read G s, Gi ls, Girls, the missing letters a constant source of annoyance and odd inspiration. The apartment—which would be no more than a tiny bed-sit with a postage-stamp-size kitchenette and a bathroom with barely enough space to crouch over the chipped toilet—would be Spartan in its decor. She'd be thrifty with what money she had, but that wouldn't be why she hadn't even put any posters on the walls. Rather, it would be because she preferred to let her imagination be whipped by the teeming life below her. I knew, thanks to Don Henley, just how much could change in a New York minute. Of course, Mona's book was about London minutes, so that blew that theory of asceticism all to hell.

Okay, so maybe what she had then, no matter how else her apartment was furnished, was the huge display of bookcases I'd always envisioned her having, all crammed full with all sorts of diversions for the committed Anglophile. She'd have her Dickens minutes, her Austen minutes, her Fielding minutes, both Henry and Helen, plus all the authors in between and beyond. The point was, she'd have all this, but she'd still have it in New York City, a place I'd been dying to see ever since I first heard Frank Sinatra sing about it.

God! Wouldn't it be just great to live in New York? Or at least to go there for a vacation? Of course, it would take a lot of getting used to. I wasn't foolish enough to think that it was just like London, only bigger and with bad accents. No, I knew about all the bad architecture, bad taxi drivers, and all of the guns that only a completely free society could provide. I imagined myself there. There would probably be violence everywhere I looked and I'd have to take care not to get caught in one of those drive-by shootings they were always having, but the cheesecake at Lindy's—boy, was I ready for that!

Did Mona have a gun? I wondered. Was our newest, hottest commodity going to turn out to be a pistol-packing mama?

"*The Rubber Slipper* really is brilliant, Jane," Dodo interrupted my reverie, turning pages happily all the while, "even better than Tony Blair's hair."

When you've been around books for a long time, you begin to realize that all writers have one of three problems: either they don't know how to start a book properly, which is the worst flaw of all because if you can't hook the readers, then they probably won't still be around to see how brilliant you are later on; or they suffer from saggy middles; or they don't know how to end a book properly, which can be devastating in a mystery if, say, the author throws in a murderer out of nowhere, making the reader want to throw the book across the room.

Having written both the first and final thirds of *The Cloth Baby,* I was discovering that my problem as a writer was going to be a saggy middle.

Feeling a little desperate about my self-discovery, as I usually am about any self-discovery, I punched in David's number on my mobile, toying with the salad I'd been eating at my desk as I waited for him to pick up.

"Shalom?"

"I have a saggy middle!" I despaired, not bothering with the niceties of greetings, foreign or otherwise.

"Could it be the foods you've been eating?" he asked.

"That wasn't—" I was about to tell him that my own waistline hadn't been what I'd been referring to at all, that what I'd been referring to was the problems I was experiencing writing the book, when I remembered that this was one crisis David couldn't help me with. He still didn't know about the book.

"That wasn't what, Jane?"

"I'm sorry." I did that head-shaking thing even though he couldn't see me. "I forgot what I was going to say."

"Well, that makes this a good use of your free minutes. Is there anything else? I'm trying to filet a mignon here."

"Yes, there *is* something else."

"Which is?"

"Your reference to the foods I've been eating would imply that you do believe I have a saggy middle."

"I never said that. I was merely trying to come up with a logical reason for how, if you did have a saggy middle, you got it."

"I see." I put down my salad fork. "I'm tired of this diet."

"Which diet is that?"

"The one I've been on."

"And how long have you been on this diet?"

"Hmm—" I consulted the ceiling, considering, "—about twenty years."

"You know what I think, Jane?"

"What?"

"I think that mobile phones and free minutes in the hands of the wrong people are a very bad thing and should be against the law."

"Hey!"

"I'm going back to my filet now. Call me the next time you have an emergency."

My life was going so well in some ways.

Mona Shakespeare's book was bound to be a success and I was the one who'd discovered it. This meant that I'd soon have more money, power and respectability in the workplace, three things I'd always coveted before (which would be a good thing for me to fall back on if my own book didn't turn out to be the tearing success Devil Alice kept whispering in my ear that it would be). Never thinking for one second that they would be mine, I had previously conducted my work life along the lines of: Why bother? The picture of my baby that I now had on my desk—well, the phony sonogram picture—looked great; whenever I was there, everybody commented on it. And I even looked cute in my maternity clothes. Why, then, was I so glum?

"Why so glum, chum?" asked David.

The two of us were sitting around the coffee table in his living room, drinking ale, while Christopher weeded out their CD collection.

"I don't know," I whined, aware that I was whining even as I was doing it, but unable to stop myself, my voice carrying the heavy verbal equivalent of dragging feet.

"Maybe it's losing Tolkien."

Well, of course we all knew that a lot of it was that.

"Maybe it's having to pretend all the time at work or maybe it's the chronic back pain I've been experiencing what with the cloth baby and all."

I knew this was never going to win me any sympathy or any constructive criticism, save to abandon my scheme;

which, as we all knew, was really David's scheme. Well, sort of. I pressed on.

"I don't know. Maybe it's just... *Oc-to-ber.*"

"Ah, yes," said Christopher, without looking up from his task. "Whole months in autumn containing thirty-one days can be annoying in that way." He paused. "U2? Is there any reason we need to listen to U2 anymore?"

David shrugged. "I never said that there was."

"Don't you people ever work?" I asked. "I thought you owned a restaurant or something."

"We do," David acknowledged, taking a long draw from his ale. "But it's Tuesday and we're closed. You always visit us on Tuesday."

"You visit us on Tuesdays and we all get drunk," Christopher added.

"Then you totter back to your place," began David.

"But first you have to put on your fake baby and spray your breath with lots of breath spray in case you run into the Marcuses, who still think you're pregnant," finished Christopher.

"Now that you're a couple," I asked testily, "can't I ever see one of you anymore without seeing the other?"

"So-*rry,*" Christopher said, finally looking up, "but it is hard for me to disappear when I do live here now."

I just glared harder at him until he blinked first.

"*So*-rry," he said again, leaving the room to get another ale.

Well, I thought, even if he was just leaving the room for a few minutes, the fact that I'd been able to intimidate him at all made me feel as though I was getting my own back.

"I wasn't aware that you had lost any of your customary *zing,*" said David, when I intimated as much to him.

Perhaps that was what was bothering me, I thought: I'd lost my zing.

"You really think that you've been bested by life in recent months?" he pressed.

"Mmm…"

"And you're sure that this isn't some paranoid schizophrenic fantasy on your part, starting with the fact that you continually feel as though you are in some sort of verbal competition with Christopher—"

"Hello, is someone calling me?" came Christopher's voice from the kitchen.

"Finish your beer," I shouted.

"—which has oddly somehow come to parallel your need to fake a pregnancy?" David finished his question.

"You mean you haven't noticed a kinder, gentler Jane in recent months?" I countered.

"Possibly." David smiled. "But that's just the pregnancy talking."

Sophie's assurances that my nightmares were perfectly normal for a pregnant woman had done little to allay my fears that I was fast turning into a full-blown psychotic. True, I believed her when she said that the dreams-nightmares I was experiencing were brought about by unexpressed anxiety concerning my future, but they had turned into nightly occurrences and I was fast becoming concerned for my sanity. Tolkien would have been the perfect sympathetic listener, but he was sadly out of my life for good now, and while I was tempted to discuss my problem with the people at work, I feared that upon hearing in particular about the baby with the pitchfork and tail, they might begin to fear for my sanity as well.

And so it was that on a brisk autumnal day in October, I found myself wandering down to the spiritually oracular source of all things future in London—the open market at Covent Garden. Wending my way through the tourists, I made my way past all of the palm readers, the purveyors of questionable foodstuffs, the vendors of somewhat legitimate goods and the sidewalk artists.

But, on that day, I wasn't looking for silly tea-leaf readers or cheap fashion accessories or another concrete Mona Lisa; I was looking for the last resort of all twentysomething female Londoners in a pinch: I was looking for an authentic tarot card reader.

Finding the real deal though wasn't as easy as one would think.

I turned my nose up at all of the supposed tarot card readers who displayed other methods of divination, like crystal balls or ancient runes, alongside of their seventy-eight-card decks of the Major and Minor Arcana; the way I figured it, if the practitioner didn't have perfect faith in the unbelievable, then why should I? Similarly, I bypassed all of those who had patently trumped-up Eastern European accents, figuring that if I was going to hand over my money to a fraud, I'd prefer not to be able to detect the perpetrator until after the fact. When you got right down to it then, me being as picky as I was, there really wasn't much left to choose from.

Not much left to choose from turned out to be a pudding-figured dwarf of a woman with a body that was like a couple of margarine tubs stacked one on top of the other. She was of an indeterminately older age, with wire-like coils of gray hair sticking out from under her gaudy head covering, her swirling skirts of different colors doing nothing to enhance her form while her gold chains, bracelets and dangling earrings kept up their own racket. She had a hooked nose, creased skin that looked like she'd been living out in the cancerous elements all her life, and the most astonishingly beautiful sapphire-colored eyes peering out from the deep folds around them. Her most astonishing feature, however, was an impressively sizable wart on the point of her chin, a wart that had a single rather long dark hair growing out of it.

She gave me a smile that would have scared small children. "Read your fortune, missy?" she oozed at me, with an attempt at a Romanian accent that sounded more like

Greek to me and that I deemed to be as fake as her jewelry.

I couldn't help myself, couldn't resist. As if my hand had a mind of its own, I watched as it reached out and tugged on the single hair first before trying to pull off the wart whole. Apparently, my brain had been whispering to my hand something to the effect that the lady before me was another fraud, her wart just a part of an elaborate costume designed to scam the unsuspecting.

She swatted my hand away with one hand. Then, with the other, she began massaging the red mark that my pulling had left in the area where I had endeavored to remove what I now recognized to be a very real wart.

"Whatsamatta with you, missy?" She glared at me. "Are you crazy?" Then her eyes traveled downwards to my protruding belly, a gleamingly satisfied look coming over them, not dissimilar to the one that I imagined I had worn when I'd first passed judgment on her hairy wart.

She didn't wait for me to answer her rhetorical question. "Never mind that," she said. "Sit, sit," she instructed, indicating a folding chair at the card table she'd set up to ply her trade from and taking a seat across from me when I'd done so.

"For you," she said, pulling out the smallest deck of cards I'd ever seen in my life from some pocket that was hidden among the folds of her skirt, "for you I will read the future for free."

I couldn't contain myself. "What the hell are these?" I demanded, referring to the insultingly miniature cards that she'd handed me so that I might shuffle my own fortune. "You can't be serious."

"It's called the Connolly Mini Tarot Deck," she huffed.

"The mini *what?*"

"Look," she sighed, growing exasperated, "even I get the shit scared out of me whenever I try to use the Aleister Crowley Deck. Trust me on this. If you don't mess with the Dark Arts, the Dark Arts won't mess with you. Still—" and here she waved her hand in the direction of a heavily bearded and sinister-looking gentleman that I hadn't noticed before "—if you insist on courting the possibility of dead goats left hanging from your wrought-iron fence, I'm sure Hector will be only too glad to assist you."

I shrank from Hector's menacing gaze, which came at me from beneath the kind of bushy eyebrows which were really just one long unit, and turned back to my dwarfish friend. "Fine," I relented, "I'll take my chances with the mini."

"While you shuffle the cards," she instructed, "concentrate on the question you most want them to answer."

I thought to myself that what I wanted to know was what the future would bring. Isn't that what everyone wanted to know?

I finished shuffling the cards, handing them back to her.

With no more ado, she began to turn over the first of the ten cards that would form the Celtic Cross Spread. "This card covers you," she announced, a tarot phrase I'd never quite understood, as she placed the card in the center of the table. "Ah! Missy!" She looked delighted. "The Nine of Cups!"

I studied the tiny card. On it was a picture of a man who looked an awful lot like portraits of Jesus at the Last Supper. Before him were nine gold cups, one with a flower in it, while above his head, strung between two Ionic columns, was a length of flowering vine.

"And that's good," I prompted, "the Nine of Cups?"

"Oh, ye-ess!" She dragged out the words. "It is known as the Wish Card and can mean that your wish will come true." But then she began to qualify her remarks. "Of course that's most especially true when it falls in the tenth position. When it falls anywhere else, you have to wait for the rest of the reading to see what it all means."

She then turned over the second card, laying it crossways over the first and saying, "This card crosses you for good or bad."

There were two dark-haired men in long robes who were facing each other. David and Christopher, perhaps? One was rubbing his chin and looking away while the other carried a drum and wore a red-colored cap of a shape similar to that which Scrooge wore with his pajamas. Behind him was a tent, while beside him was a tree stump with two swords stuck into it.

"The Two of Swords," she intoned. Then she shook her hand from side to side, making an AC-DC gesture as she shrugged in an almost Gallic fashion. "It means that the choice is between six of one, half a dozen of the other. You must grab your sword of individuality and march to the beat of your own drummer."

Wasn't that what I'd been doing all along? Who else in London had a fake pregnancy scam going on so that they could get a publishable book out of the deal? Still, I thought, maybe she was referring to the monkey-see, monkey-do path that I'd been trodding upon for most of my life.

She turned the third card up, placing it directly beneath the first card. "This card is the basis, it is the root of your present situation. It is the Two of Pentacles."

This one looked somewhat like a harlequin standing between the parted curtains at center stage on a black-and-white tiled floor. In each of his hands he held a purple disc upon which there was a five-pointed golden star, while above his head there was a glowing pink infinity sign.

"This card symbolizes trying to cope with two situations. If you make a decision, more will be achieved. This can be accomplished."

Two situations. Could she be talking about the way that, for a time, I had been pretending to be pregnant with everyone else while with Tolkien I had appeared as myself, creating a situation in which it was impossible for the two areas of my life to be reconciled? But how could I ever bring the fake baby and Tolkien situations together by making a decision?

She placed the fourth card to the left of the first, only this card came out upside down and I had to crane my neck a bit to make out the picture. Depicted was an elderly gentleman with buttons on the side of his pants who looked not unlike the solemn grandfather in the Swiss Alps in *Heidi*. On the half-opened door to his rustic hut were eight of the discs with the five-pointed stars in them that I now knew to be pentacles.

"This card is behind you," she said, "or in the process of leaving. It is the Eight of Pentacles. In the reversed position, it means that you are going about things in the wrong way and have a need for guidance."

"But that's good!" I crowed. "I mean, if I'm leaving this 'going about things in the wrong way' behind me, that's got to be a good thing, doesn't it? It must mean that, in the future, I'll go about things in the right way."

She pursed her lips at me, the wart twitching in her irritation. "The fourth card is only indicative of what is behind you, in the past. It predicts nothing about the future."

Before I could say anything further, she placed the fifth card, which also came out upside down, above the first.

"The fifth card crowns you and could come into being."

My crane's-eye view revealed a fair-haired young man, a feather sticking out of his cap and a golden cup in his hand. A flower was at his feet and behind him a fish jumped out of the water.

"The Page of Cups in reversed position means that you will be offered help in the future, possibly by a young person."

Odd. I didn't really know any young people, since I tried very hard not to, not unless one included all of the babies I'd been meeting lately.

She placed the sixth card to the right of the first, this time right side up.

"The sixth card is before you. In this case, The Tower."

"Does it have to be?" I asked fearfully, as I stared at the picture of a monolithic structure being struck by lightning, causing flames to burst from it as two people fell from its height. The woman, for there was a man and a woman, looked oddly as I might have done had I never dyed my hair.

"It's not as bad as it looks," she eased my fears although I sensed reluctantly. "It merely means that you must take a good long look at your life. Your situation will change rapidly and you must be prepared."

To the right of the base of the Celtic Cross, she placed another upside-down card, showing a man in a gray stone tower. In one hand he held a wand, while in the other he held a small globe of the Earth. In the air floated a second wand with two birds perched on top.

"The seventh card represents your own apprehensions, in your case the Two of Wands reversed. This indicates that the foundations that you have laid will not yield your desired results."

That certainly sounded ominous.

The eighth card also came out reversed as she placed it above the seventh. This one was also a wand card, only this time, among the reeds, the rowboat, the two men and the sailboat in the distance, there was one more wand than in the last.

"Hey!" I said. "I recognize that! It's the Three of Wands, the card right after the last. Are you sure you haven't fixed this somehow?"

"You shuffled them yourself."

"Oh. Right."

"This card represents the feelings of those around you. In this position, the card indicates that your talents, skills and efforts are being wasted, that a new direction is needed."

"Oh. That's a real comfort, knowing that that's what others secretly think of one."

She shrugged again.

The ninth card, as she placed it above the eighth, looked rather attractive compared to what had gone before. It was a regal-looking woman seated on a throne among flowers with a tiara on her head, a scepter in her grasp and a butterfly floating around a fountain in the background.

"The ninth card, in this case The Empress, represents your own positive feelings. The Empress offers the promise of growth, prosperity and fertility. She symbolizes needs fulfilled with joy and satisfaction."

Well, that was a big improvement. Maybe this fortune-telling stuff had something of substance to it after all.

But then she turned over the tenth card, my final outcome card.

Even I, with my limited tarot experience, could recognize that silly-looking male with his ridiculous yellow stockings and a dog that looked oddly like a pitbull at his feet as he stood at a four-way intersection at a flowered path not far from a cliff. The fact that the legend underneath the photo bore the number zero (all Major Arcana cards have a Roman numeral attached to them), followed by the prophetic words The Fool, only served to bring it home to me.

"How dare you!" I cried, rising, the awkwardness of my cloth baby nearly overturning her card table. "I will not be called a fool by you!"

"I do not say it, the cards say it. And they do not call you a fool. They merely depict *The* Fool. What this means is that you will find yourself at a crossroads. Your decision, once you arrive there, may be very important, so you must think carefully."

"I don't care what you say about the cards. I've never been so insulted in my life. *The Fool? The Fool* as my final outcome?"

She spread her hands open. "The cards..."

"I demand my money back."

"Well—" she shrugged, gathering up the cards of my fortune and putting them back in her deck "—you never paid me anything, so we're even. Anyway, the cards don't lie," she added, looking with that meaningful gleam upon my belly again, "not like people do."

Fat was being deposited on my fetus. For all I knew, at any given moment, it might be sucking its thumb, hiccupping or crying. It could definitely distinguish sweet and sour. It was capable of responding to light, sound, pain, and other stimuli. Placental function was beginning to diminish—whatever the hell that might mean—and the volume of amniotic fluid was diminishing as well, what with the three-pound fetus filling the uterus. The bottom line was that were I to give birth to my baby as early as this, at the end of the seventh month, there was a good chance it would survive.

As for the mother, she was having plenty of difficulty sleeping, although not at all from any reason that any reputable obstetrician might guess.

the eighth month

"What are you planning on doing about the pain?"

"Excuse me?"

I was seated in my office, mild-manneredly reading through the *London Review of Books* and wondering why certain publishers' books always seemed to garner favorable review attention no matter how abstruse the topic while the rest of us continually fought an uphill battle merely not to be treated as fish-in-a-barrel sport, when Dodo'd burst in upon my ruminating with her strident question about pain.

"Why, when you go into labor, of course," she said now as though I were the most obtuse person in the world. "I realize how inexplicably attached you've become to the advice of your Madame Zither person, but even you must recognize the possibility of your having one of these multiday labor periods that you sometimes hear about happening to first-timers—you know, the ones where, no matter how Pollyannaishly one has determined to go without artificial assistance ahead of time, the expectant mother finds herself screaming for drugs from anyone she thinks might listen. You've mentioned before that Madame Zygote doesn't even believe in pain control and, anyway, I doubt any reputable medical community would allow the woman you describe to come close even to touching a bandage." I took it as a small blessing when I realized that her shortness of breath meant that we were nearing the end of her diatribe. "So what, Jane, do you plan to do if the pain gets to be too much?"

"Well," I answered calmly, "I'm going to let her perform hypnosis on me, aren't I?"

"*What?* Do you mean—" and here she adopted a remarkably good imitation of an Austrian accent "—'Look very closely at my pocket watch' and 'You are getting very sleepy' and 'When you wake up you won't even remember making a complete arse out of yourself in front of all of these people'?" She continued in her own voice, "Just like those charlatans on variety television programs and the ones who try to convince you that they can help you quit smoking?"

I sniffed. "You don't have to make it sound so much like a scam or like cannibals in the jungle, you know. Suggestion and the power of the mind over matter are taught in every good parentcraft class. With hypnosis, it's merely a matter of a higher level of suggestion being achieved. Madame Ziggurat says that, despite the fact that only about twenty-five percent of adults are hypnotizable to some degree, I'm more susceptible to suggestion than anyone she's ever encountered and that she should be able to completely eliminate any awareness I might have of pain. We've been practicing. You know," I concluded, "despite what you might think, Madame Ziggurat is a very well respected professional in her field."

A puzzled frown came over Dodo's face. "I thought her name was Madame Zora."

I shot her a look. "Yes," I replied dryly, "and isn't it a

good thing that this pregnancy's nearly over, so you won't have to worry about running out of *Z* names to call her before it comes time for me to deliver?"

And I suddenly realized that it *was* a good thing that my pregnancy was nearly over.

Lately, I'd been of two minds. On the one hand, I was experiencing an increase in apprehension, not dissimilar to what a real mother might feel when faced with the prospect of labor and delivery, and experiencing long periods of solitude when I worried about what kind of mother I would make, as if that might matter somehow. On the other hand, even though I knew that the end of my so-called pregnancy would also mean the end to life as I knew it, there were times when I just wanted it all to be over.

Knowing that the restaurant was closed because it was Tuesday, and knowing that David had gone out for once to pick up takeaway, I cornered Christopher in their flat. It was high time we two had a showdown.

"Why don't you like me?" I demanded to know, hands on hips.

He didn't even bother to look up from his place on the floor, where he was selecting an evening's worth of CDs. "Whoever said I don't like you?"

"Oh, come on," I said, exasperated. "David loves me, always has done, while you...you...you barely tolerate me."

"Yes, well..."

I moved closer until I was standing over him. "I want to know," I said, "and I'm not leaving until you tell me."

"You really want to know, Jane?" Now he finally looked up and it was startling to see features so similar to David's looking up at me with such hostility.

I thought about it. "Yes," I decided, "I really do."

"Fine." He rose to his feet, so that now we were more

than evenly matched with the nearly one-foot advantage all his. "I'll tell you. It's because you're a self-absorbed, self-involved, self-centered woman—and believe me, all of those *self-* words do mean slightly different things—who is demanding, unreasonable, and pigheaded."

"Oh, is that all?" I asked, trying for blithe but not quite hitting it.

"No. No, Jane, that isn't all."

"What else then?"

"You behave terribly to David."

My voice rose enough octaves to create its own stratospheric scale. "I—?"

"You ring him up at all hours, with no regard for his schedule, you burden him with your problems, without ever bothering to enquire into his."

"I—?"

"For chrissakes, Jane, you don't even pronounce his name right!"

"What?" Okay, maybe he'd a point with some of the other things he'd said, but this?

"His name, Jane. His name is pronounced Duh-*veed,* accent on the second element."

"You're joking, right?"

"No. I'm not."

"And what do I say?"

"*Duh*-veed, as if the *duh* part is the most important part to you."

"Ahem," I heard behind me, whirling to find David standing there with a takeaway sack in his hand. From the look on his face, he had to have been there for a moment or two.

I looked at my best friend. "He's joking, right?"

David, for no apparent reason, reddened. "No," he said. "I'm afraid he's right."

I was bewildered. "Why didn't you ever correct me?"

He put down the sack. "Because it truly never mattered."

"But I've been a dreadful friend to you."

He shrugged it off.

I swallowed. "I could try to do better."

He hugged me. "If you do, that's fine. If you don't, it still doesn't matter."

I pulled back from his embrace. "Why doesn't it matter? What is it you see in me?"

"Yes," said Christopher, coming to stand beside us like a minister presiding over a kissing bride and groom. "Tell me, too. What is it you see in her?"

"I see someone who's spent most of her life looking for love in spectacularly wrong places," David said.

"Perhaps," said Christopher, "but she's not very nice to the women she works with, she's not very nice to her family, and she wasn't very nice to Trevor."

"So?" David shrugged, looking at me, not Christopher. "Did any of them give her reason to be nice?"

"Well, Dodo," I conceded.

"Yes, there is Dodo," said David, "but I'd say you've returned her kindnesses in some way."

"Maybe," I said.

"Is there anything else you see in her?" Christopher prompted.

"Yes," said David. "I see a woman who is more lively and alive than any woman I've ever known, flaws and all."

"Oh. Well." Christopher threw his hands up. "You should have explained that all to me sooner. Christ, I'd have loved her, too."

"You're not going to believe this!" Dodo crowed a few days later.

"Believe what?" I asked, tossing down in mild exasperation some line edits that I hadn't really wanted to do anyway as Dodo sailed into my office.

She waved an e-mail printout at me. "It's from Mona Shakespeare! And you'll never guess—what I'm holding in my hand explains why she's been refusing to come to us all these months, no matter how we've tried to tempt her!"

"Well? Are you actually going to tell me?"

"She's a bleeding agoraphobic! The reason why our newest whiz kid can't come to us is because she can't even make it as far as her own mailbox!"

Suddenly, the pieces all snapped into place, like the fact that an American had refused an all-expenses-paid open-ended stay at the Connaught and the fact that every communication we'd ever received from Mona Shakespeare, *everything,* including her 252-page manuscript, had come in the form of an e-mail or a file attached to an e-mail.

"So what are you going to do about it?" I asked. "After all, you've been saying all along that you think the book is a surefire bestseller, but only with some serious hands-on editing, the kind that was given to that *Cold Mountain* book several years ago. Come to think of it, though, I do seem to remember reading an article in their *Times* that said that the editing job on that was also done long-distance."

"Oh, you know me, Jane. I can never do anything long-distance, no matter if other people have done it with phenomenal success before. No. You know I'm only happy editing if I can be practically peering right over the author's shoulder while he or she tries to follow my suggestions."

"True. So the question remains, if she won't—or, I guess in all fairness to modern definitions of psychiatric illness, I should say, *can't*—come to us, what can you possibly do?"

That's when she waved two Virgin Airways tickets in the air, all excitement. Without even being close enough to read the printing on them, I could guess that they were two round-trip tickets to New York.

I leapt out of my leather swivel chair, oblivious of the way my eight-month belly jumped as I did so. "You can't be serious!" It was my turn to crow, as I began to do the girl-jumping-on-a-trampoline routine that I'd learned from the girls in the office. "I've always wanted to go to New York! I can't believe this!" I stopped jumping, grabbing on to Dodo's elbows. "And what I really can't believe is that someone would be foolish enough to allow herself to become agoraphobic in New York City of all places. What the hell's the matter with Mona Shakespeare? Is she nuts? Oh, well, it doesn't matter. Not so long as it serves as an excuse to finally get me there!" Seeing the startled look on Dodo's face, I immediately sobered up. "What's wrong?" I asked.

"While it's true that *I'm* going to New York next month, you're not going with me." She said it as gently as possible. "You can't go. Your pregnancy's too far along and I'm sure that even Madame Zanzibar wouldn't let you fly on an airplane at this point. What would happen if you found yourself at 35,000 feet, somewhere over the middle of the Atlantic Ocean, and suddenly you went into labor?"

"I'd hold it in until we touched down on the other side!" I cried desperately.

"That's not good enough. You might not have as much control over it as you'd like to think. After all, if women could control the onset and duration of their labor, don't you think that the vast majority of them would opt for about thirty seconds on a rainy Sunday afternoon?"

"Well, I can control it!" I shouted, ignoring the obvious truth contained in her rhetorical question. "You'd be bloody surprised how much I can control about this pregnancy and delivery!"

"Yes, I'm sure I would, Jane. You've always been one of the most self-determined women I know. Nevertheless, *if* you went into labor over the Atlantic and *if* even you couldn't do anything to control it, what would you do if it turned out that there was no one on the plane equipped to deliver a baby?"

"I'd deliver it myself!" It was so much a day for exclamation points. "I'd do it myself in the bloody aisle if I had to!"

"Yes, and I'm sure the rest of the passengers would find that just a treat. No, I'm sorry, Jane. I'm afraid it's out of the question. Even if you're willing to risk the health of yourself and the baby, I'm not." She delicately pried away my fingers, the ones that had been gripping her elbows too tightly. "Besides, I've already asked Constance to accompany me and she's been kind enough to accept."

"*Constance?* That little troll? The tiny little thing with all the different shades of retina to match each outfit, the one we always want to send for coffee, *if only we can find her at her bloody desk?*"

"I think you must mean the lens," said literal Dodo. "The retina is something else entirely. As a matter of fact, I would think that the reason they are called contact lenses in the first place is because—"

I windmilled my arms in exasperation. "Do I look like I want a bloody science lesson?" Then I let my arms drop in sheer exhaustion. "Why, Dodo, why Constance of all people?"

Dodo studied her perfectly practical nails as opposed to looking at me. "It may have escaped your notice, Jane, you being so preoccupied with other things, but our Constance has been improving lately. She's been showing real get-up-and-go."

Our Constance? "Fine." I folded my arms. "Then she can just go if she's getting so good at it."

Dodo chose to ignore me. "And I've even taken the liberty of approaching Dexter Schlager about it. He agrees with me, and so, at the next editorial meeting, we'll be announcing her as my new Assistant Editor."

"But I'm your Assistant Editor!"

"Yes. I know that. But once the baby comes, even though you haven't committed to an exact time frame yet,

I know you're going to want to take some time off. Of course we'll keep your job open for you here indefinitely, but while you're gone I'll still need someone who can do the things for me that you do so well. And, here's the good part—" and now it was her excitedly grabbing onto my arm "—Dexter Schlager was having such a good hair day when I spoke with him about it—you know, one of those days where he doesn't notice that he hasn't got any—that he also agreed to make you a full Editor upon your return from maternity leave! Well? What do you think? We'll practically be on equal footing!"

I sank back down into my chair. What I thought was that this would have been one of my wildest dreams come true, if only I could be around in a few months' time, or whenever my "maternity leave" was over with, to enjoy it. What I thought was that Constance, who would never be *my* Constance, was getting to go on the trip that should by all rights have been mine. And now, instead of getting to go, I'd have to spend a large part of my last weeks at Churchill & Stewart training someone I kind of loathed to do a job I kind of loved.

Some lifetimes, it just didn't pay to try to out-trick the world.

Oh, well, I tried to tell myself as I sucked on my sour grapes, once *The Cloth Baby* was published and it became a huge international bestseller, translated into more languages than Jean Auel or Karl Marx, I'd be able to afford to hop over to the Big Apple any time I chose. Why, by that time, I probably wouldn't even care about working as an editor anymore.

I had decided to drown my sorrows, over not being able to go to New York to meet with an author whom I alone had discovered, with tea at the Ritz Palm Court. Of course it was an impossibly touristy and expensive thing to do— 17 pounds, 50p for a snooty waiter, china-cupped tea and an assortment of teeny sandwiches, scones with jam and Devonshire cream, and minuscule pastries that proved better on sight than on tongue—but it was something I had never done before. Sure I had lived in London or its vicinity for my entire life, but like the New Yorker who never bothers to go up in the Statue of Liberty, I'd never been to a lot of places that tourists would be sure to visit if they knew that they were only going to be in London for one week.

I don't know what I'd expected from the Ritz, but I certainly hadn't expected a maitre d' asking me if I had a reservation.

"*Reservation?* No, of course I don't. I just want a cuppa."

"*A cuppa?*" Clearly we were each having our share of problems understanding the other's Queen's English. "No, I'm sorry, madam, but the Ritz is very popular and it is customary to reserve far in advance."

"Oh. Fine." I was exasperated. "I'll just go to, oh, I don't know, Claridge's, I suppose." I'd never been in Claridge's either. "They're always happy to serve me."

I moved to step away and let the next person in line be abused by Mr. Surly.

I guess it's possible that, before that moment, the little podium that served as the maitre d's station might have blocked my eight-month belly, because suddenly his attitude lightened. "Madam, are you expecting a baby soon?"

"Well," I said, vaguely insulted, patting my protruding belly, which that day was sporting a navy-blue jumper with a decorative red anchor on the front to enhance the nautical theme, "this isn't exactly a pile of wadded cloth I've got under here."

I moved to go again, but now he came around the podium, delicately taking me by the arm.

"But, madam, why didn't you say something before?"

"Well, it's not as though I begin every conversation by saying things like, 'I'm pregnant, which table would you

like me to sit at' or 'I'm pregnant, do you carry olives without the pimientos' or—"

"Yes, I can appreciate that—" he was leading me to a
table now "—but still, had I but known, well, I know how
important it is for that unborn baby of yours to get all of
the food he or she wants. Oh, I just love babies!" He held
a seat out for me, pushing me in so close to the table that
my belly became completely tucked underneath, my
breasts practically resting on the table itself as though displayed on a ledge. "I'll send Henri over right away with a
trolley of our best delicacies. Now, mind you, don't
forget—" and here he wagged his finger in my face
"—you're not to select any of the teas that have caffeine.
Caffeine is very bad for the baby."

I think I liked him better when he was Mr. Surly.

So, no, I hadn't expected to be attacked for not having
made a reservation, but I had expected the marble steps,
impressive columns and baroque fountain, all of which I'd
seen before on film and none of which was disappointing
when viewed up close and in person.

But there was to be a second thing I hadn't expected,
one that made its presence felt when I was halfway through
my first cup of decaffeinated tea and my scone, slathered
with jam and clotted cream.

"Jane?" a voice asked from my side. "Jane Taylor? Is that
you?"

Even though I hadn't heard it since I'd told him I
wouldn't marry him a couple of months before, I'd have
known that voice anywhere.

"Tolkien!"

He looked perfect. He looked absolutely the same.

In my overwhelming excitement at seeing him again, I
practically leapt in my seat. This action, in turn, caused me
to spill some of the tea in the cup I was still holding onto
my jumper, which action, in its turn, caused me to make
another chair-leaping action, only this time backward.

With this smooth move, I succeeded in revealing my eight-month belly and dripping some of the jam from my scone onto my jumper, all in one go.

Tolkien, ever the gentleman, was in the process of helping me wipe the jam off of my anchor decoration, all the while saying, "You know, Jane, I can't tell you how often I've thought of calling you these past few months. Every day I look at that phone…" when suddenly he noticed what he was dabbing at. "Good God, Jane. Are you pregnant?"

I giggled nervously, giving the same answer that I'd given to the maitre d', the one about me not having a pile of wadded-up cloth under my jumper.

"But what are you doing here," I asked, "at the Ritz?"

"Oh that." He waved off my question, still stunned at my appearance, and sank into the chair beside me. "I'm doing some undercover surveillance work. They've got a pasha who's been staying here forever and who they've become convinced is robbing them blind in silverware. Guess even the Ritz has to think about cutting down on the overhead at some point."

"My, how interesting," I genuinely enthused. "Will you be wearing one of your undercover getups like the one you had on the night I first met you?"

"Never mind that, Jane." He sounded a trifle exasperated. "This," he gestured towards my belly, both palms up, "this baby, you've got in there—is it by any chance… mine?"

I couldn't be sure, but I thought the wondering look on his face was one of hope.

"Good God, no! I mean," I added more gently, covering one of his hands with mine, having seen the crestfallen expression overtake his face, "how could it be? Think about the last time we were together and do the math. If this were your baby, and I was already this big after just something like two or three months, then by the time our baby was born I'd be a shoo-in at Ripley's." Of course, I realized then that if I didn't come up with any further explaining, what I'd just said wouldn't make much sense either, given my present size. "You see, some women don't begin to show until fairly late into their pregnancies, so that when we last saw each other even though I was five months along—" which was just a one-month-off lie from what I'd been telling everyone else, but he'd have never believed me if I told him that I'd been six months along the last time we were together "—I hadn't started to show yet, but then when I did, well, as you can see I pretty quickly made up for all that lost time."

But he wasn't paying any attention to the last part of what I was saying anyhow. "Of course you're right. I see that now. I mean, not that I think you look inordinately big or anything—as a matter of fact, I don't think you've ever looked more fantastic—it's just that I see now what you mean about it not being possible for your baby to be mine." He studied me closely. "Was that it, Jane? Was that why you wouldn't say yes when I asked you to marry me?"

Oh, how I wished now that I'd answered him differently before. Now all I could think of to say was, "Well, I couldn't very well say yes, now, could I? Not knowing what I knew and you didn't. How could I possibly say yes to your question when you were asking your question without full possession of all the facts?"

"Oh, Jane. You still have the power to utterly confuse me. I still don't understand why you behaved as you did. Did you think that if you'd told me that you were pregnant with another man's child from before you even met me, did you think I'd run out on you, that I'd love you or your child any the less?"

I could see by the look on his face that would never have been the case. I swallowed hard.

"Did you mean what you said before," I asked, "about thinking to call me every day since last we met?"

"Yes, Jane." He ran his fingers roughly through his hair. "I think about you all the time. I think about you every day. I think about you when I'm dreaming at night." He sighed. "I think about you when I don't even know that I'm thinking about you."

God. How much I had lost. How much I had allowed to just walk away.

But what was there that I could do about it now? If I whipped the cloth baby out from around my belly, shouting, "See! It's okay now! I was just having the world on," would it make things any better? Would he still want to marry me if he knew that I was something of a pathological liar, perhaps not dangerous like one of those serial-killer types they manufactured over in America, but capable of dreaming up a whopper of a lie to tell my family and friends just so that I could: first, trap a man; second, get what I thought of as my fair share of TLC; and third, sell a universal bestseller based on my experiences as a wacko? Would he consider it a mitigating circumstance at all, that I had at least been unable to bring myself to say I'd lost the baby when the fake baby became no longer convenient for me?

I just couldn't see it.

Arguably, Tolkien Donald was the best man who had ever lived—he was certainly the best man I had ever met—but I just couldn't picture him shrugging off the stream of lies I'd trailed behind myself these past several months.

And so I did the worst thing I'd ever done in my life for the second time: I let him go again.

Oh sure we talked for a while longer, making small talk about my job, his job, how the holiday season seemed to pop up closer in one's face each year older one got. But when the chance had been there to say, "I made a mistake, I should have believed in you enough to give you the truth," I hadn't taken advantage of it and then that window had closed and the rest was just pain for both of us.

At one point, he did say, "You haven't said anything about the father's involvement in all of this, whether he's planning to be involved or not or even knows, but I remember that you'd just broken up with some bounder when we first met. Anyway, what I want to say is that if you ever need anything at all, anything that you think would be best for a man to provide or anything that you just need a friend to do for you..."

God. After all that had happened, he still loved me.

I've always known that I'm not the most lovable woman in the world—maybe that's been a big part of my problems, that knowledge—and there's certainly no explaining why fools do fall in love with who they fall in love with, but for whatever reason, this stupendously, monumentally wonderful man had chosen to love me and hadn't yet been able to teach himself to stop. I had to bite my lip to keep from crying, to keep from speaking the truth.

When the time came to pay for my tea, I refused to let Tolkien do it, despite his comments about my needing to save money where I could these days. Instead, I proudly paid my own 17 pounds and 50p, wished him luck with his pasha, and waddled out of the Ritz as quickly as my bulk would allow before I did in fact burst into tears.

You expect a gay wedding to be different somehow, but it never is.

Save for the fact that the impromptu nuptials of David and Christopher took place in the middle of Meat! *Meat!!* *MEAT!!!,* and that I was the tuxedoed best man in a room filled overwhelmingly with gay men, it was just like any other wedding really; the only other difference being that, given the degree of openness and generosity of spirit they each brought to the union, it seemed more likely that they would attain a happily-ever-after.

As their relationship had progressed over the last several months, and as David grew more and more sure of

Christopher, I had begun to have second thoughts. I'd begun to tell myself that I didn't think that Christopher was the one. How could he be, when merely being around him made me feel so unaccountably testy?

But then I began to account for it and the pieces finally began to fall into place in what passes for my tiny little mind.

Watching David and Christopher exchange their vows, surrounded as I was by scores of the most beautiful men in London, I recognized my feelings toward Christopher as being a smallness of character, as being the nakedly jealous thing that they were. I'd blown my own chance with Tolkien and here my best friend was facing his great chance at happiness, while all I could do was stand as living proof that maybe Gore Vidal was right: that all I could see in my best friend's success was the chance for me to die a little death.

"Well, to hell with that," I said fiercely, not intending to speak the words aloud, certainly not right smack in the middle of David and Christopher's exchange of vows, but doing so nonetheless.

"What do you mean, Jane?" David turned to me, concern etched on his face. "Why are you objecting to the minister inviting everyone to stick around for wine and pastries, and filet mignon of course, after the ceremony?"

"I didn't mean that," I said with a sob, hurling myself into his arms. "I just meant that I do love you and I truly want you to be happy always. Always."

He patted my hair, not dismissively, but lovingly, a caress like a benediction. "I do know that, Jane."

"And," I sniveled, "I do know that it was never really your scheme about the…well, you know. I do know that it was all my fault."

"Yes, Jane." He smiled. "I did know that, too."

"Ahem," coughed the minister. "May I…?"

As he pronounced them a couple—so I guess maybe

there was another small difference between this and other weddings I'd been to—I beamed my approval on the proceedings, hoping it didn't look forced.

At the reception afterward, my best friend was generous enough to steal some moments away from his own beloved to minister to my needs. As we stood in a quiet corner, sipping expensive champagne—okay, so maybe I was guzzling mine—he spoke:

"You know, Jane, I do have some sense of what you must be going through today."

"You do?"

"Yes. You must be looking at Christopher and me, at our nuptial happiness together, and recognizing that you could have had the very same thing with Tolkien, if only you'd been willing to give up your plan to remain falsely pregnant for nine months so that your family and the girls at work would be nicer to you."

"Well," I said, "I did want to experience that whole 'rosy world' thing."

I could see he was exasperated with me. "'Rosy world, rosy world'—for nine months now, you've been going on and on to me about this 'rosy world' thing. There is no 'rosy world,' Jane! There's *life*. There's *life* and then there's make-believe. Take your pick."

That was when I finally came clean with him. I told him the whole truth about my book deal with Devil Alice.

"So you see," I finished up, speaking in an overly excited, French grapes-induced rush, "I couldn't very well walk away from all that, now, could I? Not when my book is destined to be an ultragalactic bestseller and—"

"An ultragalactic bestseller? Is there even such a thing as an ultragalactic?"

Odd, but instead of the sympathy I thought I'd see on his face, he looked angry with me.

"You gave up a chance at true love for an ultragalactic bestseller?"

"It didn't seem to bother you any," I defended, "when I gave up true love so that my family and the girls at work would be nicer to me."

"Did I ever *say* it didn't bother me?" He shook his head. "Besides, giving up true love for those reasons is perhaps insane, but insane is okay as a defense. But for *mercenary* reasons? For an *ultragalactic bestseller?*"

"Well, I—"

"Do you have any idea how rare true love is? No, clearly you don't. True love is what human beings live for, Jane, and it's rare, very rare, *ultragalactically* rare. Most people wind up settling in their relationships—settling for someone just to have a companion, settling with someone who isn't totally abusive either physically or emotionally, *settling*—or else they convince themselves that they have love when what they really have is something somehow less. But you had a chance, Jane, a real chance to live rare, and you gave it up. And for what?"

I started to tell him about my other reasons, about how I hadn't been willing to admit my lies yet, about how I couldn't bring myself to hurt Dodo et al. by inventing a grim end to the pregnancy. But David waved me off.

"I don't care what your reasons or what your *other* reasons were." Then he grabbed me, firm yet gentle hands cradling either side of my face. "Promise me something, Jane."

I nodded.

"Promise me that…if you can't bring yourself to do it right now, then promise me that *one day,* even if it's years from now, you'll go after Tolkien. You'll tell him everything you did, everything you really felt in your heart for him, and let him decide what happens next."

What choice did I have? It was his wedding day. You can't deny someone what they ask for on their wedding day, certainly not when that someone is the best friend you'll ever have.

"I promise." I spoke fiercely, but my eyes must have started to water, because David reached for a handkerchief and wiped them for me.

"Please don't be sad, Jane."

"I'm not sad," I said, and I wasn't, not at that moment. "I'm just so happy. My very best friend has managed to find himself that rare true love and he's even smart enough to do something about it."

And as I waved them off on their honeymoon several hours later, the bouquet I'd caught in hand, I endeavored to maintain that smile of pure joy at their good fortune in having found one another. Perhaps those psychological theories are right—that if you let a smile be your umbrella, you begin feeling happier on the inside as well or some such rot—because I felt my spirits lifting, at least momentarily.

I finally felt ready to take responsibility for another being, but who? After all, Tolkien was out of the picture and David no longer needed me as he once had.

My purpose when I originally went to the Ritz had been to get over my disappointment at not being able to go to New York. My falsely hearty devil-may-care attitude at David's wedding had been meant to help me get over the experience of seeing Tolkien at the Ritz. Now I needed something to get me over my best friend's happy wedding.

I'll never know where my stamina came from that day; I'd never been one for walking long distances, certainly not when there was a cab or a tube station handy. Then, too, it was the kind of gunmetal gray, insidiously damp, November in London, a can-never-get-quite-warm-enough sort of day that makes a person begin to understand what Guy Fawkes was on about, it being the kind of weather that could provoke any sane person into starting a rebellion. Still, I pulled my coat more tightly around myself, turned the collar up and continued placing one booted foot in front of the other. Before long—well, actually, it probably took me a fairly long time to get there from Piccadilly—I found myself in front of Royal Hospital, not quite knowing how I'd gotten there, as though I'd been conveyed there on a moving belt rather than by my own two feet.

For some odd reason, the hospital seemed to me to be a far more interesting place than any of the shops in the neighborhood. Oh, well, I thought to myself, feeling a bit like Alice in Wonderland as I struggled to pull open the heavy door, I'm here; might as well go in and have a look around.

The last time I'd been in any kind of medical facility was when I'd tried to get the women at that clinic to sell me their sonogram photos. This time, however, with my badge of honor entering the room a beat or two ahead of me, my reception was far warmer.

"Can I help you?" asked the nurse at the information desk, her smile telling me that, given my condition, there was nothing I could ask that could be too great a burden.

"The nursery?" I asked, tentatively at first, then, more definite, "The nursery. I wondered if you might direct me to the nursery, please."

"And the name of the baby you're here to see?" she asked, cueing up the appropriate screen on her computer.

Good God, I thought. Name? I had to come up with a name? "Smith," I blurted out after a long moment's thought. Well, they had to have one of those, didn't they?

In fact, they had two. "Would that be Robert or Julia?"

"Oh, Julia," I said. "Definitely Julia."

"Just go straight down the hall here and take the lift up to seven, then take a right and soon you'll see the window."

"Thank you."

I set off to follow her directions, half of me wanting to

hurry toward my destination, the other half reluctantly dragging its feet as though once I got there, there would be no turning back, as if were I to stop now, I'd be able to halt some kind of unstoppable train from being set in motion.

The floor on seven gleamed with high polish as I made my way toward the window to the nursery. I stepped up to the glass, still both attracted and repelled at the same time.

"You won't hurt them, by standing there, you know," commented a passing nurse. "You can move closer."

I turned toward the sound of her voice, nervous half smile at the ready, but she was already bustling down the corridor.

I took that one step closer.

My heavens, they were odd really, weren't they, babies? The way they scrunched up their little faces and you never could tell if they were fixing to cry or squeezing out gas or maybe they were even already thinking complex thoughts in their own prelanguage sort of way. I mean, who knew?

I thought for sure that the caps they'd be wearing to keep their little heads warm would be in shades of pale pink and blue, like on the television, but it wasn't like that; they all had the same cream-colored caps and I found myself squinting at the names at the end of each bassinet to see if I could find Baby Julia Smith.

There she was! And she was a good-looking baby all right, not the best in the bunch maybe but by no means as off-putting as that chronic face scruncher down the row from her. The chronic face scruncher they could keep. After all, I might be ready to snap out of my W. C. Fields phase, ready to start thinking of these tiny life forms as something more than mere poop machines, but I wasn't about to become one of those silly creatures either, the ones who coo at miniature clothing and think that anyone under the age of six should be granted the benefit of an angel.

Still, if given the chance, I suppose I might have cooed at Baby Julia, touched my finger to her cheek just to see if it really was that soft.

Weird: no one I knew was even looking and yet I felt something stir, something that was downright uterine, as I looked at these babies.

Suddenly, they didn't seem so much like alien beings anymore.

They were hope.

It wasn't so much what they looked like, and I really, really, certainly, definitely was not going to become one of those gaga people who claim that they're all cute, but looking at them was like viewing a small sea of individual potentials. They were possibilities, that's what they were. I guess I wasn't the first person ever to have the thought, but I wasn't romanticizing things: I knew that they wouldn't all grow up to be Saint Augustines; I knew that one might be a Jack the Ripper. But that was the beauty in looking at them, knowing that they were each still a blank slate and that what they were to become had yet to happen.

Oddly enough, and tough as it was to tear myself away, I left the nursery feeling better than I had all day. I still felt saddened, more like wistful, I guess, that in losing Tolkien, I'd somehow let my own best chance of the kind of happiness I'd seen there float out the door. But I was gladdened, too, and that made up more than half the measure of what I was feeling, gladdened at the notion of the sheer numbers of potentialities there were out there on any given day, loose in the world.

My baby was now statistically eighteen inches long and weighed five pounds, just like a sack of flour. Its brain was growing a lot. It could see and hear. (Can you imagine what it would be like if I really did have a baby in there, one that could see and hear all of the·crazy things its mother was up to? I'd probably wind up with the first case ever of a fetus suing its mother for divorce on my hands.) Most of its systems were well developed, but it was possible that its lungs were still immature. Should the baby be born now, there was an excellent chance of its survival.

Still, from where I was sitting, having come as far as I had with the thing, I figured I might as well carry it the whole term if at all possible.

the ninth month

As I moved inexorably toward the inevitable culmination of what I had so blithely begun nearly nine months before, I now found myself in a state that I imagined was not unlike schizophrenia. I seesawed between extreme stages of enervating fatigue and manic energy, feeling more excited and, at the same time, more apprehensive than ever before. I was having an increasing amount of difficulty sleeping and, when I did sleep, my dreams were so oddly blissful that they terrified me. I was impatient, restless for it all to be over with, and feeling severely put-upon by the impatiently expressed desire on the part of others to just see me get it over with. Mostly, however, I was simply relieved myself to be nearly at the end.

The final preparations were now being made for the birth, which could safely take place at any time. The lungs were mature. Another two inches and two and a half pounds had been added to the baby's length and weight. The average statistics on babies showed that they were approximately twenty inches long and seven and a half pounds in weight, at birth. Of course, since I was petite and since I had been so sensible about not gaining too much weight during my pregnancy, hopefully my baby would be slightly smaller and therefore more easy to bear, although I don't suppose I'd want it to be too small; like Thumbelina, say. The fetus might seem less active at this point but, like a calm before a storm, it was simply that, being possibly engaged in the pelvis, it was more confined at the moment.

The storm itself could really come at any time now.

I was shopping the grocery store in the basement of the Marks & Spencer closest to my flat when the domino effect of my unwieldy nine-month belly pushing into the edge of my shopping cart propelled the cart into the bum of the tall man in front of me who'd bent over to study the tinned foods. Since I'd noted from studying pregnancy magazines and the women I'd encountered in my life that when a woman grew near to term she suddenly seemed to have a surge in size, taking on that overripe look of a balloon puffed up to near popping point, I'd used my rudimentary sewing skills to sew extra padding into the back of my cloth baby in an effort to ensure authenticity. Apparently, though, I'd taken things too far, as evidenced by the fact that I had turned into the walking embodiment of one of America's SUV-driving soccer moms: I never seemed to have any awareness of how much space I was taking up, my condition gave me blind spots, and I was always bumping into the unsuspecting, wreaking havoc in other people's existences like a mad Bobo doll gone out of control. The angry face of the man I'd just rear-ended, as he turned to confront me, would have confirmed this fact in case I'd been too obtuse to have sensed it already.

"You stupid cow…" he began, before lurching backward as though I'd tried to bump him again. Then he saw who the stupid cow was. "My God!" shouted Trevor. "Jane!"

"My God! Trevor!" I lurched backward as well, in my case causing irreparable damage to a display of creamed corn. "What are you doing back in town so soon? I thought you were going to be doing some sort of stock thing in Asia somewhere for the next several months."

"I thought so, too, but home office called me back. Seems they need me more here than there." He couldn't seem to tear his horrified eyes away from my bulging belly. "My God! Look at you! I can't believe you've taken this scheme so far! I was sure that after I'd left you'd come to your senses, perhaps tell your family and friends that it'd just been a big mistake, like one of those phantom pregnancies that you hear about every now and then. I certainly never dreamed that even you'd go all the way with such a thing."

"Yes. Well." I had the good grace to look embarrassed at myself. But not much.

"What are you going to do when the nine months are up, which looks to be about any minute? I mean, you can't stay pregnant for the rest of your life—people can count, after all. And I think it might be a little too late in your game to pull the oops!-just-another-phantom-pregnancy act now."

"I'm sure you must be right, but I haven't gotten that far yet."

"You haven't gotten that far yet?" His voice rose to near screaming pitch. "YOU HAVEN'T GOTTEN THAT FAR YET???"

"Will you keep your voice down," I admonished sternly. "Do you want everyone to hear?"

Passersby were giving us funny looks but, thankfully, more so at Trevor than at me. So far they'd been unable to suss out what we were arguing about—a fraudulent pregnancy—and, apparently, it was considered bad form for privileged-looking men to shout in public at women who looked as though they were going to sail into labor at any second.

"Do I want everyone to hear?" His desperate-sounding voice was a notch down on the volume level; thus, still pretty loud. He put his hands on his hips, his nodding head confirming to himself his own words. "Well, maybe I do. Maybe that's *exactly* what I want. I think it's high time you were exposed for what you are. You can't be allowed to go on like this, playing with the minds and emotions of the people around you. Someone has to stop you!"

I shoved the shopping cart out of the way and got right up in his face. "Thames Waterways," I said smugly, squinting my eyes up at him to play out the final showdown at the O.K. Corral.

"What did you just say?" His voice squeaked a bit as he blanched and tried to step away from me.

But I wouldn't let him. I matched him forward step for backward step. "Thames Waterways was what I said, you toffee-nosed git."

"But how did you…?"

"Behind the bed. You must have fallen asleep one night while reviewing your illegal scheme."

Now it was his turn to plead for discretion. "Please, Jane, keep your voice down."

I ignored him, still on the prowl. "Then, when you decided to abandon me and my baby…"

"You know that's not what happened!"

"…you were so eager to leave in a hurry that you must have forgotten you'd ever had those papers in the flat with you."

"Please. What will it take to shut you up?"

"Shut *me* up? I'll bet that Inland Revenue would love to get a look at the information I've got on you. I'm sure they'd love to know about all of the extra money you've made and not reported *and* I'm sure your employer would love to find out that you've made it with insider information."

"You wouldn't do that to me!"

"Oh, wouldn't I?" I watched him squirm. "Tell you what, Trevor, you and I are going to make a deal. You keep quiet about my little secret and I'll be good enough not to have you thrown in jail for yours." I grabbed my cart and bumped him with it again. "Now get out of my way. My baby and I have some shopping to do."

It was that magical hour in London that occurs only on Christmas Eve.

Okay, Christmas morning, technically, since it was after midnight and long past the hour when all of those Christmas masses would have let out.

It was two in the morning and I was all alone, unable to sleep, had been alone in fact since I'd left work early with everyone else that afternoon. Oh, I'd had plenty of holiday offers—everyone wanted to keep me company, no one wanted me to be alone, as my delivery date neared—but I'd turned them all down. I just couldn't face more well-meaning maternal advice from my mother and Soph for a baby that didn't exist and I couldn't deal with Dodo's kindheartedness now that she'd returned from visiting Mona Shakespeare in the States. As for Constance, who knew what color contacts she'd be wearing on this of all nights? The idea of her staring solicitously at me with red-and-green eyes just made me shudder.

It was a good night for being alone, actually, for taking stock. Why, I hadn't even been tempted to drink any alcoholic cheer. No, instead I'd spent the last several hours reliving the last nine months. And, as I relived it, I saw how in some small way my fake pregnancy had changed me. Maybe all pregnant women change. Maybe it's hormones, maybe not—who is to say?

What I did also see, however, was that David had been right: the only way for me to move forward was to come clean...with everybody. It no longer mattered if *The Cloth Baby* was published, even if it was an ultragalactic success.

Correction, it *did* still matter, but not in the same way, because I realized now that my ultragalactic success as a novelist and taking responsibility for what I'd done were mutually exclusive things.

There was only one thing for me to do, only one thing I *could* do.

"Please be there, please be there, please be there," I whispered to myself as I dialed the phone.

The phone rang once, twice.

"Hello?" he said, not sounding groggy at all, not like you'd think he'd sound at that hour.

"It's Jane," I said. "I need to talk to you. Can I come over?"

Supposedly the Eskimos have something like seventy-two words to describe the different variations on the theme that we English refer to as snow, while here we have just the one. Still, despite having just one word for it, a Christmas snow in London is much more benevolent than the snow that James Joyce chose to bury his Dubliners under in "The Dead," and the slowly drifting fat flakes that were coming down now, coupled with the red, gold and green lights of the closed shops I hurried past, made for a perfect study in the Dr. Jekyll side of Charles Dickens.

I was on my way to see Tolkien and I'd decided to walk.

London is a walking city and he didn't live very far, not to mention that I didn't think it would be very easy to flag a cab at that hour on that night. Plus, it would give me just a little more time to think about what I wanted to say: the truth, of course, surely that, but there was no harm in working on the presentation of it.

One thing I was sure of, and that was that he deserved to hear the truth before anyone else. Just like a real father deserves to be the first to hear he's going to have a baby, Tolkien deserved to be the first to hear that I wasn't. I'd come clean with him, then everyone else.

On the phone earlier, before we'd rung off, he'd explained that he, too, had turned down holiday offers, preferring to spend it alone. He'd even offered to work that night and had just gotten off at midnight but wasn't tired yet.

"I'll see you in a little while," I'd said hesitantly, torn because while I was anxious to see him in person, I was reluctant to sever the cord that was enabling us to talk right then and there; it was that good to hear his voice.

After putting the phone down, I'd gotten ready, getting the cloth baby out; not for deception now, but for safety's sake.

The streets of London, at this magical hour that only occurred once a year, would be practically deserted. Nearly everyone would be with loved ones or drinking alone because they weren't; everything would be closed. The only people out would be cops, people looking for trouble, and troubled souls.

It was the ones who were looking for trouble that a girl had to worry about.

Oh, sure, the way I figured it, even if everyone was supposed to be feeling all "God bless us, every one" on this one night, if I were to go out as just myself, I still might get accosted. But, having long since learned that everyone—even those who are nice to no one—treats pregnant ladies more kindly, I had strapped on my cloth baby one last time beneath my clothes.

Thus, I was Pregnant Jane, out for a holiday stroll.

I figured that I would start at the very beginning, tell Tolkien how I'd originally just wanted to be married like everyone else, whether Trevor was the right man for the job or not, how I'd first thought I was pregnant, then pretended I was while hoping to become so, then decided to go on pretending, again just so I could be like everyone else, have what everyone else had. I'd tell him about the book deal, although that part had come later.

It was hard to finally admit that I had become the very kind of person that I would normally laugh at: just like so many others, I wanted to have certain experiences—marriage, a baby—not because I genuinely wanted them at the time I was striving for them, but because the having of them would make me somehow normal.

I was just wondering how I could say all of that to him without appearing like an impossibly small person, and realizing that it was impossible, as I neared a stone church along the way.

I suppose if I'd just kept my head down, focusing on my own progress even as I focused on my own thoughts, I might have missed what happened next. But I didn't. I looked up. Was it the soft cry that drew my attention from out of myself? Perhaps. I can't say for certain. Anyway, I did look up and what I saw was a huddled figure with its back to me, bending over to gently place something on the church steps.

I stopped, watched.

The figure straightened, paused, then bent over once more, reached out a hand and appeared to caress what it had placed on the steps. Then it straightened once more and began to walk off, up the street, away from me.

I started to walk again myself, passing the church, returning to my thoughts.

She must have heard my footsteps—I saw now that the figure was in fact a she, because she'd turned to look at me. Then, a look of fear and sadness came over her face and she turned and began to run, moving faster as she went, looking over her shoulder occasionally to see if I was following, moving faster until she'd turned the corner and was gone.

I returned to the church steps to see what she'd left there. Well, I had to, didn't I? It could have been something dangerous; it could have been a bomb. Even I have some sense of civic responsibility. In case of a bomb, the proper authorities would need to be notified.

It wasn't a bomb, of course, I could see that clearly as I cautiously bent over what I now saw to be a basket with a soft blanket inside. I reached out a hand, tentatively pulled back a corner of the blanket.

There was a sleeping baby inside, a very tiny baby from the look of it, a very new baby. My movement must have wakened it, for it slowly, sleepily opened its eyes and gazed up at me with what evolved into a curiously considering expression.

"Hello," I spoke softly, running one finger against its cheek. "How could anyone possibly bring themselves to leave you here?"

I realized that I didn't even know yet if it was a boy or a girl. God, whatever it was, it sure was cute.

"Coo," it cooed at me.

"Coo yourself," I cooed right back. Good God! I hadn't known I was capable of such a sound.

I know I should have taken it to the proper authorities right away, but I don't imagine I was thinking straight right then. Or maybe I was thinking straight, thinking straight for the first time in my life.

I realized with a sudden lurch that I was finally ready to have a baby. I was ready to put another human being ahead of myself.

The proper authorities could be properly dealt with in good time. What was really important was that now I had a baby to raise, a baby who, from the looks of things, needed me just as much as I needed it.

I slowly lifted it, blanket and all out of the basket, slinging the basket over my wrist, in case I needed it for something later. Well, you never do know when a basket might come in handy, do you?

"Coo," I whispered again, nestling the little body close to my breast as I gazed down at it. "You don't want to stay in that basket forever, now, do you? You want to come out here where it's safer somehow. There, there," I soothed, "I've got you now."

Then I began to walk, holding the baby close, walking step upon step until I reached my destination.

He held open the door as I stood on the stoop before him, the fake baby pushing my clothes out, the real baby in my arms.

"Tolkien," I said, "I have something to tell you."

ACKNOWLEDGMENTS

If you're still reading this book, after having finished what was clearly the last page of the last chapter, then it must be because you expect to be thanked. So here goes:

Thanks to my editor, Margaret O'Neill Marbury, for bringing me to this moment in time; and thanks to Zareen Jaffery, editorial assistant and hand-holder extraordinaire.

Thanks to Baratzes, Logsteds, DelVecchios, and Simonellis everywhere, with special thanks to: my mother, Lucille Baratz, for providing me with an unmatchable model of what a great lady should be; my aunt, Sadye DelVecchio, for a seemingly endless supply of ancient ruled paper, without which I might have given up long ago; and Grace Logsted, Kathy Baratz and Vera Logsted, all of whom never failed to ask and always with expressions that clearly showed that they fully believed that one day the answer would be "YES!"

Thanks to my first readers: Jason Kessler, Greg Logsted, Robert Mayette, Kathleen O'Connor, Joan Philpott, Andrea Schicke-Hirsch and Sue Ann Siegrist.

Thanks to Livia Ryan and Stanley Klein for giving a little girl a little job in a big bookstore a long, long time ago.

Thanks to Bethel Public Library for providing me with shelter during my pregnancy, which curiously coincided with the writing of this book; special thanks to BPL Director Lynn Rosato for her gracious support of my "other" career.

Thanks to MOMS Club-South of Danbury, with particular thanks to Cindy Iazzetta, Alexis Scocozza and Vera Solovyeva—great women, great mothers, great friends.

Thanks to Laura Wininger for over a quarter of a century of friendship: I would do anything for you; you have done everything for me.

Thanks to Greg Logsted for twenty years of patience; for the use of his last name since 1989, thereby making my own that much more interesting; and for our daughter, Jacqueline Grace, the inspiration for all things bright and beautiful.

If your name does not appear on the above list, and you feel that it should have been included, feel free to call me and complain. Otherwise, thanks to everyone who has ever stood in my way, because you only made me more determined; and thanks to every single person who has ever even done so much as smile, because you've made my life easier.